I, Dreyfus

BERNICE RUBENS

I, Dreyfus

LITTLE, BROWN AND COMPANY

Rhoda Swindells.

A *Little, Brown* Book

First published in Great Britain by
Little, Brown and Company 1999

Reprinted 1999

Copyright © Bernice Rubens 1999

Illustration on page 149 © Rebecca Nassauer

The moral right of the author has been asserted.

A CIP catalogue record for this book is
available from the British Library.

ISBN 0 316 64809 4

Typeset in Ehrhardt by M Rules
Printed and bound in Great Britain by
Clays Ltd, St Ives plc

Little, Brown and Company (UK)
Brettenham House
Lancaster Place
London WC2E 7EN

For Zack, Matty and Dylan

Author's note

In 1894, it was discovered that somebody in the French military had passed state secrets to the German defence attaché in Paris. The honour of the French army was at stake and a scapegoat had to be found. Alfred Dreyfus, a Jewish army captain, was the obvious candidate. The conspiracy to frame Dreyfus was prompted by the virulent anti-Semitism prevalent in France at the time. Dreyfus was tried, found guilty, stripped of his rank and sentenced to five years' imprisonment on Devil's Island. In 1901 a new trial was held in which he was pardoned, but his name was not wholly cleared until 1906.

The novelist Émile Zola pleaded Dreyfus's case in a pamphlet entitled *J'accuse*, in which he pointed the finger of guilt at high-ranking officers in the army. He was sued for libel and spent one year in prison for his pains.

The Dreyfus affair was reported worldwide. It was a cause célèbre in France. It emphasised the conflict between the

republicans, who were pro-Dreyfus, and the right-wing monar-
chists, abetted by the Catholic Church, who, with no proof,
insisted on Dreyfus's guilt. But above all, it was the power of
anti-Semitism in France that dictated the initial trial and its
outcome.

This novel makes no attempt to update the Dreyfus story.
Rather it is concerned with the Dreyfus syndrome, which alas
needs no updating.

B.R.

PART ONE

1

Jubilee Publishing
London House
Sen Street
London W1

6 June 1996

Alfred Dreyfus, Esq.
7609B
HM Prison Wandsworth
London SW18

Dear Mr Dreyfus

I write to express the interest of Jubilee Publishing in an
account of your unfortunate story, told from a personal

viewpoint. We know, as you do, that others have written about it. But we are more than interested in your own version. We would be honoured if you would give your earnest consideration to our proposal and communicate your thoughts to us.

Yours truly
Bernard Wallworthy
Managing Director, Jubilee Publishing

Jubilee Publishing
London House
Sen Street
London W1

6 August 1996

Alfred Dreyfus, Esq.
7609B
HM Prison Wandsworth
London SW18

Dear Mr Dreyfus

We communicated with you some two months ago and as yet we have received no reply. We have ascertained that our letter was delivered into your hand and we do hope that you are not indisposed. We would appreciate a swift reply to our suggestions in our first letter.

Yours truly
Bernard Wallworthy
Managing Director, Jubilee Publishing

Jubilee Publishing
London House
Sen Street
London W1

6 October 1996

Alfred Dreyfus, Esq.
7069B
HM Prison Wandsworth
London SW18

Dear Mr Dreyfus

We have again ascertained that our letter of two months ago was delivered into your hand. And we have likewise ascertained that you are not indisposed, that is, not additionally indisposed, given the conditions of your present confinement. It occurs to us that the delay in answering our letters is possibly due to the question of remuneration for your work. If this is so, we would be glad in our next communication to enclose a contract for your perusal. Please let us hear from you very soon.

Yours very sincerely
Bernard Wallworthy
Managing Director, Jubilee Publishing

I sit and look at these letters. I read them over and over again. I know them by heart. I don't know how to respond. Do I want to write my version of the story? More to the point, do I need to write it? But most important of all, should it be written? Even if I could answer all those questions and finally and with difficulty pick up my pen, I would still be faced with many

problems. I would have difficulty, for example, with the very
first sentence. In it I would have to write down my name. Isn't
that how autobiographies begin? But my name is a problem. I'm
not too sure of it any more. It used to be Alfred. That's how I
was known as a child, with the occasional 'Freddie' in my infant
years. I answered to Alfred during my years at school. In the
cadets, I swore allegiance in that name. Then suddenly,
overnight almost, and all over the world, my name evaporated.
I was not a person any more. I was a 'thing', an 'article' with a
tag somewhere about my frame. In France for example, the
label carried the legend '*L'Affaire Dreyfus*'. I had been rebap-
tised. My Christian name was now 'L'Affaire'. In Germany it
was 'Fon', in Italy, 'Affare'. Here in England Dreyfus had
become my Christian name, followed by a new patronym,
'Case'. So it is hard for me to tell you my name. You must
make your own choice. I myself cling with some desperation to
the name my mother gave me. But I have less and less confidence in its sound. The trial robbed me of any sense I may have
had of myself, of my own entity. 'Alfred' is the name of a
stranger I have not seen for some while. The name 'Case' suits
me adequately I think, and I am sadly beginning to grow used
to its sound. Its hollowness exactly translates my lack of self.

So my name is 'Case'.

My age you know. You will have seen it in the papers. I am
forty-eight years distance from innocence. But I find my age is
as questionable as my name, for in the last months I have aged
greatly and yet, at the same time, I have become a child again.
For it is in the recall of those childhood years that I find solace
and comfort. So, for my part, I am of any age. I am in infancy
and dotage at one and the same time.

My profession too you know, from the journals and the stories they have told. A headmaster. And of the finest school in
the land. But what you do not know, either from newspapers or
from hearsay, is my view of the case. Can you see reader, how

I already regard myself as a case, an 'affare', a 'Fon', an 'affaire'? Even I have difficulty in seeing the flesh and blood behind the story, of seeing the body that is parcelled in my own labelled frame. So perhaps after all I should oblige this publisher with my own version, in the hope that I will thereby reassemble the pieces of myself from out of their several strands, to learn that which I truly am, to enable me to whisper 'Alfred' to myself, and to know that it is I. Why not? I ask myself. Let others make do with the 'affaires', the 'Fons', the 'affares' and the 'cases'. And let history make do with them too. I care little about posthumous labels. It is now, in the tide of my forty-ninth year, and in this nightmare of a dwelling, that I must learn to call myself by name. Let the words Alfred Dreyfus echo across the confines of my cell and rebound from the walls into myself again.

HM Prison Wandsworth
London SW18

12 October '96.

Bernard Wallworthy, Esq.
Jubilee Publishing
London House
Sen Street
London W1

Dear Sir

Yes.

Dreyfus

2

It did not take long for the news to spread along the publishing grapevine. Jubilee exalted in its coup and excited the envy and anger of other publishing houses that had lacked the imagination to take the initiative. It was now too late. The publisher was sewn up. A *fait accompli*. But as yet there was no talk of an agent and in the course of the following week, despite questioning headlines in the press, a shoal of letters arrived at Her Majesty's Prison in Wandsworth, the honeyed words of which were but the subtitles of their calculations; the foreign rights, the paperback sales, the serial possibilities and the film and television tie-ins equalled a ten to fifteen per cent that was very fat indeed. So they wrote, enclosing their stamped addressed envelopes, which postage would hopefully be added to their commission.

But not Sam Temple. Sam Temple didn't write. He phoned. He phoned the governor of Wandsworth Prison and made an appointment to pay Dreyfus a visit. He arrived at the gates hot-foot, and long before Dreyfus's mail had been sorted.

Sam Temple was not popular amongst the literary agents' fraternity. Not least because he was too successful. He was pushy, it was said, and unscrupulous. Most likely they considered he was a closet queer. But what's more, he was one of 'those'.

But Sam Temple wasn't pushy. He simply got things done. Neither was he without scruple. His dealings, compared with most literary agents, were offensively straight. As to his sexual proclivities, he kept a wife and two children in the country and was rumoured to have a mistress in London. No. Sam Temple was neither pushy, unscrupulous, nor a homosexual. But certainly he was Jewish. As was Dreyfus, the other agents reminded themselves in a whisper over a pre-prandial sherry. For the English are known to be of a polite persuasion and their anti-Semitism is of the most courteous kind. Sam Temple himself did not believe he could reap any advantage from the common factor between himself and his hoped-for client. Dreyfus was known as a closet Jew and might well bristle at any reminder of this aspect of his identity. Temple would skirt it. The purpose of his visit was business. If that could be settled to both their satisfactions, friendship might well follow, as it often did with many of his clients. He sincerely hoped so in this case, for he was convinced, like many others, of Dreyfus's innocence.

Alfred Dreyfus would not be the first of Temple's prison clients. He had two of them on his list, and one of them, a convicted murderer, had begun his writing career in Wandsworth. Temple had been a frequent visitor and their business connection had led to a firm friendship. During that time, Temple had had reason to discuss his clients' cases with the governor of the prison and those meetings too had developed into a strong relationship that continued outside the prison walls. It was through the good offices of this governor that Temple was able so quickly to secure a meeting with Dreyfus.

He sat in the governor's office.

'Is he going to write his story?' the governor asked.

'He has agreed with a publisher.'

'It will be interesting to read. I think he is an honest man. I think he might even be innocent. That's off the record of course.'

'I had that same impression when I went to his trial,' Sam Temple said. 'There are rumours of an appeal.'

'There have always been rumours. Ever since he was sentenced. But you need new evidence. And people are frightened.'

'So he could spend the rest of his life here?' Sam Temple said.

'It's possible. Come,' the governor rose. 'I'll take you to him. It'll have to be in his cell. You're way outside visiting hours. He's in solitary, as you know. That is his choice. You can have fifteen minutes. You'll be doing most of the talking, I'm afraid. He's a pretty silent man, our Dreyfus.'

The governor led the way through the main block, then climbed the spiral staircase. Sam followed, flicking his pen along the upright metal supports in order to break the terrible silence of the place. Thus he orchestrated their climb to the top, and once on the landing he put away his pen and followed the governor to Dreyfus's cell.

A warder stood outside the door and unlocked it as they approached.

'Fifteen minutes, Sam,' the governor said again. 'The warder will see you out.' He shook Temple's hand. 'I'll see you again no doubt. And no doubt,' he smiled, 'quite often.'

Sam slithered into the narrow cell opening allowed by the warder. Dreyfus rose from his cot and, as Sam heard the cell door close behind him, he had a sense of sharing a confinement. It somehow put him at his ease. He smiled.

'My name is Sam Temple,' he said. 'I am a literary agent.' He put out his hand. Dreyfus took it and Sam felt how limp was his grasp, and he tried not to be affected by it. 'May we sit down?' Sam said.

Dreyfus nodded and Sam sat on the cot since there was no other seating. Dreyfus sat at his side, though at a distance.

'I'm not acquainted with your profession,' he said. 'Indeed I don't even know what a literary agent does.'

'It sounds more pompous than it really is,' Sam said. He noticed that his companion's face was shadowed by a pall of indifference. Nevertheless, he laboured to outline the functions of an agent, and under certain headings in order to shorten his recital, but at no time during his explanation did Dreyfus show a flicker of interest. Sam then moved on to the earnings potential of such an autobiography, hoping perhaps that that aspect might stir a little enthusiasm. But Dreyfus's apathy persisted.

'I had not given a thought to contract and monies,' he said. 'I shall write it in any case. Not out of any desire for wealth or out of moral compunction, but simply as a personal need.'

Sam Temple marvelled at the length of the sentence. They were the first words Dreyfus had spoken for a long time. Such a reticent man might well be a good writer, he thought. 'That's a good enough reason,' he said. 'Would you then leave all the accounting to me? I will get the best deal I can for you.'

Dreyfus nodded, but with little interest.

'Money is always useful, Mr Dreyfus,' Sam said.

'It cannot clear my name.' Dreyfus stood up, signalling that he wished the visit to be terminated. Sam doubted whether at any time he could woo the man's friendship.

'It only remains for you to sign the contract,' Sam said. 'It gives me authority on your behalf.' He handed Dreyfus a pen which the prisoner took, and without the least perusal he penned his signature on the dotted line. Then he went to the door and called the guard.

'Is there anything I can do for you on the outside?' Sam asked.

'Thank you,' Dreyfus said. 'There is nothing.'

Sam Temple returned at once to his office and put in a call to Jubilee Publishing. He had no intention of conducting any discussion on the telephone. He knew that instrument served as a convenient cover for dishonesty and prevarication, the speaker safe in the knowledge of the absence of visual give-away. He simply used his call to make an appointment and, as casually as possible, to plead its urgency. The secretary obliged him with a meeting that very afternoon.

When Bernard Wallworthy was appraised of Sam Temple's appointment, he regarded it as an irritation in his otherwise orderly day. Wallworthy was the head of Jubilee Publishing; its chairman was absentee and nominal. He had been with the firm all his working life, starting as a tea-boy, and over the years working his toiling laddered way to his present eminent position. As a boy he had chosen a publishing career because it was an honoured and honourable profession, a respected wing of the establishment ranking with law, medicine and politics. But over the years the profession had been eroded. Now it was riddled with arrivistes, parvenus and upstarts, accountants all of them, whose activities gave off a faint odour of commerce. Literary agencies too had proliferated and had been invaded by the same flavours of 'trade'. In Bernard Wallworthy's offended mind, Sam Temple epitomised this alien invasion and he did not look forward to his visit. Yet he could not ignore it. Temple was known to be one of the best agents in town and as such he enticed the best writers. In the old days it had seemed to Wallworthy that agents had rightly been on the publishers' side. But now men like Sam Temple were speaking out for their writers and the old and comfortable order seemed to have been destroyed. He could not imagine what Temple wished to see him about but, whatever it was, he expected an uneasy hour.

And such expectations were fully realised. Once in Wallworthy's office, Sam Temple lost no time in declaring himself as Dreyfus's appointed agent. The news struck Wallworthy below the belt. The joy he had felt in his Dreyfus coup slowly soured. The interference of Sam Temple rendered his triumph into a mere deal.

'Congratulations,' he said, with as much enthusiasm as he could muster. But he couldn't manage a smile.

'I've come to discuss the contract.' Temple came straight to the point. 'Have you given it any thought.'

'In which way?' Wallworthy parried.

'Well let's start with the matter of the advance,' Sam said.

'Well – er – we have to remember that we're taking a big risk,' Wallworthy said.

Sam had expected such an instant defence and he was prepared for it. He simply laughed in Wallworthy's face.

'The name Dreyfus a *risk*?' he said.

'Well, you can't say he has a track record as a writer.' Wallworthy had raised his voice. 'No doubt Dreyfus will require a ghost.'

'I doubt it,' Temple said. 'I have just come from him. He is most articulate.'

'You've *seen* him?' Wallworthy asked. These upstarts get everywhere, he thought. 'How did you manage that?' he asked.

'The prison governor is a friend of mine.'

For a moment Wallworthy considered whether the governor was Jewish too.

'You have the name Dreyfus,' Sam was saying, 'a name that nowadays surmounts all risks.' Then without taking breath he said, 'I'm asking for an advance of a quarter of a million pounds, excluding all foreign rights.'

Now it was Wallworthy's turn to laugh. 'You're talking fantasy. Besides, to pay out a single penny might well be considered unlawful. Dreyfus has been found guilty, after all,' he said.

Sam Temple shifted in his chair, gathered his papers and made to rise. 'You know, as well as I,' he said, 'Dreyfus has as yet signed nothing with you. I could auction this book tomorrow and every publisher in London would put in a bid. And the final offer would be much larger than that which I'm suggesting to you now. I'm doing you a favour, Mr Wallworthy.'

The publisher knew he was cornered. He was seething with hatred for the man. 'Don't be hasty, Mr Temple,' he said. 'We can discuss it. Would you like some coffee.'

After ten minutes of argument – Temple would allow no longer – Wallworthy yielded.

'I'll put a contract in the post,' he said miserably. 'You drive a hard bargain, Mr Temple.'

Sam smiled. He left the Jubilee office with no sense of triumph. Simply with satisfaction. He reckoned he had made a fair deal.

Though Wallworthy would have wished to keep his surrender quiet, he doubted that Temple would hold his tongue. But he was wrong. Temple was well aware of the envy rampant in his profession and he did not want to nurture it. Nevertheless, within hours, the news crept and then sprinted along the grapevine. Its provenance was that of a whisper of a simple secretary whose eyes bulged as she typed nought after nought in the signature payment of the contract. It was murmured in the coffee break and passed on to the first outside visitor, a freelance editor, who, in his turn, took it to his club and bounced it on to the snooker table. Thereafter it was a free-for-all, and before the day was out it was sensationalised across the London evening paper without Wallworthy or Temple having uttered a single word.

In her kitchen in Pimlico Mrs Lucy Dreyfus read the news. And it did not please her. She did not see it as a bonus. On the contrary, it offered yet another source of anger and envy to her husband's persecutors, and even those who silently sympathised might well now find their sympathy turning sour. She hid the paper in a drawer in the vain hope that the news could be kept from the children.

3

I see no point in waiting for the contract to arrive. I have made my decision to write my side of the story and it is not dependent on legal clauses, fees or royalties. Moreover I am anxious to make a start. Excited almost. It will be like a voyage of discovery. Besides, it will give me something to do.

Since it is my name that I seek in these pages, I shall begin with my baptism. It's not what the publishers want, I know. They will fail, and rightly so, to see the relevance of my baptism to the events that led to my trial. But it is relevant to me. My baptism is the very source of that elusive label I seek in these pages. Let them skip them if they will, or read with patience until I get to the trial, the heart of the matter. For that is what they are after. The heart. But I seek the soul. Bear with me.

I have read sundry autobiographies in my time. At one point it was my favourite form of reading. I was fascinated not so much by the matter itself, but by the simple fact that anyone on earth would wish to frame himself in pen and ink, and moreover to presume that anybody else would be curious enough to read it. Autobiography is confession. But it is more than that. It is an act of arrogance. I need the first, it is true, and if the former entails the latter, I make no apology. I am by nature, with or without writing, an arrogant man. You will have relished that titbit from the journals. And now I thank God for it, for arrogance is what one needs in a hell-hole like this. It is a means of survival. But I digress. I was writing about my baptism. I don't remember it. I know from my reading that many writers claim total recall. I suspect they lie. Births, christenings, first words, and sundry childish pearls of wisdom are learnt by hearsay or told in hindsight. This latter by its very nature is a lie, for all events told in hindsight are far from the truth. They are misted over by acquired wisdom. So I will be honest with you. It was my mother who told me about my baptism. It is her point of view, for mine was no doubt blurred by holy water. But whosoever's view it was, my baptism was undoubtedly the first lie of my life. Some years later my brother Matthew was subject to the same deception. But that lie was not of our doing. It was thrust upon us and neither Matthew nor I can be held responsible. It was a lie because we are Jewish, and responsible Jews are never baptised.

But in my early years it did not worry me. I did not know that I was Jewish. Occasionally we went to church *en famille*, and we celebrated Christmas and Easter along with our neighbours. Until one day at school I accidentally broke a pencil belonging to another boy, who turned on me with a ten-year-old's spitting fury and called me a bloody Jew. I didn't understand him, but I understood even less the hurt inside me. I couldn't fathom the tears that welled to the rim of my eyes, nor the twisted offended knot in my stomach, and I suspected with fear and trembling that perhaps I was a Jew after all. I did not tell my parents of the incident for I feared their confirmation. I wanted to be like everybody else and no target for anyone's abuse. So for many many years I was a closet Jew, even though I grew to understand that being Jewish is in the eye of the beholder, no matter how I paraded myself. My trial convinced me of that. But I resented the lie my parents had thrust upon me and it was only in later life that I began to understand it and was able to forgive them.

You see, my parents were children born of fear. Fear was their nursemaid and tutor, and so schooled were they in terror that they felt shadowed all their lives. In 1933, they were just starting school. It was an ominous year for European Jews. In that year in Germany the bell tolled the first chime of the impending genocide. Their parents were neighbours and close friends. When in 1940 Paris fell and the German occupation began, it became clear that there was no advantage to be reaped from being a French Jew. But they could not escape. So my mother's family moved into their neighbours' apartment. Together they felt safer. They rarely risked the streets. My grandfather bribed the concierge to keep our residence quiet. She accepted the hush money with pleasure as in those days did many of her kind. But her son was more to be feared. Fourteen-year-old Émile knew how to turn a pretty franc. The Germans paid informers well. Émile would have sold his own grandmother for the twenty francs they paid him. Instead, he sold mine.

Life was difficult and food was in short supply. One day in July 1942 my mother craved a cup of milk and both my grandmothers went to the dairy in the hope of finding some. They never returned. Since that time my mother never touched a drop of milk. The taste and even the look of it soured her heart. It was an aversion she passed on to me, a survivor's inherited guilt. That night when it grew dark, their husbands, both our grandfathers, defying the curfew, went to search for them and they too were never seen again. It was later known that they were all spirited away to Drancy, that site of the round-up of French Jews, and from there they had been railroaded to Auschwitz. They had gone the way of much French-Jewish flesh at the time. Melted to the bone.

After the grown-ups' disappearances, my parents were somehow gathered into a miraculous children's transport which risked the Channel to Dover, and thence into the surrounding countryside and an orphanage. Since their births, my parents have never been separated. I know little more about them. They spoke rarely about their childhood and something forbidding in their manner withheld my questioning. But I do remember a frightened reference to the name of Émile. Like most of those who got away, my parents' tongues were stilled by survivors' guilt.

In the fullness of time, each at the age of nineteen, they married each other and after I was born, they took me, uncircumcised, to the church, where I was baptised. That is the lie that I have now forgiven, for I realised that, in the light of their history, they had had enough. Now they wanted peace, both for themselves and for their children. So as I grew up, despite other people's labellings, I joined them in their silence, out of respect for and understanding of my parents' denial. It might even have been the reason why I chose to teach in a Church of England established school as a way of underwriting their disavowal of the past. I make no apology for it although now I see how vain was that pursuit, how futile, and finally, how lacking in self-esteem. Perhaps during this exploration of myself, I shall find my beginnings and happily acknowledge them, and learn to walk with my grandparents who, like six million others of their kind, walked alone.

4

I must stop now. My supper has been delivered, though outside these walls it is only tea-time. I imagine that my two children, Peter and Jean, will be sitting around the kitchen table. My wife, Lucy, would insist on the kitchen. The dining-room, if there is one, would be too painful for all of them, with my patently vacant chair at the head of the table. The kitchen has no special seating arrangements. They are random and it is safer there.

Here I eat alone in my cell. With the exception of breakfast I usually manage to dine alone. That is my choice and the governor has not objected. There is little to say about the quality of the food except that I have eaten better in my time. But I do not complain. The food is ample, if not tasty. Tonight I am glad of its respite. This writing business is entirely new to me and the sudden introspection it requires. Such is not my nature, but in my present circumstances, such reflection is forced upon one.

In my days of freedom, the notion of self–confrontation never occurred to me. I had no interest in such examination. I loved life and all aspects of it and I simply got on with the living of it. But nowadays I am strangely unbusy, and I find myself thinking of my childhood and of my parents, which is surely the first step into a reconnaissance of one's past. And this writing business promotes such reflection, and in such a pursuit I am green and unpractised. So tonight I am glad of my supper. It is a diversion of sorts and may help to take my mind off my mind.

5

If only my mother had not had a craving for milk that day, my grandparents might have survived. Or might not. They could of course, through the accident of history, have been born in Austria in which case they would have been second in line in the Auschwitz queue. Their French provenance gave them a slightly longer lease on fear, longer than a Dutch, Romanian, Hungarian, Polish or Czech mortgage on the terror of capture. But in the end it made no difference. All joined the multilingual line, bewildered, enraged, and full of futile prayer. All of them. Milk or no milk.

My parents were haunted by their grievous orphanhood until the day they died. They rarely talked about their private secret. They died three years ago, each within a month of the other, as if the burden of that secret, even in death, was too heavy to bear alone. Mercifully they were gone before all my troubles began. Had they lived to witness them, they could hardly have survived. For my situation gave the lie once and for all to their years of denial, and irrefutably demonstrated its futility. I loved them, both of them, yet I have to confess to a certain measure of solace when they died. In my weeping and my mourning I could not suppress a sigh of relief that they had at last been freed from a lifestyle of denial and painful deception.

As a child I was unaware of all this subterfuge. My parents had been fortunate in their fostering procedures. As refugees, they had landed on the Kentish coast and for the rest of their lives they remained in that county. It became their natural habitat. They had not been separated and were able to continue a joint childhood in the care of a kindly village schoolmaster, John Percy, and his wife, Elaine, who themselves were childless, although their days were filled with children. Mr Percy was the headmaster of the village school and they lived in the school house itself, in a small village near Canterbury. Few Jews lived in the region – cathedral cities have never been the flavour of the month for Jewish settlement – and the nearest synagogue, if ever needed, was some twenty-five miles away. The village church was a few steps down the road from the school, a far more veiled venue, and it was there that my parents were married and where Matthew and I were baptised.

I never knew the Percys. They had both died before I was born. But my parents never tired of talking about them. Their verbal memories made up for the strict silence they kept in respect of their natural parents, a silence that was never broken. The Percys had raised them as their own and both were taught at the village school in which they lived. At eighteen, my father was sent to a teacher's training-college in Canterbury and my mother to a domestic science school. When qualified, they were able to slowly relieve them of their school duties, and eventually they cared for them in their retirement. Before their deaths some years later, the Percys requested my parents to take over the running of the school, and they lived and worked in that village until they died. Then the local vicar buried them in the village churchyard and a Jesus tomb leant over them both, the final confirmation of the lie that they had lived.

Now, in the confines of this cell, it sickens my heart to think of it. They lay within comfortable earshot of the Canterbury Cathedral bells, a million miles from the oven-tombs of their parents. But I understand them and, because I will no longer walk in their vagrant path, I forgive them. But unlike them, I can afford to keep the memory of my mother and father alive, and from time to time I took my children back to that school house where I spent such a happy childhood. And yes, we visited their grandparents' graves in the churchyard and they did not question the Jesus that protects them. For they too have never seen the inside of a synagogue, and although they know about the ovens, they are unaware of any personal connection. And this I swear, that if ever my innocence is proved, and I am once again a free man, I shall tell them how Drancy, the freight-trains, the multilingual lines and the ovens are their own personal legacy.

It occurs to me now that possibly Wallworthy will be getting rather fed up with this Jew bit of mine. But I don't care. It is after all, the core of my tale. It is what I, Dreyfus, am all about. It was what the trial was about, it was the nourishment of the accusation, it was the sickness of the whole society that condemned me. So bear with me, Mr Wallworthy. There could be no book without it.

Matthew and I were village children, and though we were only two hours' journey from London, it was not until my eighteenth year that I first saw the capital. And it frightened me. My parents too. Mostly village-orientated, they were as uncertain as I. And as for Matthew, he couldn't understand it at all. The London visit was a treat, my reward for having gained a scholarship to Oxford to read English. My parents were overjoyed, for to them Oxford spelt the English establishment, and my admittance to its historic and revered portals annulled once and for all their alien provenance. Their son had arrived, and by osmosis, so had they. A year later Matthew would be in Manchester in his first year of an engineering degree. And my parents were very proud of him. They had not been ambitious for either of us. They were happy for us to fade into an accepting background, as they had done, and to earn a decent living. And that is exactly what we did. Both of us. Until my fall, of course, which they did not live to see.

My years at Oxford were pleasant ones. I encountered no hostility and I mixed easily with my fellow students. I joined a number of societies but I gave a wide, almost anti-Semitic berth to the Jewish Students Club. And I admit to being ashamed. But I did not wish to draw attention to myself. To do so would have been to let my parents down. Though I did make one Jewish friend, Tobias Gould. He was reading law and we saw much of each other. He went to work in Canada and for many years we lost touch. Until my trial, when he flew over to give me his support. Of all the friends I made during my Oxford sojourn, Tobias was the only one who acknowledged and backed me during my trial. Most of the others claimed not to have known me. After all, when the prosecution is part of that very establishment to which they belong, they could hardly be expected to take the side of the defence, especially when the accused was not of their kind. On his last visit to my cell, Tobias told me that he had made a nostalgic visit to his alma mater, and he had heard 'Dreyfus' whispered in the common room. 'Well, what d'you expect, after all,' a Fellow had said. 'He's one of "those".' Tobias was eavesdropping, so he could not argue with the man. In any case, what was the point? Scapegoating is a compulsive neurosis and you don't argue with bedlam. We laughed about it, Tobias and I, and when he had gone I relished that proof of his friendship.

Every Christmas Matthew and I would come together again in the village school house. My parents made a big production

of Christmas. It was their annual plea of 'count us in' to the village community. And so our Christmas tree was bigger than
anybody else's, and the presents more lavish. The holly wreath
covered half our front door and our many visitors had to search
for the doorbell. During the holiday my parents entertained on
a large and generous scale. One Christmas especially stays in my
memory. The village had a new resident. I thought he was from
foreign parts, though he professed that he was English-born.
But he spoke the language rather too well, with that perfection
that a foreigner often cultivates. Did he too want to be 'counted
in'? His name was John Coleman. He was an engineer and he
had secured a post with an industrial plant near Canterbury. He
had chosen to live in our village, similar, he said, to the one
where he had spent his boyhood. He was a bachelor, in his
twenties, and my parents thought he might be lonely. Especially
over Christmas. So the newcomer was shortly invited to take tea
in our drawing-room. From our front window, I watched as he
searched for the doorbell. I let him look. I did not like his
appearance. It was stiff and obedient. At last he found the bell
and rang it triumphantly. Matthew answered the door and led
him into the drawing-room. He shook hands with my parents
and introduced himself to Matthew, who passed him on to me.

Now that I know exactly who John Coleman was, and the evil
that attended him, I find it difficult to find words to describe
him. In any case I am tired, and bewildered at my fatigue. All
I have done today is to move my pen across the page. Yet I am
physically exhausted. It seems that the price of every word I
have written has been a press-up, a knee-bend or a toe-touch. I
shall sleep well tonight. I know it. And even maybe, for the first
time in my cell-life, with a modicum of pleasure.

6

Sam Temple was an agent who strove to know his clients 'in the round'. And, to this end he needed to meet with Mrs Dreyfus. He sensed she would not receive him without permission from her husband and he was not too confident of Dreyfus's consent. He rang the prison governor to make another appointment, but this time he stressed that Dreyfus should first be asked whether he would receive him. Later that afternoon a call came from the prison saying that Dreyfus would welcome him, but only for a little while, since he was seriously occupied. Sam Temple smiled at the response. 'Seriously occupied' was a writer's phrase. He did not doubt that Dreyfus had started on his story.

The same warder let him into the cell. Dreyfus sat writing at a table, a table that he had acquired together with a chair. He did not rise to greet him. He merely lifted his head in acknowledgement, and mumbled that he would attend to him shortly.

Sam Temple felt that he was applying for a vacancy. He did not sit down on the cot. He stood and waited to be seen to. He watched his client as he wrote. The man had changed. He looked relaxed, almost at ease with himself. His lips were mouthing the words he wrote and a hint of a smile played around his eyes. At last he put down his pen, rose from his chair and put out his hand.

'Good of you to come,' he said.

In that moment Sam Temple felt sure he could become the man's friend. He smiled.

'I see you've made a start,' he said.

'I'm telling myself a story,' Dreyfus said. 'A true one.'

'I never ask to see work in progress,' Temple said, 'but some writers need to show instalments. If you wish it, I would be more than happy to look at it.'

'Absolutely not.' Dreyfus was adamant and for a moment Sam feared that he would never at any time allow a reader to look at his work, even when it was finished. He'd come across other writers with the same reluctance. But he would cross that bridge when he came to it, and meanwhile he would try to gain the man's confidence.

'I don't want to disturb you,' he said. 'I came just to keep in touch and to find out if there was anything I could do for you.'

'There is something,' Dreyfus said. 'I would be grateful if you would visit my wife. I fear she is very isolated. She is allowed only one visit a month and it would be a relief if you gave her news of me from time to time.'

Sam Temple was delighted. It was as if Dreyfus had read his mind.

'I'd be very happy to do so,' he said. He put out his hand which Dreyfus took, first with one hand then covered it with the other, and he actually smiled. 'You can read it when it's finished,' he said. 'But I want no doctoring. This is my story and the truth that I am telling. I do not want the truth diluted, nor subject to grammar. Especially grammar, which is often nothing but decoration.'

Though spoken in a friendly tone, Dreyfus's words were those of dismissal. Sam Temple took his leave, wishing him well with his story.

'I'll come again soon, if I may,' he said.

'I am always here,' Dreyfus said with a smile.

Once back in his office, Sam Temple wrote to Mrs Dreyfus, appraising her of her husband's request and asking if he could pay her a visit. Her answer was prompt and by telephone. She eagerly asked him to tea that very day.

He brought flowers and chocolates, more out of gratitude than etiquette. He was looking forward to the visit. He was curious. Little was known about Mrs Dreyfus and her children. She had daily attended her husband's trial and newspapers had managed to secure her photograph. But she had never opened her mouth with a comment. A meeting with Mrs Dreyfus was almost as big a scoop as securing her husband's story, but he would not let his visit be known. If the press were to discover it, he would be hounded by their hacks.

She opened the door herself. She was an attractive woman and totally unadorned. She wore no make-up or jewellery. A simple black dress proclaimed her grief, and its white lace collar postponed her mourning. She ushered him into a small parlour that served for sitting and dining. A visible kitchen led off one side. A tea-table was set in the middle of the room. The furnishings were utility and the walls were hung with tasteless prints. No attempt had been made at a personal stamp on the place. It was drab and depressing and clearly represented nobody but the landlord's idea of minimum accommodation. It was anonymous and rented.

When Dreyfus had been charged, the family had lost its residence as well as its income, and it seemed that Mrs Dreyfus had settled into the namelessness that she craved. Alongside one wall was a sofa that in its time had taken the weights and shapes of many a tenant and its uncut moquette was smooth with use. It was dirty too, but those who sat on it were well kempt and scrupulously clean. Two young children and a man, who looked unnervingly like Dreyfus himself. He was introduced as Matthew, Dreyfus's brother, and the two Dreyfus children as Peter and Jean. Sam regretted the lavish bouquet he had bought. It lay on the table like an insult. But all of them were welcoming. Their visitor had been with the one who was nearest and dearest to all of them.

The family gathered round the table and Sam took the place that was offered him. The children sat opposite. They were solemn, both of them, and wore that hopeless look that Sam had seen on their father's face the first time he had visited him.

'Your father is well,' he said to them. 'I saw him only yesterday.'

How could he be well, they must have thought, for they showed no response.

'I'll make the tea,' Mrs Dreyfus said and she went into the kitchen.

There was no word at the table, and all eyes were fixed on the plates and it was a relief when the whistle of the kettle broke the silence. Shortly Mrs Dreyfus returned with the teapot and there were things to do to occupy those seated. Then, when they were all served, Sam felt he ought to initiate a conversation. He started with the children.

'What school do you go to?' he asked. Then immediately regretted the question.

But Peter answered. 'We don't go to school.'

'They say terrible things about Papa,' Jean contributed.

'So we don't go,' they said together.

'Well,' Sam rallied, 'if that's the case, we could all go to the zoo one day. Any weekday and we won't have to queue and fight our way through the crowds. I haven't been for ages.

D'you want to come with me one day soon? If your mother will let you. In fact we can all go.'

He delivered his invitation in almost one breath and each word nurtured his own excitement. He couldn't wait to make a positive arrangement.

'We would love that. All of us,' Matthew said.

They were the first words he had spoken, and he gave a smile with them as if relieved that he had opened his account at last. And after that there was no stopping him. He itemised all the animals that he loved and why, and then went on to defend the principle of zoological gardens against those arguments that would see them closed. Sam noticed how the children gazed at their uncle Matthew in astonishment as if they too were hearing him speak after a long silence. And they joined in the debate, laughing, and so did Mrs Dreyfus, and Sam had the impression that his presence in the house had loosened the rope that tied them all into silence, the silence of the dire unmentionable, and that in the company of a third unrelated party they could once again savour the taste of normalcy. In a slight pause in the debate, Sam took the opportunity to organise a definite date for their proposed visit which they all agreed could be early in the following week.

He turned to Mrs Dreyfus. 'It will be something to tell your husband about,' he said.

'I think I can leave that to the children,' she said. 'We're due for a visit in two weeks' time.'

It was a cue for silence to take over once more and Sam allowed it, accepting a biscuit that was offered him.

'Why don't we take Jean to the park, Peter?' Matthew asked. He sensed that his sister-in-law needed privacy. When they had gone, Mrs Dreyfus set about arranging the flowers that Sam had brought.

'I'm very grateful to you Mr Temple,' she said. 'I think you've given my husband a purpose at last. His last letter was almost merry. And, of course, the money is very helpful. Now it will be much easier for me.' Suddenly she put her hand on Sam's arm. 'It's hard for the children, Mr Temple,' she said.

'I imagine so.'

'I daren't send them to school. They are bullied and insulted. Even by their teachers. I know my husband is innocent. And so do they. But they cannot protest. Their father has been condemned.'

'We must hope for an appeal,' Sam said. Then, after a pause, 'Do you have any friends?'

'I *had* friends,' she said, 'but now no one wants to know us. Matthew is wonderful. He comes as often as he can. But he tells me that he is now friendless too. Dreyfus is not a good name, Mr Temple.' She took her hand from his arm and started to stack the tea things.

'I'll help you,' he said.

She did not dissuade him, and once they were in the kitchen he said, 'D'you think of getting a tutor for the children? They would be happier if they were occupied.'

'I've thought of it, of course,' she said, 'and since we now have money it should not be difficult. But where would I find a tutor for the Dreyfus children? I'm too frightened even to enquire.'

'Would you leave it to me?' Sam asked. 'I think I know somebody. Someone sympathetic. Someone who believes as I do, in your husband's innocence.'

She gave him a radiant smile. 'I would be so grateful,' she said. She started to wash the dishes and she handed him a tea-towel. She wanted to keep his company. 'Will you come and see us again?' she asked.

'Of course. And you can ring me any time.' He picked up a plate. 'How did you meet,' he asked, 'you and your husband?'

'Through my friend, Susan. My best friend. Or at least she was. Though not any more. Not any more,' she repeated.

Sam refrained from enquiring further on the subject of that lost friendship. He sensed it was a private affair and had little to do with Dreyfus's present predicament. But he was wrong. It had everything to do with it, and Lucy Dreyfus seemed willing enough to throw light on that loss.

'I met Alfred one evening at Susan and Matthew's flat, and it went from there. It seemed a blissful arrangement at the time. We were a happy foursome. And remained so. Until the troubles. We used to take holidays together, the four of us, and later on the children as well. It seemed that our friendship would be eternal, cemented now by our kinship and the closeness of our children. Then when Alfred was arrested and the name Dreyfus became a curse across the world, she quietly changed her name by deed poll together with those of the children. Susan Smith she is now. Unaccusable. She won't let her children see Peter and Jean, and she's none too happy about Matthew's loyalty. He's been absolutely wonderful. All the way through.'

'Are they still together?' Sam asked.

'They live in the same house, but the marriage is over. He daren't move out. If he did, can you imagine what the newspapers would make of that story?'

'Does your husband know of this?'

'No. And he mustn't know. It would upset him terribly.' Lucy put the dishes away. 'I don't know what I'd do without Matthew,' she said.

'What work does he do?'

'What work *did* he do, you probably mean. He's an engineer. He had a highly responsible executive post. But after Alfred's arrest, they began to drop hints of redundancy, and after a few weeks he was told to leave.

'How will he manage?'

'He has some savings. And we shall share the book money. Alfred insists on that.'

They returned to the table. 'I'm glad I came,' Sam said. 'And I hope you'll let me come often.' He arranged a date for their trip to the zoo and promised to organise a tutor. 'When we go to the zoo, I'd like to include Matthew's children,' he suggested.

'Susan wouldn't allow it,' Lucy said. 'You know Mr Temple, sometimes I think she believes my husband is guilty.'

Sam shuddered. 'How torn that family must be,' he said. He rose to go, taking her hand. 'Any time, Mrs Dreyfus, you can call on me. Matthew too. Please tell him.'

She took him to the door. 'I shall see Alfred soon,' she said. 'He will be happy that I have your support.'

'You'll find him changed I think,' Sam said. 'He's more at ease with himself. I might go as far as to say that he has the odd happy moment.'

On his way back to the office, Sam passed the local park. In the distant children's playground, he discerned Matthew, Peter and Jean on the swings, swinging in rhythm, higher and higher, as if nothing in their orbit had changed in their lives. They whirled in a time when there were no stuttered breaths, no sighs, no secret tears, and that only when the swings had run their course, would they notice the clouds that had begun to gather.

7

It was natural that Matthew and I attend our parents' village school. We did after all, live on the premises. And though we were in no way favoured, we were happy there. Matthew is younger than me, and throughout our childhood I was his natural protector. Now the roles are somewhat reversed. Since my arrest he has guarded me with as much indignation as my own. He has petitioned, he has pleaded and above all he has protected Lucy and my children. I love him more and more. Do you have a brother, Mr Wallworthy? If so, you will know of that love. It is like no other. In its gentle language are no words of expectation or disapproval, no censure of any kind. The fraternal affection is a God-given implant at birth. One can no more ignore it than deny a gene.

When I was eleven, I went to the high school in Canterbury where most of the village schoolchildren continued their education. A year later, Matthew followed me. It was a Church of

England school and much emphasis was placed on religious instruction. Every morning at assembly we sang at least two hymns. The word Jesus was an inevitable ingredient of each song. But I never sang it. The word seemed to me to be too exclusive. I said 'God' instead, even though it didn't scan, but it was a word that covered anybody and everybody. But I said it in a whisper. I think Matthew did the same. I wonder now where that word-aversion had come from. It must have been from my parents. I had never heard the word from their mouths but perhaps I may have noted its conspicuous absence. Somehow they had managed to avoid it, and it saddens me now to reflect on how, all their lives, they arranged to pay lip-service to a god whose name they could not even utter. In some corner of their minds their parents dwelt with a chronic permanence and stilled their tongues on that forbidden word, and that taboo must have passed into our genes. Invincibly.

We did well at that school. Both of us. We struggled with and often relished those disciplines which today are not even taught. Grammar, sentence analysis, parsing, those fields of exciting exploration seem to have no place in today's curricula and I am sad for my children's loss. Do you have children, Mr Wallworthy?

From Canterbury I managed a scholarship to Oxford, and then I entered a teachers' training-college. A year later Matthew left for Manchester to study engineering. It was the first time in our lives that we had been separated. Until that time I hadn't realised how much a part of me he was, and I think he felt the same. We wrote to each other regularly, but I missed his smile, his shrug, his nudge, those movements that use no alphabet. I looked forward to every Easter and Christmas and summer breaks, when we could all be together in the village school house. In time he married, and a few years later so did I. But the bond between us remained unshakeable.

In the course of all that schooling, I made many friends. And we kept in touch over the years with letters, parties and reunions. It all looked so permanent. Until my troubles. Then the letters stopped. It was as if they were denying ever having known me. Except for some, who profited by my fall. Who advertised their acquaintance. Who sold their pathetic stories to the newspapers. I WAS AT SCHOOL WITH THE VILLAIN, was the headline of one of them and DREYFUS – SOME PREFECT! another. They hurt me, those stories. The matter of them was for the most part pure invention and its interpretation vicious and baying for blood. I was hurt most of all for Lucy and the children. But they didn't lose faith. Not for one moment. It was I who crumbled. It was I who lost hope. Why, there were even moments, terrible moments, when I actually believed myself to be guilty of all those sins of which I had been accused. I had a strange feeling that it would be *easier* for me to be guilty. That it would be a relief almost. That my guilt would validate my cruel punishment. So for many days, I sat in my cell and told myself that I had done what they had said I had done. I repeated it to myself until it became a daily mantra. But it never carried any conviction. So I replaced it with the phrase 'I am innocent'. But though that phrase carried conviction with ease, it did not give me hope. It simply enraged me and I paced my fury up and down my cell for many days. Then, God be thanked, Lucy was allowed a visit and I felt a traitor to her trust and radiant faith. She saved me from my deeply destructive self and I am whole again, whole in my innocence. Unshakeable.

From time to time, the governor gives me a newspaper, and he has allowed me a radio. For the first few weeks I never switched it on. It was my arrogance that ignored it, for I couldn't imagine that anything in the world was happening that was more significant than my own incarceration. But in the occasional newspaper I read items that slowly stirred my interest and I was curious as to how they developed. I was forced then to switch on the set, and since that time it has rarely been silent. So I am *au courant* with current events. I am currently following the American election, but my main interest lies in the Middle East. Every night I listen out for that news item, and when there is nothing, I feel relieved. For from my point of view, there is rarely any good news coming out of that area. And by good news I mean that which is on my side. The side of Israel. After all that has happened to me I could surely be on no other side. Not that that side is always in the right. I am appalled by some of the wrongs that it perpetrates. But I want Israel to survive, otherwise those who accused me will, in some roundabout way, be vindicated.

My trial and its unjust verdict coincided with a fearful Israeli attack on the West Bank, in which many Palestinians, some of them children, were maimed and killed. The newspapers rightly condemned it; there were demonstrations in the streets. But others got on the wagon, and all those inbred, inborn, engrained anti-Semites suddenly found a new word for their hate. That word was anti-Zionism, and that translation made their Jew-hate respectable. And I was the spark. The name Dreyfus was the dynamo.

I digress. But do I? These ramblings of mine are part of my story. Are they not the very core of the accusations against me? Are they not the summary of my condemnation? No. I do not digress. On the contrary, I am moving towards the centre.

I must pause now. I expect a visit from Mr Temple. He will have seen Lucy and the children and, loath as I am to stop writing, people are more important than the pen.

8

Sam Temple came straight from the zoo. He had deliberately asked for that appointment time so that his report would be fresh and credible. He hoped that the odour of the monkey house where they had spent most of their time still clung to him, so that Dreyfus could be a vicarious participant in their outing.

When Sam entered the cell, he noted the strewn papers on Dreyfus's desk and he was heartened by their untidiness. They somehow hinted at a greater freedom. Dreyfus rose quickly when he entered, and smiling he stretched out his hands in welcome. Sam could not help but compare this openness and warmth to the rigid frigidity of their first meeting. He assumed, and with a certain satisfaction, that the change was due to work, to the writing, to the unburdening of his onerous load. They sat side by side on the cot.

'I've just been with them,' Sam said. 'We went to the zoo. All of us. Lucy, Matthew, Peter and Jean.'

'Where were Susan and the children?'

Sam had prepared himself for this enquiry. 'She had to take them to her mother's,' he said. 'It was a long-standing arrangement. Next time, perhaps.'

Dreyfus seemed to accept the explanation but Sam wondered how long he could remain ignorant of his sister-in-law's treachery.

'Tell me all about it,' Dreyfus said. He oozed the excitement of a little boy who'd been too young to be invited to a party.

So Sam faithfully recorded their zoo itinerary, from the elephant house to the monkeys, to the aquarium and the snakes, and then again to the monkeys, the pandas, the bears, the birds, and the monkeys once more. At each port of call, he reported on the children's enjoyment, especially Jean's, and how Peter took care of her, lifting her up to read the signs on the cages. He described their imitation antics but he did not mention the occasional comments of the passers-by. 'Look, look. Aren't those the Dreyfus children? And their mother. What a nerve!'

Dreyfus said not a word, but he chuckled and smiled the while. 'And how is Matthew?' he asked when the story was told.

How can I tell him how Matthew is, Sam thought. 'He's well,' he lied, picturing his saddened countenance and how he had forced himself to be part of the treat.

'What does he do all day?'

'He sees a lot of Lucy and the children. He and Susan,' he lied. 'I like him a lot. He's a decent man. He's passionate about your innocence. Every day he's seeing people and pleading for an appeal.' This latter part was true. Matthew had shown him a list of all those names that had the power to re-open his brother's case. He was petitioning them all.

'I miss him you know,' Dreyfus said softly. 'Lucy too of course. But Matthew is a blood absence. Somehow it's different. Tell me about the children,' he said after a while. 'How do they look?'

'They look like Lucy. Both of them. Beautiful.' Sam smiled.

'I managed to get them a tutor. His name's Tony Lubeck, a son of a friend of mine. He's working on a thesis for his Ph.D. He goes to your house every day. He has a shaggy appearance and he's rather eccentric. Peter and Jean love him.'

'You have been good to me, Mr Temple,' Dreyfus said. 'I hope one day to repay you.'

It was a good moment to move on to the second purpose of Sam's visit. He was curious as to the progress of his client's book, though he didn't want to push him.

'How's the book going?' he asked as casually as he was able.

'I've discovered I enjoy writing,' Dreyfus said. 'I look forward to it every day. I don't know whether it's good or not, from a writing point of view that is, but it's certainly good for me.'

'Would you like me to read it?' Sam asked. 'Just for an impartial opinion.'

Dreyfus hesitated a while. 'I think not,' he said. 'I feel it would be like giving you my diary.'

Sam was disturbed by this response. If Dreyfus already regarded his work as a private confession, he might well baulk at its final publication. But he did not want to make an issue of it. It was too soon. Yet it worried him. He felt he had to make some comment.

'It may well be a private pursuit,' he said, 'but in the end its purpose is to vindicate you, to prove your innocence, of which thousands of people are already convinced. It's not only for them that you are writing, it's for your own accusers to prove to them their miscarriage of justice.'

'At the moment it's for me,' Dreyfus said.

Sam decided to let the matter rest. He would ask no further questions about the book's progress or its matter. In his time he had come across many writers with a similar initial reticence and in time that reticence was overcome by simple vanity. And Dreyfus, for all of his integrity, was human like the rest of them and subject to that same failing.

'I'm not yet quite sure of its shape,' Dreyfus volunteered.

Sam was relieved for he thought he saw a shadow of conceit.

'Perhaps next time you visit,' Dreyfus suggested. 'But I don't want to change anything,' he said. 'Not for the sake of better sales or more money. I won't have a single word altered.' His tone was faintly angry.

Sam smiled. Here was his client with but a few infant steps into his first book, and already he was talking like a writer with all the swagger and arrogance that was simply a veil for a crumbling lack of self-confidence and self-esteem. Sam was satisfied. His new client might well turn out to be a best-seller.

'Does it have to be chronological?' Dreyfus ventured.

Sam was now beginning to hope that he would leave the cell with part of the manuscript under his arm. 'There are no rules,' he said. 'If your mind is working in a non-chronological way, and this is common in confessional writing, then it is right for you. In the end, the logical progression manifests itself. I wouldn't worry about chronology.'

Dreyfus seemed relieved. And even grateful. He crossed over to his desk – it required only a few steps – and he tidied the pile of papers he had written. Sam felt a surge of hope, but Dreyfus quickly returned to the cot empty-handed.

'I keep going back to my childhood,' he said.

'Naturally,' Sam assured him. 'That time was seminal.'

'Then out of that comes a thought or an event that belongs to adulthood. I – I'm not sure that it's right.'

Sam allowed a pause. 'Would you . . .' he started.

'D'you mind reading it?' Dreyfus asked.

His surrender had come sooner than Sam had expected. 'Of course,' he said. 'I would be happy to.'

'But I don't want any criticism, I just want to know if it works.'

Sam expected that warning too. 'No criticism,' he repeated. 'Just does it work.'

'I'd be grateful,' Dreyfus muttered. He went to his desk again and gathered up the pile. 'I don't want anybody else to see it,' he said nervously. 'Only you. I want your promise on that.'

'You have it,' Sam said taking the pile. He put it in his brief-case trying to hide his excitement, as if this were part and parcel of his daily routine. 'I shall make a copy of it,' he said, 'and see that it is returned straight away.' He rose to leave. 'Is there anything I can do for you on the outside?' he asked.

'You are doing enough,' Dreyfus said. Again he put out both hands.

'Come again soon,' he said. 'And please call me Alfred.'

'Only if you call me Sam.'

They shook hands again and Sam felt that on his next visit even an embrace might be on the cards. He called the guard. As the cell door opened, Dreyfus whispered in his ear.

'Take special care of Matthew,' he said.

Sam Temple hurried back to his office. On the way, Dreyfus's last request echoed in his ear. He sensed that Dreyfus knew of Matthew's torment and if not the details of it then of his overwhelming despair. He must have suspected it in Matthew's last visit, or perhaps Lucy had inadvertently hinted at it. It was hard to keep such betrayal a secret. He was moved by Dreyfus's concern. He resolved to be in touch with Matthew. And on his own. Take him to dinner perhaps. He would ring him from his office. But first he had to make a copy of the manuscript. This he did himself, mindful of his promise to show it to no one else. As he ran it through the machine, he tried not to look at its content. He was saving it up for himself as a treat. When the copy was made, he sent the original by courier to the prison. Then he settled down at his desk and told his secretary that he was not to be disturbed.

'But Mr Wallworthy has phoned twice,' she said. 'He said it was urgent.'

'I'm not in the office,' Sam said, 'and you don't know when I'll be back.'

He knew why Wallworthy was calling. He was becoming nervous of his investment. He wanted to see something on paper. That Dreyfus man had had long enough to make a start. He would insist on seeing a sample. 'I have to arrange a jacket,' would be his excuse. 'I have to fashion a blurb.' Sam Temple had heard it all before. Wallworthy could wait. He, Sam Temple, had no doubt that Wallworthy's investment was in safe hands. He poured himself some coffee from his thermos and settled down to read.

There was not too much of it. Merely a beginning, written in a neat and confident hand. There were no crossings-out, no side-notes. It was clearly a first draft that was intended to be the last. He took a sip of coffee and started to read. Within the hour he had finished and there was no doubt in his mind that Dreyfus was a writer. His words were driven by rage, bewilderment and an offended understanding, and he had no doubt that all those forces would be maintained. He had to confess to some uncertainties about the occasional polemic, but he would not offer it as criticism. Indeed, as Dreyfus had wished, he would offer no criticism at all and he would assure him, and quite sincerely, that the lack of chronology in no way disturbed the continuity. Then he wrote to Dreyfus, calling him 'Alfred', and added lines of fulsome praise and encouragement. Before he signed the letter, he phoned Matthew to make a dinner appointment, so he could pass this news on to Dreyfus as proof that he had taken note of his last whisper. He signed himself 'Sam' and had the letter posted right away. Then he poured himself some more coffee and lit a rare cigarette and, leaning back in his chair, he inhaled with pleasure.

Then the phone rang. 'It's Mr Wallworthy again,' his secretary said. 'Are you in or out?'

'I'll take it,' Sam said. There was no point in stalling the poor man any longer. As he expected the publisher was anxious about his investment.

'Are you in touch with him, Mr Temple?' he asked.

'I saw him this morning,' Sam teased.

'How is it going?'

'He's writing.'

'Yes. But how much has he written? And have you seen any of it?'

'I don't know how much he has written,' Sam lied, 'and no, I've seen nothing. I don't think he wants to show it to me yet.'

'Well, that's not good enough,' Wallworthy spluttered. 'I'm entitled to see at least a sample of what I have bought. I insist on it, Mr Temple.'

Sam was patient. 'There is nothing in the contract, Mr Wallworthy, that entitles you to view the work before it is finished. Unless of course it is Mr Dreyfus's wish that you do so.'

'But surely, as his agent, you are curious as to its progress?'

'Indeed I am, Mr Wallworthy,' Sam said, 'but again it has to be my client's wish. And I must respect that.' He could smell Wallworthy's exasperation down the line.

'Well I hope I haven't made the most terrible mistake,' the publisher said.

'I'm not in the least bit worried,' Sam assured him, 'and I ask you to have the same faith.' He felt slightly sorry for him. 'I assure you, Mr Wallworthy,' he said, 'I shall try to persuade Mr Dreyfus to show his hand.'

'I'll leave it to you then,' Wallworthy said.

But Sam had no intention of hurrying Dreyfus. A deadline would unnerve him. He had most of the day to work in. But he needed diversion. An amusement of sorts that would not tax his mind. He was due to meet Matthew in an hour's time. He would remember to ask him if his brother played chess.

Sam reached the restaurant well before time so that he would be ready for Matthew's arrival. He had chosen a small unknown bistro off the Kings Road. Even so, when Matthew entered, Sam distinctly heard the whispers of 'Dreyfus' around the occupied tables. Matthew's face was as well known as his brother's. Every petition he made – and there were many, to influential people in sundry professions – was documented and photographed and the public viewed him with as much disdain as they did his brother. He was brave to venture out at all, and to be seen with him, especially in pleasant exchange, rendered one vicariously stained. But Sam was not phased. Indeed he showed off his friendship. He shook Matthew's hand warmly and rested his other hand on his shoulder as he sat down. Then, before seating himself, he gave a challenging look to the other diners. The waiter showed no sign of recognition, and they ordered quickly to get it over with so that they could enjoy conversation. Sam reported on his latest visit to the prison, but he said nothing about the manuscript. There was a silence while their orders were placed before them. They wanted no eavesdropping.

Then Matthew spoke. 'You know about my problem,' he said.

'I know the bare bones,' Sam agreed. 'Lucy told me.'

'I'd like to tell you about it if I may. It is, of course, of vital importance that it is not known.'

'You can trust me,' Sam said, 'as I think your brother does.'

Matthew looked around him. He spoke in a whisper, fearful of being overheard. 'It's not only that Susan has changed her name. And those of Adam and Zak, my children. That would be bad enough. But there's worse.'

Sam saw the man's distress and he wondered what could be worse than his wife's betrayal.

'I'm almost ashamed to tell you,' Matthew said. 'I haven't even told it to Lucy. It would break her heart.'

'Are you sure you want to tell it to me?'

'I have to tell somebody,' Matthew said. 'You're the only one I can trust. There is absolutely nothing you can do about it, but it would be a relief to unburden myself a little.'

'I'm listening,' Sam said.

Matthew put down his knife and fork and leaned across the table. 'It's that Susan actually believes that Alfred is guilty. She told me so,' he whispered, and Sam noticed a flush of shame budding on his cheek. 'She actually believes that he did it. To imagine that Alfred would be capable of such a heinous crime. It's unthinkable.' His voice was breaking. Sam didn't know what to say. He would have liked to meet with the woman and give her a good talking-to. Even if she believed that her brother-in-law was guilty, it was her bounden duty to stand by him. In any case he could not argue with her. He had no more proof of Dreyfus's innocence than had Matthew. It was just that he could not begin to believe in his guilt and he knew that many, many others shared his opinion.

'I'm so sorry,' he said. Then after a pause, 'Have you tried talking to her?'

'We're beyond dialogue,' Matthew said. 'Or conversation of any kind. I come from a silent house, Mr Temple,' he said. 'Even my children look at me with suspicion as if they have caught the verdict from their mother. I don't know what to do,' he said helplessly. 'I can't leave her. That would set tongues wagging. And she can't leave me for the same reason.'

It seemed that he was talking to himself, setting forth the pros and cons of his choices, though he knew that he had no choice at all. Sam allowed a silence and then he said, 'There is nothing you can do. Nothing.'

Matthew looked at him. 'It has helped to tell you at least,' he said. Then as an afterthought, 'And Alfred is so fond of her. He thinks the world of her.'

'And he must go on thinking so,' Sam said. Then after another silence, 'What about the children?' he asked. 'And their schooling?'

'Well, they have a new name now. They're even getting used to it. They practise it aloud as if to taunt me, and I feel betrayed.'

Again the flush on his cheek. 'I think Susan has made enquiries at another school. Over the river. She'll cook up some story or another.'

'She's taking a risk,' Sam said.

'She knows that. I think she almost wants the name change to become public. Then she could openly leave me and take the children. Then Alfred would read about it in the papers and that would be the end for him.'

Poor Matthew was at the end of his tether, and Sam feared for him.

'You must keep yourself strong for your brother,' he said. It sounded like lame advice, but he was at a loss as to how to comfort him. He wanted to kill Susan for the extra torment she was causing. Then he had an idea.

'Perhaps you should get away for a while. I have a cottage in Surrey. There's no one there at the moment. My family are in London this week. It's quiet and peaceful. You could put a little distance between you and your problems. Take walks, listen to music, read. I'm sure it would help. Come back to the office with me. I'll give you the keys and the address.'

Matthew smiled. 'You're taking a risk too, you know,' he said. 'Lending your cottage to a Dreyfus.'

'No one need ever know,' Sam said.

'Why are you so good to us?' Matthew asked.

'I believe your brother is innocent.'

As they left the restaurant, they heard the whisper of 'Dreyfus' once again, but this time Matthew reacted.

'Yes,' he said, to all and sundry, 'I am Matthew Dreyfus, and my brother is innocent.'

9

After I had trained as a teacher I was offered a post at a grammar school in Bristol. My parents were proud of me. I was, after all, following in their footsteps. When he graduated, Matthew stayed in Manchester and took a job in a large engineering company. But we still met up at Christmas and Easter in the old school house.

I was none too happy in Bristol. The school had earned a high and well-deserved reputation, but its headmaster was little short of a villain. He was a man of little learning, though he had sundry degrees, and he was given to violence of the 'this hurts me more than it does you' category, which he dealt out with sadistic pleasure. It is no exaggeration to say that I hated him. Every morning after assembly I would pass by a line of terrified boys, usually first-formers – the headmaster favoured the young – waiting to receive that punishment that would 'hurt him more, etc.' Sometimes I waited with them. I said nothing, but I hoped they would sense my support. Then I heard the crying from behind the door, and in spite of the head's dictum, I knew that it was not the sound of his pain, nor his tears. During all my time at that school, apart from staff meetings, I managed to avoid him. Then, mercifully, God forgive me, he died. He was not much over fifty, but I did not pity him. He was an evil man and children were safer without him. I attended his funeral with joy.

The deputy headmaster, who was close to retirement age, took over as stand-in principal. I was already the head of the English department, and when, after about six months, the post of headmaster was officially advertised, I thought I stood a reasonable chance of stepping into the head's unhallowed shoes. But I was only thirty years old at the time, and though I suspected that my relative youth would not be in my favour I nevertheless decided to file an application. I let it be known in the staff-room, and I noted the lack of reaction. There was neither discouragement nor dissuasion. I let it lie. I heard on the grapevine that there were half a dozen serious applications. I waited to be summoned for an interview. I waited in vain. I was not even called upon. The appointment was finally made and given to a man scarcely older than myself. I began to feel uncomfortable in my job, bewildered and humiliated. I decided to look around for a new post.

Matthew had secured a new job in London and I was anxious to move to the capital to be close to him. There was a deputy headship vacancy in Hammersmith, and I lost no time in applying. I was successful and, overjoyed, I left Bristol with little scruple, leaving only a few friends behind.

It was Christmas and time for our family reunion. Matthew arrived with a companion. Her name was Susan Cohen. An interesting name, I thought at the time. It was a name that spelt indecision. The surname gave no doubt as to its religious origins, but the Christian name was exactly that – Christian. It was as if her parents had started off on the same road as mine, but unlike them, had not gone the whole way. Susan was a beautiful girl and of a kindly and attractive disposition. She and Matthew were well suited and I was happy for them both.

'It's time you settled down as well,' Susan teased me.

Until that time, I had not seriously thought about marriage. Occasionally I had taken a woman friend to dinner or a theatre. I liked women's company, but none of them had yet stirred me beyond friendship. Now I wanted to be of equal status with Matthew. I feared that, if I continued as a bachelor, the edges of our bond might be blurred. My parents teased me too. They wanted to see us both settled down. They looked forward to grandchildren.

That Christmas was the last we spent in the village school house. At the end of the next summer term my parents retired and bought a small cottage close by. They would not be persuaded to move to London. Despite being born in a capital city, they had become village people. Possibly because of their perilous childhood, they had no longings for a big city.

I had taken a flat in Hammersmith, near my school. Matthew lived a short distance away in Notting Hill. He and Susan were making marriage plans. We saw a great deal of each other in those days and one evening, at their flat, I met Lucy, Susan's closest friend. Over the next few weeks we were a happy foursome. One day I ventured to take Lucy out on my own and over the weeks, I grew to love her. I was wary of asking for her hand for I feared refusal. But it was she, in 1980, a leap year, who proposed to me, and all my life I shall thank her for that.

My new school was much to my liking. I intended to stay there for a while to gain administrative experience. I was ambitious. Shamefacedly so. I had my sights on a headship. But not just an ordinary headship. I wanted to rule at the finest public school in England.

In 1981, Lucy and I were married and we settled into a

larger flat in Hammersmith. Matthew and Susan had married too and their first child was on the way. My parents were happily settled into their retirement and all was well with the Dreyfuses. Now when I think back on those years, I can hardly believe that there was a time in our lives without torment. Those days are gone for ever, and I must try not to think of the future.

But I do think of it. I cannot help myself. On the outside, they are working for an appeal. But they cannot hope for one without fresh evidence. I know that Matthew never ceases to collect signatures that claim a miscarriage of justice. Poor Matthew. It's how he must spend his days. For he has no work. He was made redundant soon after my arrest. I have destroyed my whole family. No I have not. I must not think that way. For I shall start once again to believe that I am guilty. It is they who have destroyed us. Those scapegoating hunters. It's envy and fear that has destroyed us. I had no part in it. I am tempted to name the man who hounded me. Who set out in full cry, who stalked and gave chase until I was finally gone to earth. I shall shut my eyes and write it down. Eccles. Mark Eccles.

I am not feeling too well. I think that name has stuck in my throat. I must rest now. This writing is not good for me. Yet I have come to the point when I could not bear to be without it. I wonder whether all writers have such moments. Confessional writers I mean. But none of them are Dreyfus. Yet surely in every writer's life there must be Dreyfus moments, times of awareness of a gross injustice to their person. Do they then put down their pens as I do now and wonder where the next sentence will come from, or whether it will come at all? In moments like this I think of Lucy and the children. They will help me with the words I must write and they will tell me that they must be written, for without the words, I have no future.

Apart from my short exercise period, I have been writing

most of the day. I have not even glanced at the newspaper that the governor passed on to me this morning. I shall lie on my cot and scan the headlines. Just the headlines. They will help to keep me in touch. The details and comments are at present beyond me.

At the same time, in Surrey, Matthew was scanning the same headlines. Sam in London was doing likewise. And this is what they all read. 'MATTHEW DREYFUS LEAVES LONDON TO HIDE HIS SHAME. BROTHER GIVES UP ON BROTHER.'

Matthew, white with rage, packed his bag and hurried back to London. Sam Temple simply put his head in his hands.

Alfred Dreyfus once more picked up his pen.

10

It's a lie. All lies. Poor Matthew. He would never desert me. He simply needed a break from all his protest. But will it never cease? This muck-raking, these false reports, these foul innuendos? And will they dog me for the rest of my life, and after my death, will they tag my children with their infamous Dreyfus label? But I must not entertain such thoughts. I must get back to Hammersmith and my safer and happier days.

I loved teaching. Especially poetry. I found that even the most recalcitrant pupils, the bullies, the ruffians, the unreachables, even they could be touched by verse. They would learn it eagerly and recite it with such pride as if they had written it themselves. If only mathematics could be taught in rhyme. I suggested after-school drama classes, expecting few volunteers, but the response was overwhelming and in time Shakespeare no longer frightened them. I looked forward to every day at that school and the discovery of the first light in a new rogue eye.

I had been at Hammersmith for five years when the headmaster was due to retire. I wanted his job desperately. I felt that
that school was mine. But my failure at Bristol still left a sour
aftertaste. It was clearly not my age that had hindered me, nor
my teaching record and qualifications. I suspected it was some
factor that I was loath to acknowledge – that a long-established
traditional English grammar school was unlikely to appoint a
Jewish head. But I had never advertised my faith. I had
attended prayers with the rest of them. I had even knelt when
it was necessary. I had kept my head uncovered and – the ultimate blasphemy – I had uttered 'Jesus' a thousand times. I
could have fooled even a Jewish god. But somehow I must
have been suspect. Perhaps they had smelt the outsider on me.
I could think of no other reason for my disqualification at
Bristol. I decided that I would not let it happen again, and in
order to avoid it I resorted to a means of which I am so deeply
ashamed that I can barely bring myself to write it down. If ever
these words are published, they must appear in the tiniest of
prints, so sullied am I by their matter. Indeed as I write them
down, I shall close my eyes, thus pleading myself invisible, as if
the story happened to someone other than myself.

There were a number of applications for the post, but as yet
no shortlist had been decided upon. I felt that if only I could
make that list, I would have proof that prejudice had not pre-
vailed. I had to act quickly. I waited until the luncheon bell.
Then I loitered outside the staff cloakroom until I caught sight
of the headmaster on the turning of the stair. I took my time as
I pushed open the door. I found several members of the staff
inside. Ellis from maths was there and I chatted cheerily to him
as I carefully chose my placing. Along one wall, two adjacent
urinals were empty. I took the one at the end and before I could
prepare myself the headmaster entered and took the one beside
me. I thanked God (the Jewish One) for my good fortune.
When my business was finished, I took a step backwards before

adjusting my dress and in that moment, as inadvertently as possible, I exposed my uncircumcised member. It was my
declaration, futile as it might have been, of belonging to their
tribe, proof of my qualification for headship.

I buttoned myself with a trembling hand, and tried not to
think of my grandparents. Perhaps they would have forgiven
me, because I was eventually appointed to the post, but I doubt
very much whether they would have been proud. The memory
of that shameful incident stays with me always. It haunts my
dreams. If I am guilty of anything in my life, it is of that gross
trespass, not only of the sin itself, but of the fact that I profited
by it. But since that time, though I haven't advertised it, I have
never denied my faith, much less contradicted it. Indeed, since
my trial, I have had the urge to shout it from the rooftops.
Loud and clear. But others have done that for me. Not so loud
and not so clear. For English courtesy still favours the whisper
and ambiguity.

I settled happily into my new post. Very gradually I introduced changes in the administration. I activated a long dormant
Parent-Teacher Association and I banned any form of corporal
punishment. In staff meetings I encouraged opinions, arguments and open debate. My door was always open, to staff and
students alike. I did less teaching of course. Administration
took up much of my time. But I continued with extra-mural
drama and poetry readings and invited any parent who wished
to attend. Over the years we became a community school and a
model one, to the extent that we welcomed visitors from departments of education in Britain and abroad. Slowly I acquired a
fine reputation, and though I belittled that fame, it did not
diminish my ambition. But I had to curb my natural arrogance
and avoid falling into complacency.

By now I had two children, Peter and Jean. And with
Matthew's two sons, my parents were very happy. It was a good
time for all of us, and I had moments when I sensed it would

not last. But I sensed it in terms of parents' deaths, natural terms. I never envisaged a calamity of such devastation as that which now faces me. And all my family. Let me dwell on those happy times for a while with words that are easy to find, for the lexicon of my future is elusive. And besides, there are yet some years before my fall.

One summer holiday I organised a family trip to Paris. I had never been to that city, but I had always nurtured a longing to seek out my roots. My parents took a little persuasion, but their presence was essential to my purpose. And for my sake, they agreed. I understood their reluctance. Any *recherche* would simply illuminate the lie that they had lived since their escape, and they wanted no reminders. But they appreciated the importance of such a visit for their children and grandchildren and they accepted the invitation with grace. So together we were ten and of three generations. My parents travelled with trepidation, their two sons with curiosity, and their grandchildren with the excitement of a treat.

Our first port of call was to the Rue du Bac, where my parents had been born and had spent their short-lived childhood. Before calling at number seven, we wandered in the surrounding streets. Perhaps I was trying to shadow the steps of my grandparents as they went foraging for milk and each other. My parents registered no recall. Nor even curiosity. Their faces wore a look of pure disdain and contempt, and they dragged their steps as we approached number seven.

It was a four-storey dwelling and there were many bells attached to the front door. I pressed the one marked '*concierge*' and I saw my mother shiver. The intercom buzzed and the front door gave way. I pushed it open and allowed our whole family to enter. I think we all had a sense of propriety about the place and I could feel a rising of common rage. On the right of the vestibule was the porter's lodge. The door was open, and without invitation, I led my conquerors inside. The man who sat at the desk had his head down in a pile of letters and papers and did not at first notice the invasion. But when he looked up, he showed a distinct irritation at our intrusion.

'What do you want?' he almost shouted.

He was a man in his sixties, thin, and of wiry build. His skin was deeply pock-marked, and his half-bare arms, below his rolled-up shirt-sleeves, displayed numerous tattoos. An opened bottle of wine, half empty, stood at his elbow but there was no sign of a glass. He looked like an ageing thug who'd seen better thugging days. I noticed my father staring at him, and he seemed to grow pale. He moved towards the desk, leaned over and peered into the man's face. 'Émile?' he whispered.

The porter screwed his thick eyebrows. 'How d'you know my name?' he said.

I detected a hint of fear in his voice. For the first time since we had arrived, my mother was roused from her indifference.

'We lived here,' she said. Her voice was strong and confident. 'In the forties. During the occupation. Your mother was the concierge.'

The porter trembled and offered a lame smile. 'What do you want?' he asked.

'Nothing,' my father said. 'We have seen enough. Come.'

It was an order to all of us. The family followed him outside. But I stayed, holding my own in front of the desk. My father said nothing. He was happy to allow me my say, whatever that say might be. But it was not words I wanted to exchange with Émile. All his life his words had been in his fists and I wasn't about to introduce him to vocabulary. I moved around the desk. 'Get up,' I said.

He reached for the bottle but I tipped it on to the floor. I opened my account with a fierce punch into his pig-face. It occurred to me to tell him that the blow was for my grandparents, but I didn't want to personalise my attack. I thought of all those grandparents, parents and children that he had so profitably shopped, and that thought fuelled my anger and gave me strength. I was physically fit, and some years younger than my adversary, not that he put up too much of a fight. He was too frightened, too cowardly, and too utterly astonished. I punched and I pummelled him, his nose, his eyes and his lips, until he lay sprawled on the floor, bleeding profusely. Through his swollen bleeding mouth, he begged for mercy, but his plea only served to enrage me further. He sank to the floor, spread-eagled, and I waited for him to regain his breath. Then I began to kick him in his nether regions; I wanted to increase his pain. I watched him with pleasure as he curled up on the floor, groaning his agony. I had to curb myself from killing him. So I picked up the bottle and poured the remains of the wine into his split lip, and with a final and vicious kick in his groin I took my leave.

The family were waiting outside the house. They said nothing though they must have guessed what had kept me. I had booked three nights in our hotel, and it struck me that my parents had already had enough. They wanted to go home. They wanted to be safe. The fear that had tailed their daily Parisian lives seemed to have returned. But they were mindful of their grandchildren who still regarded the venture as a holiday treat. So for the rest of our stay, we became tourists. We viewed the sights, we visited the museums, we took a trip on the Seine. My parents maintained their silence throughout, but now it was tinged with sadness. I began to regret that I had ever suggested a *recherche*. I thought it might have been an exercise in catharsis, a coming-to-terms with their past. Instead it had been a defilement.

It was not until we were settled on the Dover ferry that they relaxed and assumed their former cheer. But we did not talk about our visit, and until their deaths they never referred to it. But there was no doubt that the visit had affected them profoundly. Gradually they reinforced the deception that had

clothed their lives since their childhoods. They went regularly
to church. My mother joined the flower-arrangement group
attached to the Cathedral and I am sure that they pronounced
'Jesus' above a whisper but equally sure that the word stuck in
their throats.

Since that time I have been often to Paris, but I have avoided
the Rue du Bac. Instead, I hang around the Jewish quarter, and
begin to feel at home.

After that summer I returned to school with new vigour. Our
A level results had placed our school at the very top of the
league tables; in second place was that prestigious seat of learning where my ambitions lay. I had a full timetable. I was in
much demand as a public speaker at educational conferences all
over England. And I was invited to America to propagate the
values of our English system. I had come a long way from my
parents' little village school, but in essence I had not moved one
step distant from my French legacy. And then, one year later,
I was awarded honourable recognition.

I remember the day well. It was a Saturday, a day always
reserved for my children and their entertainment. When the
letter-box rattled with the post, Peter rushed to collect it. He
was expecting his comic. He handed me a sheaf of envelopes,
and I shuffled through them. There seemed little of interest
except for one envelope which was clearly of a finer quality than
the rest. It felt like linen. I turned it over and my heart stumbled. It was from the Palace. Lucy was in the kitchen, preparing
omelettes, and I was glad that I could open it in private. As I
read its contents, my hands trembled, and my face must have
flushed for Peter said, 'Are you all right, Papa?'

'Of course,' I said. 'I'm hungry, that's all.'

I waited for Lucy to return and for the serving to be done.
And then I said, 'Did you sleep well, Lady Lucy?'

I heard the title and relished its noble ring. I had not yet
tried it on myself. Lucy looked at me with a worried smile. I am

not given to small talk or tease and my question was entirely out of character.

'Are you all right?' she asked.

'More than all right,' I said. 'Sir Alfred Dreyfus is very all right, thank you.' Then before she could suspect that my mind had turned, I handed her the letter. She glowed as she read it. 'For services to education,' she said aloud and then repeated it with pride. She actually rose from the table to embrace me. My wife is not a demonstrative woman and this was a rare gesture. She handed the letter to the children, and they too, like Lucy, of natural reserve, embraced me. We were to keep it a secret it seemed, until my acceptance was accepted and it was officially announced. But I could not keep the news from my parents. Or from Matthew.

'Let's drive down and tell Grandma and Grandpa,' Peter said.

'And can Uncle Matthew come too?' said Jean. 'And Aunt Susan and Adam and Zak?'

'We'll take champagne,' I said, 'and surprise them.'

So it was that we spent that Saturday in my childhood village. And the celebrations were secret and intense. The children kept practising our new titles and were happy to be sworn into the common secrecy. But we made plans for the investiture and the party that would follow.

Oh the words for happiness are so readily available, and as I write of this event, I wonder where I will find the alphabet for my fall. But for the while I must stay in the happy arena. My banishment will come soon enough.

Lucy and the children accompanied me to the Palace. At the time, Matthew and Susan lived in a grand mansion flat overlooking Hyde Park, and I had arranged a small luncheon there for family and close friends. And they had gathered there, toasting my honour, while I knelt before the Queen. I was not worried about the kneeling – heaven knows, I had had enough illicit practice – but this genuflection had nothing to do with Jesus even though my benefactress was head of the established Church. It was all over in a few moments. The excitement and intoxicated anticipation of the plain Mr Dreyfus waned with the rising of Sir Alfred. Somehow it was all an anticlimax. The journey had been more dramatic than its arrival.

We posed for photographs in the Palace yard, Lucy, the children and I. At the time I did not know how famous that photograph would become, and how often it would be used in newspapers all over the world. In it, my face bears a bewildered look which turned out to be apt and fitting for the odious and vicious captions that would underline it. They would not even single me out. They would use the original grouping, including Lucy and the children, so that they might be contaminated with my infamy. But I must not think of that. All that belongs to the future, which requires an altogether different grammar.

They were waiting for us at Matthew's flat, our friends and family. I had invited some of my colleagues from school and a handful of my old-time friends from the village. We were a mixed group but all were united in doing me proud. As I sit here, in my cell, I often recall that gathering. It is a welcome light in the darkness of my surroundings. I dwell on it and wonder how it could ever have been real, or whether I had dreamt it, and it is a momentary but false relief in my continuing nightmare.

The following day I returned to school to much teasing, bowing and tugging of forelocks from the staff. Even some of the boys risked it, but I let it lie, knowing that the novelty would soon fade. I concentrated on my work and the preparation of speeches for a lecture tour of training-colleges. I was even called in to speak to the Minister of Education to appraise him of the differences between state and private schooling. The knighthood helped of course, and through it I made many useful contacts. One of them even suggested I stand for

Parliament. But politics was not my ambition. I still nurtured the hope of ruling the best school in the land.

But it was to be almost five years before that opportunity arose. By then, I was forty-five years old and a knight of the realm, with an established reputation in an academic field. I considered myself highly qualified. The headmaster of that great school was about to retire and I decided to wait until the vacancy was advertised. But they came to me. In other words, I was approached. And faintly overwhelmed. I was invited to the school to dine at High Table.

About twenty of us were seated, most of them members of staff. I sat next to the reigning headmaster, with the head of music on my other side. We adjourned to the great library for coffee and I mingled with those with whom I'd had no opportunity to converse at table. The headmaster led me across the room to meet Smith of geography.

'You've got something in common,' he said. 'You're both village boys.'

'I grew up in a village in Kent,' I said.

'Mine was in Yorkshire,' Smith offered. 'My father was the curate in the village church.'

Smith was amiable enough and I wondered why I suddenly felt cornered. I suppose that the words 'church' and 'curate' were reminders of those origins that I was disposed to conceal. I decided to play along with him.

'We had a beautiful church,' I said. 'My parents were married there, and I was baptised by the same vicar who married them.'

I needn't have given them all that information. I wasn't exactly telling them I was a Christian. But I was giving them enough reason to believe that I was nothing else. I was shamefully satisfied.

It was a pleasant evening and not for one moment did I sense that I was being interviewed. I had the impression that the job

of headmaster was mine for the taking. And indeed, within the
week an official letter arrived offering me the post.

When I think of it now, it was an eccentric appointment. It
is true I was English-born, but I wore no trimmings of the
church, to which the school was closely linked. On the other
hand, I bore no obvious signs of my true origins, and if they
had guessed at them, they must have chosen to pay them no
attention. Or they may well have been seduced by my title and
reputation. Whatever their reasons, my appointment was cause
for yet another family gathering and celebration.

I sense that my readers might well be fed up with all this
success and happiness, and in their irritation are entitled to
asked, 'For God's sake, who gets cancer? And when?'

The answer is my father. And the time is now.

I was due to take up my new posting in September at the
beginning of the school year. I was still seeing out my last term
at Hammersmith and we were wholly occupied with examina-
tions. I was at work in my study when a call came in from
Lucy. I knew it must be urgent for she rarely rang me at the
school. I feared for the welfare of my children. I took the call
immediately. My mother had phoned from Kent. 'Papa is desperately ill,' she said. I feared to ask the nature of the illness and
I hoped that Lucy would not inform me. But her silence told
me that, whatever the diagnosis, it was fatal.

'Does Matthew know?' I asked.

'Yes. He's going down after work. He wants to know if you
want a lift.'

'Tell him to pick me up,' I said. I wanted the call to end. I
was afraid that Lucy might elaborate. And for the same reason,
I refrained from calling Matthew. And again, for the same
reason, our journey back to the village was a silent one.

My mother had heard the car and she was on the doorstep to
greet us. She walked down the rose-throttled pathway, and
waited. I studied her face for clues. But I saw only her usual

smile of welcome. And then, as we reached her, my father surprisingly appeared on the doorstep. He looked pale it is true, but I so firmly expected him in a bed and moribund that I was overjoyed at his presence. My mother stretched out her arms to hold us, an unfamiliar gesture, and I was afraid.

'It's bad news,' she said. 'Papa has cancer.'

I looked at my father, and on his face was a look of deep shame. As if he had sinned mightily and was asking for forgiveness.

'Let's go inside,' Matthew said.

Silently we all stepped into the kitchen. My mother had prepared the table for supper and we sat around it wordlessly. I held my father's hand. I had expected it cold, but he squeezed my fingers with its warmth. My mother set about serving. She had clearly spent time with its preparation, and the dishes were complex and delicate. It was as if we were once again celebrating. I noticed that my father ate slowly and with little appetite, but he relished the wine, raising his glass to drink to our health, a toast which broke my heart. We were silent throughout and it was not until the dessert was served that the silence was broken.

'I have three months,' my father said.

I thought, in three months he could travel the world. In three months he could write a book. In three months he could compose a symphony. He could plant a tree and see it bud. Three months was all one needed for a lifetime.

'Is there no treatment?' Matthew dared to ask.

'It's the pancreas,' my mother said. 'It's inoperable.'

'But there must be *something*.' Matthew was almost weeping.

'There's chemotherapy,' my father said. 'It's a horrendous treatment, and even if it works it would give me only a little more time. And that time would have no quality. I've decided against it,' he said.

'But you must try it,' Matthew pleaded. 'Please Papa.' He spoke like a child begging a favour. Even his voice had rebroken.

'It's Papa's decision,' my mother said.

My father took Matthew's hand. 'Don't worry,' he said. 'They will look after me. They have promised I shall feel no pain. I am prepared. And I shall go gently.'

I felt my anger rising. His going, gently or not, was simply not allowed. But I knew too, that only he could make the choice. That was his inalienable right.

'You must come back with us to London,' Matthew said. 'You must stay with us. We'll all look after you.'

'I want to die at home,' my father said.

He used the word with no hesitation. 'Die' was the very last word I was prepared to use. He could have cancer, an inoperable one, an untreatable one, but he didn't have to die. Dying was in another department altogether. My father was setting the pace and I didn't want to follow him. But his decision had been made and was unarguable.

'Let's say no more about it,' my father said.

'What about you, Mama?' I asked. 'How will you manage?'

'The nurses will come daily,' she said. 'And at night. Whenever I want them. We'll manage,' she said helplessly. 'I just hope you will come as often as you can.'

'I'll stay here,' I said. 'I'll commute daily.'

'So will I,' Matthew said.

My father laughed weakly. 'It will be like old times,' he said.

And so we commuted, Matthew and I, silently, twice daily by train. We said little to each other on those journeys. We both held our tongues on that shared sorrow, and close as we had always been to each other, our bondage was now indissoluble.

During the weeks that followed, Lucy and Susan and our children came down to the cottage for the weekends, and we all sat with our father and shared tales of the past. In time, he took to his bed. The daily paper lay unread at his side, and his favourite music was unheard. During his last weeks, my term came to an end, and all day I lay beside him and held his hand.

One day I noticed that the dressing-table had been moved so that my father could not glance in the mirror that faced his bed. He appeared not to notice the change. At least he made no comment on it. And no one mentioned how his colour had turned yellow. Occasionally he spoke, but most of the time he stared vacantly, as if in deep thought. And from time to time he would turn towards me and smile. But what was most disturbing was the frequency with which he looked at his watch as if to check on how much time was left of the three months that had been promised him.

It was a Saturday and the summer days were shortening. Time crawled relentlessly, but for my father it sprinted towards his deadline. On that day, he struggled to sit upright. I lifted him against the pillows and I was appalled at his feather-like weight. He looked at his watch once more, stared for a while, and then he began to speak. His voice sounded disembodied, as if it were coming from another place and another time. Which indeed it was.

'It was Émile,' he said. 'Little Émile. He caught her with the milk.' Then he looked at his watch again and smiled.

I called everybody to his bedside and we all held on to his hands. Tightly, as if by holding him, he would not leave us. We watched as his lips began to move.

'*Shema Yisrael*,' he muttered. That was all. Then he was gone. And we sat there and looked at him. Unbelieving.

I heard the beat of my heart, which threatened to burst. It was my father's farewell that was breaking me. All his life he had refused to recall the Rue du Bac. All his life he had turned his back on the 'why' of his exile. And with his last words, he had acknowledged both.

But despite his prayer, a prayer that echoed with millions of other *Shemas* through the ovens, despite his final avowal, he was buried in the village churchyard by that same now-ageing vicar who had married him with my mother. It had been his wish to be buried there, as a final instalment of a life of deception. And as I stood by the grave and threw in my handful of earth, I recited the *Shema* in full, that prayer, never knowingly learnt, but implanted at birth in every Jewish heart. Despite the church burial, despite the vicar and despite the Jesus funeral, despite that lifelong deception, I sat on a low stool for seven days, and mourned my father.

We begged our mother to come and stay with us in London. But she refused. She would not leave my father's graveside. So we stayed with her, Matthew and I, and daily we viewed her withdrawal. She refused food, sleeping most of the time, and on the exact spot where he had left her, willing herself to join him. She prayed constantly. I don't know to whom nor in what language. It took her three weeks of ceaseless pleading to receive an answer and one morning, Matthew and I found her at peace at last. She had died of nothing else but death.

We buried her next to my father, as an acknowledgement of that lie she had lived, and that small plot of land gave the Dreyfus family a territorial right on the country of their exile.

We were orphaned now, Matthew and I, and we began to smell our own mortality. But we were not the last of the Dreyfus line. That as yet unsullied name would continue, and we found solace in our children.

I am tired now. Grief-exhausted. That recall has shaken me. My supper tray lies untouched on my table, but I have no appetite. Tomorrow perhaps I shall begin to write of my new school and take some compensating pleasure in my longed-for promotion. I shall be Sir Alfred once again, and the head of the finest school in England.

11

Sam Temple spent much of his time dodging calls from Bernard Wallworthy. But he recognised that the publisher was entitled to some information, if not proof of the progress of Dreyfus's confession, so he picked up the phone and dialled the number.

Wallworthy was cool. He resented Temple's avoidance. It fed his ever-lurking anti-Semitism. Sometimes he regretted ever having involved himself with that lot. They were always trouble. But he was mindful too of the vast profits entailed in the deal. 'I have phoned you a number of times Mr Temple,' he said. 'It would be a matter of common courtesy to return my calls.' What did Temple's kind know of common courtesy, Wallworthy thought. It was a waste of good words on them.

'I'm very sorry,' Sam Temple lied, 'but I was waiting to hear from the governor of the prison. I'm hoping to visit Mr Dreyfus this week. And then hopefully I shall have some news for you.'

'I don't want news,' Wallworthy said sharply, 'I want words.'

'I must first ascertain that he is willing to show them to you,' Sam said firmly, and added that there was nothing in the contract that obliged his client to show work in progress.

'Look here, Temple,' Wallworthy spluttered, 'I've a great amount of money riding on this deal. Dreyfus is a novice writer, if a writer at all. It would be a simple act of common courtesy' – again words wasted on the two of them – 'to show me a sample of what he has done.'

'I'll try and persuade him,' Sam said. 'But I wouldn't hold your breath.'

Sam put down the phone. He wasn't sure that Dreyfus could be persuaded and his client was Dreyfus, not Bernard Wallworthy. He rang the governor, who reported that Dreyfus had been ill. He had no appetite and spent most of his time sleeping or pacing his cell. The doctor could find nothing physically wrong with him. He had diagnosed, unsurprisingly, a state of depression and prescribed some pills. 'A visit would do him good, I think,' the governor suggested.

'I'll be along this afternoon,' Sam said.

But first he had to see Lucy. News from Lucy, though indirect, would help lift Dreyfus's spirits. She had written to Temple with her new address and had requested a visit. He rang her new number and arranged to call on her that morning. Lucy and the children had moved a good distance from their old tenancy to a flat south of the river and when Sam entered he was happy to notice that it was very different from their former home. It was more spacious and certainly more finely appointed. He noted too some significant additions. There was a *mezzuzah* on the front door of the apartment and on other doors too, and on the sideboard in the dining-room was a silver *menorah*, the candelabra for the festival of Chanukah. Mrs Dreyfus was laying her tardy cards on the table.

The children were doing their homework in the study, so

they would not be disturbed. Lucy led him into the kitchen, where Sam set out the cups for coffee.

'Matthew is living here,' she said, as they sat down. 'Unofficially, of course. He visits his boys most days but he found it impossible to stay with Susan. And though I'm very sad about what happened, I'm glad he is with us.'

Sam Temple was glad too. He couldn't tell Dreyfus, of course, but he could at least report that his brother was well.

'I'm seeing your husband this afternoon,' Sam said. 'What news can I bring him?'

'There is no bad news,' she said. 'I think we have managed to keep quiet about our move and I've seen no reporters for some time. Tell him too that the children are doing well with their tutor. Jean has made drawings for her father. You could even take them to him for her.'

'They will lift his spirits, I'm sure,' Sam said.

'Would you like to look at the apartment?' she asked, 'so that you can tell Alfred about it?' She led him into the dining-room.

'That's a lovely *menorah*,' Sam said. 'Is it new?'

'My parents gave it to me,' she said, 'when Alfred and I were married. I've never put it out before. Same with the *mezzuzah*. I decided to put them where they rightfully belonged. I think it was because Susan denied us.'

Another piece of news, Sam thought, that he couldn't carry to Dreyfus. But he could tell him about them without divulging the reason for their sudden exposure.

'I gather that the Home Secretary is looking at the trial papers,' he said.

'We must not hope for too much. When there is a petition for an appeal, it's a formality to look again at the papers. Or at least make a show of perusing them. But it *is* something. I just pray that Alfred is not setting his hopes too high. Matthew is optimistic but he never despairs. He's a wonderful support. He won't let us lose hope.'

'Is your husband kept informed?' Sam asked.

'The governor of the prison is informed. He decides what to pass on to Alfred.'

'Then I shall say nothing,' Sam said.

Lucy rose from the table. 'I'll get the children,' she said.

Sam poured himself some more coffee. He was happy to feel at home in this place. He felt that whatever he reported to Alfred regarding his family, would carry a certain authenticity.

The children rushed into the kitchen. Jean laid a large sheet of paper on the table. A crayoned drawing depicted three monkeys in a cage. 'That proves we went to the zoo,' she said, 'and Papa can hang it on his wall.'

'In his cage,' Peter added. But he said it without a smile.

'Let me look at you both,' Sam said. 'Really look at you, so that I can give your father a true picture.'

They stood side by side, stiffly, as if facing a lens.

'You've both grown since the zoo,' Sam said.

'I've lost another tooth,' Jean said. 'Tell him he owes me five pence. And give him a kiss from me,' she whispered.

But Peter did not send a kiss. He was like his father, his upper lip stiff to dam his tears.

'There's a fair at Battersea Park,' Sam said. 'Shall we go to that?'

'Yes. Please, please,' Jean said.

'Then I'll come early and we can all paint our faces for the parade. Your mother and Uncle Matthew too.' It would be a wonderful opportunity to disguise themselves, Sam thought, with no fear of the shadow of reporters.

'Can Tim come?' Peter asked.

'Who's Tim?'

'My friend.'

Sam looked at Lucy who was smiling. Peter had a friend at last. It was the best news he could take to his father.

'Of course,' Sam said. 'We'll paint his face too.'

Sam felt heartened as he made his way towards the prison. He had news, the simple domestic kind that would raise his friend's spirits. But when he saw him he wondered whether domestic news and two drawings from his children would revive him. Sam was appalled at his loss of weight. He noticed an untouched lunch tray on the table and he was surprised at the sudden sadness that overcame him.

'Alfred,' he said, daring to embrace him, 'you mustn't give in. You simply mustn't. We must hope for an appeal. And proof of your innocence. It will come. I know. You just . . . must,' he stammered, 'for your own sake, for Lucy and the children. For Matthew.' Then he paused. 'And for me,' he added. In that moment Dreyfus ceased to be his client. He needed him as a friend.

They moved towards the cot. Sam settled Alfred down, propping the pillow behind his head. Then he dragged over the chair and sat beside him. 'I've brought these from Peter and Jean,' he said. 'They want you to put them on your wall.'

A hint of a smile crossed Dreyfus's face, a smile deeply out of practice. Sam passed him Jean's drawing.

Dreyfus studied it for a while. 'How are they looking?' he asked. What small smile there was had now completely disappeared.

'Very well. I've just seen them.' Sam was about to say that they were growing up fast. But he held his tongue on that information, for it would have underlined the sadness of their father's absence.

'They're growing up without me,' Dreyfus said.

There was nothing Sam could say to contradict him. 'They miss you as much as you them,' he said. 'They have a lovely new apartment,' he went on quickly, and proceeded to describe the layout of the home he had just left. But Dreyfus seemed not to react. He kept staring at his children's pictures. After Sam's tour of the apartment, Dreyfus placed the pictures side by side on the cot.

'I've been writing about my parents,' he said. 'About how they died.' He looked up at Sam for the first time. 'I find it has shaken me,' he said.

Again Sam was at a loss for words, but he understood now the cause of his friend's depression.

'That's natural,' he said. 'I lost my parents some years ago. You think that time has healed, and then you relive it once more and it's like it happened yesterday. Then we start mourning all over again. Your cot is the equivalent of a low stool.'

Dreyfus smiled, grateful for mutual recognition.

'It will pass,' Sam went on. 'Time does heal but we have to give time, time. That's the rub. Some of us need to hang on to our sorrow. Make a cult of it almost.'

'It's tempting to do exactly that in my present circumstances.'

'But it can be dangerous,' Sam said. 'It can lead to lethargy and despair. They're working for you on the outside, Alfred. Matthew is so optimistic.'

'Dear Matthew,' Dreyfus said.

Sam allowed a silence before enquiring as to the progress of the book.

'It was going well until my parents died,' Dreyfus said. 'Then it seemed as if there was nothing more to say. By writing about my fall I felt that they would somehow hear of it. Not only do I not want to write about it, I don't want to think about it either.' He looked Sam squarely in the face. 'Perhaps I'd better give the money back,' he suggested.

Sam laughed. But nervously. Dreyfus's sudden reticence was no surprise. But it had to be overcome. 'You owe this book to Lucy and the children. To Matthew and his family. Above all Alfred, you owe it to your parents. To them above all. Dreyfus is their name as well.'

That reminder seemed to unlock him. 'I'll try to start again tomorrow,' he said.

Sam reached for the lunch tray and put it before him on the cot. 'Try and eat a little,' he said. He reached for his briefcase and brought out a small flask of whisky. He handed it to Dreyfus. 'Medicinal,' he said.

Dreyfus smiled and took a tentative sip. Then he picked up his spoon and sampled the cold food.

'You'll be pleased to hear Peter's got a friend,' Sam said. His name's Tim. I'm taking them all to the Battersea funfair.'

'Why are you so good to us?' Dreyfus asked.

'I've already told you. I believe you're innocent.' He watched as Dreyfus picked at the food. He ate very slowly, but in time he managed to clear the plate.

'I'm glad you came,' he said.

Sam took the tray and put it back on the table.

'Do you hear from Mr Wallworthy?' Dreyfus asked.

Sam laughed. 'Every day. He wants to see what you've written.'

'What d'you think?' Dreyfus asked.

'It's up to you. Personally I would show him a little something. Just to convince him that you can write. Then I think he'll be satisfied. He won't ask for more. He's not much of a reader anyway. He's just a publisher.'

'I'll give you what I've done,' Dreyfus said, 'and I'll leave it to you.'

Sam did not expect such an easy ride and he was grateful. He was anxious to get Wallworthy off his back.

Dreyfus went to the desk and gathered up a sheaf of papers, and handed them over.

'I'll copy them as before,' Sam said, 'and return them to you.'

'I'd like you to go now,' Dreyfus said suddenly. 'I feel like writing.'

'Then you must promise me to eat,' Sam said. 'Not even Tolstoy could write on an empty stomach.'

They shook hands.

'I'm glad you came,' Dreyfus said again. 'You *connect* me.'

Back in his office, Sam copied the manuscript then settled down to read. He was more than pleased with what his friend had written and he thought that Wallworthy would be satisfied too, so he selected a piece and sent it over to the publisher. He knew that Wallworthy would read it right away and telephone before the day was done. Which he did. And Sam answered immediately.

'Well, what do you think?' he asked.

'Well he can certainly write,' Wallworthy said, 'but don't you think it's a bit too . . . er . . . er . . .'

'Er what, Mr Wallworthy?' Sam asked, though he guessed what the hesitation was about.

'Er . . . well, you know, a little bit . . . er . . . too *Jewish*.'

Sam allowed a pause. Then very firmly, and with little respect, he said, 'Mr Wallworthy, I don't know whether you are aware of it, though it has been headlined in every newspaper all over the world, but Alfred Dreyfus is indeed a Jew. He was tried as a Jew, he was found guilty as a Jew, and he was sentenced as a Jew. And as a Jew he is in prison writing his side of the story. Did you expect it, Mr Wallworthy, to be a little bit . . . er . . . Muslim?'

'Very funny, Mr Temple,' Wallworthy said. 'Although they are known as the People of the Book, they are not great buyers of our products.'

'Are there statistics to prove that?' Sam asked.

'Well, everybody says so,' Wallworthy answered weakly.

When one's argument is weak, one recruits, Sam thought. 'Who is everybody?' he persisted.

'You know as well as I,' Wallworthy said without saying anything.

Sam let it rest.

'But you're pleased with it?' he said. 'You're satisfied now with your investment?'

'Yes,' Wallworthy said. 'I'm pleased with it.' And, after a pause, 'And you can tell him so.'

'He'll be delighted,' Sam said, sure of Dreyfus's pleasure because, for a writer, praise from any quarter was a bonus indeed. He wrote straightaway to Dreyfus enclosing the original manuscript and expressing his own and Mr Wallworthy's praise. He hoped that it would be encouragement enough. But he was nervous about how his friend would progress. The recall of his parents' deaths had been burdensome enough. Sooner or later he would have to recount the story of his fall from grace and Sam wondered if he was strong enough to withstand its telling.

PART TWO

Part Two

12

And now begins my fall.

The collapse itself was sudden, terrifyingly so, but its overture was slow, leisurely even, and cunningly polite. This is in hindsight, for I was not aware of it at the time. I have to state here and now that I know myself pretty well. I am both timid and arrogant, simply flip-sides of the same coin. I need acknowledgement – don't we all? – and at times I feel grossly inadequate, though I am at pains to conceal it. I am all of these things, but I am not paranoid. Yet the moment I set foot in my new school, the establishment that was the symbol of my great ambition, I sensed a ripple of hostility. I could not pinpoint it, but I knew for certain that it was there. And it took me almost a whole term to discover its source.

There was a headmaster's house in the school grounds and this is where we lived, Lucy and I and the children. The children were enrolled at local schools. Lucy was obliged to no specific duties but, as headmaster's wife, she was expected to entertain visitors and the occasional foreign academic studying the methods of English education.

Our house was Elizabethan and its character had been strictly maintained. The modern bathrooms, kitchen, and central heating were inconspicuously installed. We moved into our new quarters shortly before the beginning of the Christmas term. Matthew and Susan came down one weekend. It was a happy time for all of us. I recall that time with joy and blind myself to those as yet unseen shadows that would becloud my future and the lives of my family. But those shadows are now known, and have been ever since my fall, and it is hard to dwell in the joy that was, without sensing that lurking darkness.

But there were no shadows when my first term began, and I looked forward to a reign of benign control until my legitimate retirement.

The term began on a Wednesday, and I decided to hold a cocktail party the evening before our start. The day saw the staggered arrival of staff and pupils. I kept myself indoors during that time, as I did not want to be seen to favour any arrival. From my curtained window, I viewed the cars as they Rolls-Royced up the driveway. On the whole they were impressive. There were many uniformed chauffeurs, and it was a relief to spot a battered Deux Cheveaux as it screeched to an arrogant stop in their midst. In that sea of wheeled wealth, that filthy jalopy was a refreshing eyesore. I was not surprised to see Fenby, the music master, unfold his equally battered self from out of its chassis, and drag an equally battered rucksack after him. He viewed the building he had not seen for a while and seemed to find it good, for he smiled with approval. A few boys greeted him. One of them offered to carry his rucksack, an offer which Fenby refused, but he ruffled the boy's hair, acknowledging his courtesy.

Lucy was nervous and so, frankly, was I. We were not

practised hosts. Our occasional get-togethers were for family and close friends. And we had never given a cocktail party. But we had been invited to many, so we knew the form.

Lucy had excelled herself. The dining-table groaned with canapés catering to all tastes. I had decided against champagne, fearing it would be too ostentatious. Instead red and white wines were at the ready. Lucy had refused help from outside and insisted that I pour the wines and she herself would offer the savouries. Our guests were due at 6.30. It was only six o'clock and Lucy was pacing the room in some agitation. I insisted she take a glass of wine to calm herself and I joined her for I was none too composed myself. We toasted each other and she wished me luck. And then she said a very strange thing. Strange because it was so uncharacteristic.

'Somehow,' she said, 'I feel – I feel very alien.'

I laughed it off though she had exactly defined my own feelings. She did not elaborate and I was grateful for that and we both sat together in silence waiting for our guests to arrive.

They were early and came almost in a bunch, and by 6.30 all were present. They were a jolly lot, warm, gossipy and friendly and they welcomed me, teasingly wishing me well. I remembered many of their faces from that High Table gathering that had passed for my audition. But I had to reacquaint myself with their names and the subjects to which those names were attached. Fenby of the battered Deux Cheveaux, was memorably music, Smith, I recalled, was geography and Turner one of the sciences. I did the rounds together with Lucy and we introduced ourselves to everybody. Between us, after the party, we could perhaps summon up an authentic roll-call. I noticed that Eccles, head of the history department, was standing apart from the others. He seemed to be viewing the scene with some disdain. In my generosity, I ascribed his aloofness to shyness, though as I came to know him over the weeks, it was indeed disdain that he felt, nurtured by his sense of superiority. But at the party I singled him out for conversation, hoping to melt his shyness. He was polite but unforthcoming. I told him I looked forward to dropping in on one of his lessons, as I intended to do in all departments. His look was one of horror.

'I know it has not been the practice hitherto,' I said, 'but I wish for more contact with the academic aspects of the school. I have no intention of restricting myself to administration.'

I sensed his hostility as I sensed my own annoyance, so I moved away and left him with his disdain. I heard later from Fenby, who became a close friend, that Mark Eccles had fully expected to be appointed headmaster, which explained his hostility towards his usurper. 'He'll have to learn to live with it,' Fenby had said. I asked if he was popular with the boys. 'On the whole, yes,' Fenby had told me. 'He has a cluster of fans, sort of groupies. About a dozen of them. They take tea in his rooms. They seem to adore him. But I wouldn't worry about that,' Fenby had said. 'I do the same, though I don't have so many fans. The odd music student sometimes comes and we play sonatas or something. Nothing sinister,' he laughed. 'I'm afraid, Sir Alfred, you'll find this school virtuous to the point of boredom.'

Dear old Fenby. How mistaken he was. But he has remained a friend. One of a few. He doesn't visit, but he writes to me from time to time. He keeps me up to date with the operas and orchestral concerts he's attended, but he never mentions the school. He knows it would be too painful a reminder.

But I digress again. I must return to the party and the halcyon days. Lucy was in animated conversation with the biology man whose name I had already forgotten. So I did the rounds alone, topping up glasses on my way. Everyone seemed to be very much at home. After all, they knew the house far better than I. My predecessor had often hosted cocktail parties, and for a while I felt a stranger myself, as if I too were a guest. On my rounds I eavesdropped on the telling of holiday adventures.

In one circuit I travelled from Barbados to Cape Town to Paris and Naples, and finally settled in a small Cotswold hamlet where Dr Reynolds, the deputy head, had a cottage. And there I paused, topping Brown's glass and listening to his angling stories of the fish that got away.

When the first guest made to leave, I looked at my watch. It was just nine o'clock. I reckoned the gathering had been a success. The rest of the guests followed soon after, and as Lucy and I cleared the decks, we itemised them all by name and subject. The following morning, at the start of term, I was familiar with the handles of all its staff.

As I was finishing breakfast, Dr Reynolds knocked at the door. I was not as yet familiar with the layout of the building. I knew where my study was but I was uncertain of how to get there. Nor to the assembly room, where I was due at nine o'clock to welcome the boys, old and new, and to familiarise myself with the school song. I was nervous. I kept telling myself that I had years of assembly experience, and countless hours of public speaking, and endless confrontations of man and boy. And moreover a title to give me confidence. Yet I trembled. I was led through corridors and massive halls reeking of history, a history that was by no means mine. I passed the bronzes of saints and the portraits of ancient school founders and I felt, as Lucy had suggested, alien, and I thought of my grandparents with a certain shame. And because of all this, I trembled.

Is it in hindsight that I trembled? Or did I in fact shiver my steps down those corridors riddled with a tradition of which I was but a spectator? I cannot be sure. The Dreyfus of now, shorn of his title, is very different from the Sir Alfred of those days. My incarceration has paradoxically been a release of sorts, delivering me from a tangle of lies I have lived by, those lies of omission when I chose to ignore heritage. For those roots were a nuisance, an impediment to my progress. How futile I now see that evasion to have been. But whether in hindsight or reality, I trembled.

Dr Reynolds was leading the way and I was grateful that he gave me no potted biographies of the men who had preceded me in office, those whose portraits hung on the panelled walls. He left me in my office, promising to return just before nine o'clock to escort me to the main hall. I was glad to be alone for a while. I dialled the extension number to my house. I needed to speak to Lucy. I had nothing specific to say to her. I simply wanted to hear her voice. Simply to anchor myself to a reality that I was familiar with, in contrast to the terra incognita in which I found myself. She told me that she had discovered a secret drawer in an in-built wardrobe. It was a matter of sublime irrelevance, but she chose it deliberately to offset what she knew was my stage-fright.

'I'll see you at lunch,' I said.

Then she whispered, 'I know you'll be fine, Alfred.'

I looked at my watch. It was almost nine o'clock. Dr Reynolds knocked and called from outside the door. 'Are you ready, Sir Alfred?'

I was grateful to hear my title. It always boosted my confidence, and I strode to the door and walked by his side towards the assembly hall.

I entered from the back. I reckoned that there were about six hundred boys present, and not one head turned to view me. A few steps led on to the raised dais. There was a table on the platform and a lectern to its side. Behind it, the chaplain of the school was already in place. I stood behind the table with Dr Reynolds at my side.

The chaplain took as his text a verse from Isaiah. 'They shall beat their swords into ploughshares, and their spears into pruning-hooks.' I had expected some New Testament source, considering the Church roots of the school, and I wondered whether the chaplain was nodding to me personally in this respect and whether I had so soon been rumbled. But I did not allow it to trouble me. He spoke about the current turmoil in the world and the need to seek peace. His was a pretty homily, short and sweet. Then it was my turn. I rose to a thundering silence of expectation. I introduced myself without reference to my roots, but with a run-down on my past teaching experience. I offered the occasional witticism but I did not overdo it, for authority must affirm its place; I have in my time been confronted with a matey parson and I found it inconvenient and embarrassing. I spoke for about ten minutes, and as I sat down I noted Mr Fenby making his way towards the piano. It was hymn-time, Bunyan's 'To be a Pilgrim', a relief since Jesus played no part in it. And I joined in the singing with gusto. Then the boys sat down to listen to sundry announcements from Dr Reynolds and stood once again for the school song. Mr Fenby had rehearsed this with me the evening before and I belted it out like any old-timer. After that assembly I felt I had acquitted myself reasonably well and I was glad when Dr Reynolds shook me warmly by the hand. I returned to my office and refrained from phoning Lucy. I would see her at lunch, my next Waterloo.

I spent the morning familiarising myself with the school's routine and dealing with papers that needed my attention. Dr Reynolds called me at eleven o'clock for the morning break, and he escorted me to the senior staff room for coffee. He told me that my presence was not obligatory and that the last head had taken coffee in his room. But I expressed my wish to join members of the staff, at least on the first day.

As I entered the room, a silence fell. I felt that I had to apologise for my presence and to assure the staff that I would not make a habit of it but since it was my first day, I wished to acquaint myself with the daily routine. They welcomed me, and brought my coffee, and we settled down in the armchairs around the blazing fire.

The talk was of a story in *The Times* that morning. There had been a motion in Parliament to make Holocaust denial an illegal offence. Again, like the quotation from Isaiah, I felt that the subject was related to my appointment but I fought off such a coincidence for it threatened paranoia. Mr Fenby pronounced himself against such a move. Vicious though such denial was, its proscription threatened freedom of speech. Smith from geography agreed with him. Brown from chemistry was in favour of the motion, and cited the books of one so-called historian, a crusader of Holocaust denial, suggesting that they should be burned. Though I silently agreed with him, the notion of book-burning smacked sourly of an earlier time, and one in my own childhood.

It was then that Eccles offered his opinion. 'I think denial is a monstrosity,' he said. 'After all the evidence. After all the proof. Good God, six million. Horrendous.'

I was watching him as he spoke, though he was unaware of my gaze. As he announced the numbers I could have sworn he winked. Yes, winked. My heart turned over. I was so aghast at the wink itself that I could not finger its recipient. It could have been any one of them.

I finished my coffee and returned to my study. My stomach heaved. I wanted very much to be sick. Now that I think about it, that scurrilous wink signalled the very beginning of my fall. But, at the time, what upset me most of all was that the man taught history, and was indeed head of the department. I wanted to call him into my office but I had no grounds for accusation. I could confront him with the wink, but he might well ascribe it to a nervous tic, and then I would look a fool and word of paranoia would spread. I knew I could do nothing except keep a stern eye on him. I resolved that his twentieth-century history class would be the first that I would attend. But I would wait a while, and monitor his every phrase.

We were due to go down en famille to the cottage that weekend, all eight of us. After our parents' deaths, we had kept the cottage on by way of retaining links with our childhoods. Besides, there were their graves to visit and to tend. On my visits to the churchyard, I would whisper the news of the families. But I wouldn't tell them about Eccles. They might turn under the Jesus that protected them.

I resumed my paperwork to take my mind off the matter, but I couldn't get his wink out of my eye. And to this day, in my nightmares, it mocks me.

As I was studying the curricula, I heard the church bell toll. And again Dr Reynolds was at my door. Though I had no appetite, I looked forward to seeing Lucy who, by tradition, was required to lunch at the headmaster's table. I opened the door and found Lucy at Dr Reynolds's side. He had made it his business, on this first day, to call for her. We went together to the dining-room. More oak-panelled walls, more portraits. And something new. A roll of honour that stretched back to the Crimean War, the years when my forebears were fleeing Odessa. I took Lucy's hand and she squeezed it, but we disjoined as we entered the dining-hall. The boys were already assembled, and at our entry they rose en masse, and not until we were seated did they resume their seats.

The High Table was on a raised platform, and around it sat some heads of departments, some housemasters and the head boy. Our place settings were more refined than those at the boys' tables but the menu was the same. After the coffee-break wink, I was in no mood for discussion, so I did not initiate conversation. I looked across at the head boy, who was as silent as I. I smiled at him.

'I'm a new boy here,' I said.

He laughed. 'I was once too, sir,' he said. 'A million years ago.'

'As bad as that?' I asked.

'Not really. I shall be sorry to leave. I'll miss the treacle pudding.'

I asked him what he was going to do. He told me he hoped to go to Oxford to study law. His father was a judge, he said.

I knew that his name was Stenson. And I had certainly heard of his father, who was known as a stern judge with strong right-wing tendencies. He made it clear that he favoured the return of capital punishment. Not my kind of person, but I made allowances for his son, in the hope that he would take a kinder course. I warmed to Stenson. 'Come and see me at any time,' I said.

He seemed astonished at my offer. Clearly it was not the habit of headmasters of this school to make themselves so readily available. I intended to change that custom. I had no wish to be a mere figurehead. I hoped I had established some rapport with him. Through his office, word would leak throughout the school that the new headmaster was approachable.

After lunch, I received the housemasters in my study and discussed their reports. I had had a full working day, and I was glad to return to our school house when it was over. I was strangely tired. Lucy called it emotional fatigue. She may have been right, for that constantly winking eye exhausted me.

Over the next few weeks I followed a self-designed routine. I cocked my eye and ear continuously on Mr Eccles. I dropped in unannounced on his classes and found his teaching techniques superb. Likewise with most of the other teachers, though I found the English department less imaginative than the one in Hammersmith. Given my partiality to rhyme, I made but one innovation that term. I appointed a poet-in-residence. His job was to be available to any boy who openly, or covertly, as was usually the case, tried his hand in verse. I was not too hopeful of his appeal. But Richard Worthing, as he was called, was optimistic. And indeed, within a few weeks, a most surprising number of would-be Byrons and wannabe Dylans were knocking on his door. Once I invited him to my lunch table, but he was clearly unhappy in its stiff company. He preferred to dine amongst the boys.

My presence at morning chapel was not obligatory but I

dropped in from time to time only in order to validate my weekly visit to the Jewish prayer group. I had to be seen to balance my interests. There were only a few Jewish boys at the school, two dozen at the most, though I suspect there were a fair number of closet Jews like myself who chose the safer Jesus congregation. The school used the weekly services of the minister who preached in the synagogue in the neighbouring town. We were approaching the time of the Jewish year crammed full of Holy days: the New Year itself, followed by the Day of Atonement, and the *Simchat Torah*, which marked the ending of the reading of the Law. So there was no shortage of themes for the minister's short sermons. I enjoyed those weekly gatherings. They were noisy and informal and I didn't have to muffle a forbidden word. And though the songs they sang were entirely unknown to me, they were strangely familiar, and after a few attendances, I knew them by heart.

The term passed quickly, and on the last day Lucy and I gave a pre-Christmas lunch for most of the staff. They talked of their holiday arrangements. Fenby was participating in a music festival at Dartington; Dr Reynolds was staying put in his London pied-à-terre; Turner from physics was off skiing; and Brown from chemistry was going to San Francisco, though he gave no reason why. Richard, our poet, intended to go from party to party until he found a steady girlfriend. Eccles confessed to going to Marseilles, an unlikely place for Christmas I thought, though he insisted on having friends there. As for myself, I was going back to my village and to my first orphaned yuletide.

We were determined, Matthew and I, to make it a festive occasion, if only for the sake of the children. I missed my parents woefully, but added to that, I was slowly losing my appetite to celebrate the birth of a prophet whose name I could not even utter. For me the holiday had to be a break from the half-lie that I was living. So I concentrated on the ritual, the candles, the tree, the presents, the holly wreath on the door, the turkey, the pudding, none of which needed to have anything to do with Him in whose such abused name my grandparents had entered the ovens. Daily we visited our parents' graves, flowered them and wept. We visited their neighbours, and we picked up again on our old school friends and our children played with theirs. It was a holiday of remembrance, and in that remembrance, a celebration.

On our last night I went to the cemetery alone. I crouched by my parents' graves – kneeling was not in my nature – and I told them all about my new school. I told them I was happy there and I thanked them for their guidance. I opened my heart to them, the part that was permissible to opening. But I did not tell them about the Eccles wink.

13

'His children are growing up without him,' Matthew said. 'It's all so unfair.'

Sam and Matthew were sitting in a café beside the river.

'Is there no news of an appeal?' Sam asked.

'I don't want an appeal,' Matthew said firmly. 'I don't want a reduction of sentence. I don't want clemency. All that implies guilt. I want a retrial. Nothing less.'

How he has changed, Sam thought. He had become assertive. While hitherto he had been a patient foot-slogger, begging for support, now he was nothing less than an ardent crusader.

'I've found a lawyer,' he said, and Sam noticed a seemingly inappropriate twinkle in his eye. 'A woman,' Matthew went on, 'Rebecca Morris. She's young and not all that experienced but she is passionate in Alfred's defence. She has all the papers and she's going through them word for word. She's already discovered flaws and holes in the arguments.'

'Does Alfred know of this?' Sam asked.

'No. Not yet. And I don't want him to know. I don't want to raise his hopes.'

'How is Susan?' Sam asked after a pause. 'Are you still apart?'

'I haven't seen her for some time,' Matthew said. 'I see the children, but she disappears when I pick them up. I'm still at Lucy's. How is the book going?'

'Well,' Sam said, 'but slowly. Recall can be very upsetting, especially if, like Alfred, you are an honest man. At the moment he's writing about those events that led up to the catastrophe. It must be very hard for him. But he seems well enough. I saw him last week. I took him a cassette-player and some tapes. That pleased him, I think.'

'Lucy has a visit next week,' Matthew said. 'I've taken Rebecca to meet her and it has raised her spirits. We must hope, we must hope,' Matthew said. Then disconsolately he added, 'What else is there?'

'Just hope,' Sam said. 'We mustn't lose sight of that.'

They were silent for a while. Then Sam asked, 'Is there any chance that I might meet Susan? Talk to her perhaps?'

'There's no chance,' Matthew said. 'And even if there were, I wouldn't want you to. It's over, she and I. You can't back-track on betrayal. The damage is done. I hope one day she'll be very sorry.'

'She will be,' Sam said. Then he broached the subject that had been the reason for his meeting with Matthew.

'Did Alfred ever speak to you about a Mr Eccles? He was the history master at the school.'

'No,' Matthew said. 'I don't recall that he did. Why d'you ask?'

'I think Alfred considered him an enemy. You might well ask Rebecca to investigate his testimony.'

Sam had read the latest entry of Dreyfus's confession and

since reading it, he too had been haunted by the Eccles wink. He too sensed it as a key to the Dreyfus mystery.

They parted with promises of meeting again soon. Sam watched the back of him as he left the café. As he viewed his straight-backed tread towards the door, he thought of his brother's stoop of despair.

14

My first year at the school passed without serious hiccups. I was wary of cliques. Always had been in my whole teaching career. I discouraged them because they were exclusive and tended to lead to elitism and intolerance. It was relatively simple to disperse a group of boys who were constantly engaged with each other by diverting their attentions to other group pursuits. But when that clique is led by a master, it becomes an altogether more threatening situation. It struck me that Mr Eccles's following was more like a cabal. His groupies behaved like disciples, forever taking tea in his rooms, walking with him after school hours, and even going with him on theatre trips that, with my permission, he organised. I could do nothing about it. I shared my misgivings with Fenby, who laughed them off.

'It's always been the same with Eccles,' he told me, 'ever since I've been here. And that's about twenty years. He's always had a following. There's nothing sinister about it.' I hoped that he was right. Doubtless I had been influenced by that year-ago wink, its flickering forever in my eye, so that any Eccles activity was laced with suspicion.

It was his practice every Lent half-term to take a group of boys skiing to the same place in Austria. Again he did not want for my permission. I recognised the names of the disciples who enrolled for the expedition, about a dozen of them, but this year one of the applications came from a boy whom I had not regarded as one of the cabal. His name was George Tilbury.

Why do I need to spell it out? For George's name is as famous as mine is infamous. His name too, is known throughout the world, but unlike mine, it has not been tagged with labels. It has remained with its true baptismal title and I write it with overwhelming pity and rage.

George was the son of a cabinet minister, Sir Henry Tilbury. I'd met him once, at our speech day, an impressive man with an inherited title. His politics were centre-right and he was a devoted monarchist, at the same time favouring the European Community. In my estimation, he personified those virtues of a true Englishman, a patriot much given to tolerance. And George was exactly like him. His best friend was a Jewish boy, David Solomon, son of an orthopaedic surgeon.

I was fond of George. He was not particularly bright academically, but he was a willing boy and he possessed a quality sadly lacking amongst the pupils in general – a sense of humour and occasional mischief. I did not regard George as an Eccles follower, neither apparently did Eccles for he came to see me regarding George's request. He suggested that if he accepted Tilbury, they would be a party of thirteen, and though he himself was not superstitious, he suspected that the other boys might be wary of the number. I quickly dismissed that possibility. I felt that the superstition excuse was a cover for his own personal reluctance, so I insisted he be included in the party. I sincerely hoped I was doing young George a favour.

'You might well be right, Sir Alfred,' Eccles said.

I don't know why, but when my title was sounded by the likes of Eccles, I found it faintly insulting.

So off they went at half-term and I looked forward to George's return. Lucy and I took the children and went down to our village for the week's break. Matthew couldn't come. His children's half-term didn't coincide with ours. So I invited our poet-in-residence to spend a few days with us. Richard had not yet managed to find a steady girlfriend and he jumped at the prospect of fields and pastures new. I didn't hold out much hope for a poet in our little village. Its inhabitants were suspicious of artists of any kind, but I did not want to discourage him.

It was less than a year since my parents had died. Although I was beginning to accommodate my orphanhood, the pain of that loss persisted. Their graves were decked with flowers even in our absence, testimony to the respect that they had inspired amongst the small community. And we were always made welcome, as if they needed the link as much as we needed it ourselves. Richard too, was included in their invitations to teas and suppers and was even invited to give a poetry reading in the village hall. I was surprised that he accepted, and I was anxious about how he would be received. I expected a sparse and suspicious audience, but the village hall was full and expectant. Richard dressed for the occasion in spotless jeans, and a pink shirt with a flowered cravat. When he came on to the stage there was immediate applause even before he had opened his mouth and for the next hour he held them spellbound and silent with his magic rhymes. When he had finished there were sighs of disappointment and cries for more. And when their hands grew sore, they stamped their feet in applause. I think every girl and woman in that audience, and possibly a few men, must have fallen in love with him, and Lucy and I left the hall leaving him to his acclaim. I was sure that in the future he would not have to look further afield than our village to find his longed-for steady.

During that half-term, I thought often of George, and hoped that he was enjoying himself. Sometimes I dreaded returning to the school to find I had made a terrible mistake. But my first sight of George proved that all was well. I invited him to my table one lunch-time, together with his friend David Solomon. I asked him about his trip and he reported that it was the best holiday he'd ever had, and that he was definitely going to go again next year.

During the rest of that term, I noticed that he had joined the tea-taking group in Eccles's rooms. I saw him striding the fields in their after-school walks. It seemed to me that by the end of that school year, George Tilbury had become Eccles-hooked. I was none too pleased with this attachment, but I was more pained to notice that his friendship with David Solomon seemed to have come to an end. I don't think they had quarrelled, but the closeness was gone, and for some reason it disturbed me profoundly. George Tilbury had clearly undergone a radical change and in so doing he had sadly lost his sense of humour. I wanted very much to talk to him, but I had no valid reason to call him to my study. Boys dropped by all the time but I did not send for them. Unless there was a very good reason, it was not in my remit to solicit. And with George I had no reason. Until, that is, the summer term, when his housemaster's report indicated a serious and sudden decline in his achievement. I called George to my study and asked if he could explain his falling standards.

'I do my best, sir,' he said.

There was insolence in his tone, so unlike the George I had first known.

'You are capable of better,' I said.

'That's my best, sir,' he said in a 'take it or leave it' manner.

Then I got angry. 'You'll be sitting your GCSEs next year,

and at this rate you won't get a university place. Your father will be very disappointed.'

I hated myself for using that ploy. That I had to recruit displayed my own weakness. George said nothing. He simply looked at me with disdain. I stared at him for a moment. Then, 'Is there something troubling you George?' I asked.

'Nothing, sir. Nothing at all,' he said.

His tone had changed. He seemed a little boy again and I knew that, however he denied it, something was disturbing him.

'You can always come to me you know,' I said.

'Thank you, sir.' He backed away and I knew he wanted very much to escape. I had the impression that once outside my door, he would start to cry.

'Any time,' I added. 'Keep that in mind. You can go now,' I said, much to his relief.

He murmured, 'Thank you,' and left the room.

Later on I had a word with his housemaster. He too had noticed a sullenness about the boy, alternating with a certain arrogance. He promised to keep an eye on him.

I couldn't get the George problem out of my mind and in time, he joined the Eccles wink in my haunting nights.

Towards the start of that summer term, there was a timid knock on my door, so timid I knew it had to be a pupil. I did not call 'Come in' as I would have done to a teacher. I went to the door and opened it in the hope that my form of welcome would give the visitor a little more confidence than his limp knock betrayed. It was James Turncastle, and I wondered what he wanted of me. James was a brilliant pupil, one of the best in the school. I didn't know him well except that he was an Eccles disciple. His father was a diplomat somewhere in the Near East but I had never met his parents. Though he was part of the Eccles group, James had always struck me as being something of a loner. He was a handsome boy, who looked somewhat older than his years. He was just about to take his GCSEs. That summer though, by all accounts, he was academically ripe for university entrance. I asked him to sit down. He fidgeted in his seat.

'Take your time,' I said sensing that he had a difficult request to make. 'What can I do for you?'

'I want to take a year off. After my GCSEs,' he blurted out. He said it quickly as if he wanted to get it over and done with.

I was surprised at his request. 'Why?' I asked reasonably.

'I want a break before I do my A levels.'

'A break is very unusual at this stage,' I said. 'It's quite common to take a year off after A levels and before university. Now would not be a good time to interrupt your schooling.'

He didn't answer me and I felt I had to probe further. 'What would you do with this year off?' I asked.

'I've been invited to stay with friends in Vienna. I met them when we were skiing with Mr Eccles.'

'Have you talked to your parents about it?' I asked.

'No. I don't have to,' he said. 'They don't care anyway.'

I thought that last remark a key of sorts and I decided to investigate it. James had started at the school before my appointment. There must be records of his background somewhere. I looked at him.

'*Please*, sir,' he said.

'I'll have to think about it,' I parried. 'Come and see me at the end of the week.'

He rose. 'Thank you, sir,' he said. And again, 'Thank you.'

I was relieved at last to find an excuse to call Eccles to my study. Apart from teaching the boy history, he was also his housemaster. He came to see me after classes and was his usual sycophantic self. I poured him a sherry as I informed him of Turncastle's request.

'What do you know about the boy?' I asked. 'His background, I mean.'

'Not a very happy one, I'm afraid,' Eccles said. 'He's an only

child, and of parents who never wanted children. They are a
career couple, very rich and very selfish. He rarely sees them.
He's fobbed off to an aunt in Devon for his holidays, and since
he has been at the school, not one of his family has put in an
appearance.'

'What's this about Vienna?' I asked.

'Those friends of his are genuine. And I can vouch for them.
I know their parents. They would make him welcome.'

'What about money for the trip, his keep and so on?'

Eccles smiled. 'Turncastle has an inexhaustible allowance.
His parents' conscience money, no doubt.'

'What d'you think?' I asked him. 'Should I give him leave?'

'It's your decision, Sir Alfred,' he said.

'What do *you* think?'

'Well, he could at least come back fluent in German. Not a
bad bonus, I'd say.'

I was inclined to let the boy have his way because I felt that
to refuse him would be far more damaging than letting him go.
But first I had to write to his parents and his aunt for their
formal permission. When at the end of the week Turncastle
knocked on my door, I told him I had to await a response from
his parents. He laughed.

'Ever since I've been here, and that's almost four years, I've
never had one letter from them. Not even a card on my birth-
days. I hope you have better luck then I, sir.'

But I didn't. By the end of that term, I'd received no
response from either his parents or his Devonian aunt. I waited
for his GCSEs to be over, then I called James to my study. His
knock was still timid, and he entered nervously. I told him to sit
down and I smiled at him. He sensed that good news was at
hand, but he was still tense.

'I've decided to let you go,' I said. 'Just for the year. I shall
expect you back in school, fluent in German, a year from
September.'

James relaxed with the fatigue of gratitude.

'On one condition,' I said. 'That you write to me regularly. Just a postcard will do. But they must be regular. And I shall need your address and phone number.'

'Of course, sir,' he said.

'And I wish you luck.'

He rose from his seat. And then he did an extraordinary thing. He crossed my desk and spontaneously embraced me. I did not restrain him. I was deeply moved by his need for some affection. I put my arms around him. He felt like a son to me, and I've no doubt, he imagined that I was his father.

He moved away, turning his head. I was sure he was crying.

'Good luck,' I said to him again. 'And enjoy every minute.'

He left quickly and I stayed sitting at my desk for a while, wishing him well, as I would have wished my own son.

For the end of the school year Lucy and I gave another party. Again the talk was of vacations. This time Eccles was off to visit friends in America, Brown was making a return trip to San Francisco, and Dr Reynolds was holing up in his cottage in the Cotswolds. It did not surprise me that our young poet-in-residence was spending the summer in our little village in Kent. As for Lucy and I and the children, and Matthew and Susan and theirs, we had decided to take a cruise in the Norwegian fjords.

As I recall it now, that was the last summer we spent *en famille*. Indeed in my own life, it was my last summer altogether. I despair of seeing another. Or indeed of counting on any season at all. For my cell is deaf to the falling of leaves or the burst of buds, or the beating of the sun, or the muffled hush of snowfall. I am here in a seasonless limbo, where time is a faceless clock that ticks in the dark.

1 5

'I asked Rebecca about Eccles, Sam,' Matthew said. 'She told me that his evidence was impeccable.'

They were sitting in Lucy's drawing-room. Lucy was in the kitchen preparing tea and the children had gone to the house of friends.

'I remember it myself,' Matthew said. 'He spoke of Alfred as a great mentor with a grand flair for administration. There was not a hostile word in his whole testimony. Fenby, the music master, was the same. I can't recall that any teacher spoke against him. Except one or two maybe. I can hardly bear to think of those days.'

'Alfred is writing very well,' Sam said in an attempt to change the subject. 'Despite the painfulness of the matter, he seems to be coping well. I think he sees the writing as an act of therapy.'

'Rebecca is following all the leads,' Matthew went on, as if he hadn't heard him. 'She's even been down to Kent.'

'She sounds very thorough,' Sam said, but he refrained from probing further. He had the impression that Matthew was giving nothing away, or perhaps that Rebecca was keeping her findings close to her chest. Or perhaps both, since Matthew seemed obsessed with the search and possibly, Sam thought, with Rebecca herself.

Lucy brought in the tea, and while they ate and drank, the subject of Alfred was not touched upon. Lucy gave a progress report on the children, who were doing well with their tutor. She herself had found a part-time typing job which she could do at home.

After tea, Matthew rose to go. He seemed in a bit of a hurry. Sam was glad he was leaving for he was anxious for news about Susan which he could only prise from Lucy in Matthew's absence. He helped her clear the tea things, and when they were in the kitchen he asked, 'How's Susan? Is there any hope of a reconciliation?'

'None,' Lucy said. 'Never. Matthew is determined. And I think that he is right. In any case,' she said after a while, 'I think his interest lies elsewhere.'

'Rebecca?' Sam asked.

'Rebecca,' Lucy said.

'Have you ever met her?'

'Yes. Once.'

'I'm happy for him,' Sam said.

'So am I. He's been through a very rough time.'

'I've had a substantial offer from an American publisher for Alfred's book,' Sam said. 'Just on the basis of a few chapters. I'm wondering whether I should tell Alfred. What do you think?'

'I think not,' Lucy said. 'Firstly, he's indifferent to money. You know that. But secondly, and more importantly, I think it will make him nervous. He will feel that too much is expected of him. Let him get on with it in his own way. The only pressure should come from himself.'

Lucy was a very wise woman, Sam thought. 'I could give you a job,' he said suddenly. 'In my agency. You could work from home, and the link need never be known.'

Lucy was excited. 'What would I have to do?' she asked.

'Read manuscripts mainly,' he said. 'Fiction and non-fiction, and write reports on them. As if you were an ordinary reader.'

'I'd love to do that,' she said.

'I'll pay you in cash. Just another way to conceal the link.'

'When do I start?'

'Tomorrow. I'll bring a package over.' He could not trust a courier. Nor the postal service. Lucy's address must not be known.

'But you'll tell Alfred, won't you Sam?' Lucy said. 'It would make him very happy.'

'Of course I'll tell him. Next week when I'm due to collect his next chapter. And I won't mention the American money.'

When he returned to his office, Sam gathered together three manuscripts that had been awaiting perusal for too long a time. He was happy with his decision. It would boost Lucy's morale and it would be a great relief to himself. But above all, it would please Alfred, and Alfred was Sam's main concern.

16

When I returned to school after the summer break, the sight of a pile of postcards from James gave me much pleasure. I examined the postmarks and placed them in the order of their writing. They started off with gratitude and enthusiasm and continued right through in that vein. His German was improving day by day, he wrote. It had to, since none of his friends spoke English. He had spent the summer in the mountains, and in his penultimate postcard he told me he had enrolled in a school of martial arts. His last postcard came as a surprise. He was suddenly homesick, he said. I was pulled up sharply by that word for I wondered what or where poor James envisaged as 'home'. It could only have been the school. He intended to return at the start of the Lent term and he hoped to start studying for his A levels, with German as an added subject.

I was delighted, happy to be in a position where I would not

miss him. I wrote to him straight away, a long letter, congratu-
lating him on his GCSE results. They were, as all of us had
expected, brilliant. He had taken twelve subjects and had
achieved an A* in eleven of them. B in one subject, chemistry,
was his lowest mark. In my letter, I gave him news of the school
and how his friends had fared in their exams. I told him about
our summer holiday cruise in the fjords, and about my children
and how they were doing in their school. I realised that it was
a very intimate letter, one that a father might write to his son.
I told him that I was glad that he was making an earlier return
and that I looked forward to welcoming him back to the school.

I told Mr Eccles of James's decision, and he affected surprise.
I knew it wasn't genuine. I had a feeling that he himself might
have engineered James's return. I had absolutely no grounds for
this suspicion but, in my mind, Eccles's pronouncements always
carried a soupçon of doubt.

That Christmas term passed smoothly enough. I kept my eye
on George Tilbury and I monitored his progress, of which
there was little sign. But at least it wasn't deteriorating. He kept
to a steady pace of mediocrity. What did please me was an obvious renewal of friendship with David Solomon and that seemed
to offset and outweigh the teas he still took in Eccles's study,
and the groupie walks across the school grounds. Our GCSE
and A level results had placed our school at the top of the
league tables and it gave me great pleasure to announce our
standing to our first assembly. A great cheer went up in the hall
and good old Fenby at the piano went straight into the introduction of the school song, which six hundred boys belted out
with joy. It was a happy start to the Michaelmas term.

That Christmas vacation, we went to Kent en famille, with
Matthew and Susan likewise, back to our childhood village.
Our first invitation was to the engagement party of our poet,
Richard, and one of the village girls, Veronica, daughter of the
local smithy, and I was honoured as a match-maker. There

followed the usual rounds of Christmas parties with our friends and their children, the visit to the graveyard, the flowers and the updated bulletins. The pain of the loss of my parents sat now with greater ease. It had proclaimed its permanence, and paradoxically enough, its comfort.

That was the last Christmas I was to spend in our village. I never, never entertained the thought that I would not return. I never said goodbye to my parents for I knew that I would call on them until I died.

Spring came early that year and the daffodils were already flowering in the school grounds at the beginning of the Lent term. My first sight was that of James Turncastle, bronzed and crew-cut, waiting outside my study door. I wanted to embrace him in welcome, and I suspect from his look of pleasure that he wished to do likewise. But we both held back and instead, we shook hands.

'Welcome home,' I said. I wondered whether I had used the right word.

'It's good to be back,' he said.

I invited him into my study. Had it been later in the day I would have offered him a sherry. I had to remind myself that he was still only sixteen. I congratulated him on his exam results again and felt sure that he would be able to catch up on a lost term's teaching.

'Now tell me about Austria,' I said. 'And how's your German?'

He rattled off a string of sentences in a German that sounded native.

'It seemed to come naturally to me,' he said. 'Like a second mother tongue. Though,' he added, 'I don't have much of a first mother to shout about.'

It was an intimacy he was sharing with me, and I felt slightly uncomfortable. At the same time, I was pleased that he felt so at ease with me. I spent half an hour with him, and I felt he kept nothing back, telling me in detail about the family he had stayed with and their attitudes towards the English and the Americans, and their awareness of the past. I didn't encourage him to go into that. For some reason I didn't want to hear about it.

'I shall see them again soon,' he said, 'when we go skiing.'

The reminder did not please me. I thought again about George and I wondered whether he would be going. I asked James if he would like to lunch at my table that day. I wanted him to meet Lucy and eventually, Peter. I thought they might become friends. He was grateful all over again and he promised to put on a clean shirt.

Eccles was at my table that day. He seemed surprised that James had joined us, and I thought that surprise genuine, as was his pleasure. Lucy quite took to the prodigal son and invited him over to meet the children. I had told her what I knew of James's background and she suggested that he use us as his surrogate family.

'We should take him down to Kent one weekend with the children,' she said.

I suppose by now my readers must wonder why I have been able to write about James Turncastle with such equanimity, with such affection, why my pen does not stumble on his name. In the light of what we all now know, I should have stuttered over his mention, or even totally denied him. Dear readers, I loved that boy like a son and hindsight and its wisdom did not enter into that loving. But suddenly it interferes. It's that mention of his visit to our Kent cottage that invites the flashback. And now my pen *does* stutter for I wonder if I would be here today if Lucy, under my influence, had not offered her generous hospitality. I shall not mention his name again. Sometimes of course I shall have to, for the benefit of my narrative, but it will be only for that reason and for that reason alone.

So we all went down to the cottage, with James as our guest. Eccles once again organised the skiing trip, and once again they were thirteen. Under his housemaster's guidance, George's work had shown some improvement, and I hoped it would continue. I told him that I had noticed his good efforts and that seemed to please him. I saw them all off at the school gates, and wished them well.

I spent part of that half-term break in London with Matthew. I stayed in their flat and Matthew took time off from work to be with me. We walked around London like tourists. We sampled restaurants of foreign cuisine. And we talked. We talked all the time, recalling our childhoods together, remembering our parents, contemplating our futures. That was the very last time that Matthew and I spent serious time together. I'm glad we talked so much, and I'm glad I remember it all. For here in my cell, I hear it all again. And in his voice as well as my own.

I was sorry to leave him. He promised to come down at Easter, but for me, time was in the dark long before, and Easter never came.

17

In the course of Rebecca's investigations and her regular reports to Matthew the two of them had become lovers. But their affair was clandestine. It had to be. Matthew had told nobody. His sudden happiness was so acute that it had straightened his back. He strutted like a peacock now, but without the pride. Lucy could not fail to notice the change and arrived at the obvious conclusion, but she said nothing. Sam too, had cottoned on to the new development in Matthew's life, and he was glad for him. Unknown to Matthew, he had traced the whereabouts of Susan. He would not seek to talk to her, as Matthew had forbidden any contact. But her new flat lay only a few streets away from Sam's own apartment, and he had to pass it each day on his way home from work. One day, he crept up to the front door, and on the column of bells, he noted the name 'Smith', crisp and clear. He felt sick. He wanted to tear out the label, and replace it with its true and honourable name, but he satisfied himself by simply deleting it. For him, that flat was empty. Susan was a nothing, a hollowness in an empty space. He turned from the door, disconsolate. Some evenings later, he noted that the 'Smith' had returned, and had fastened itself inside a frame. Immovable. Permanent. And with all his heart, Sam wished Susan Smith ill.

He was due to meet with Matthew the following day so that he could be updated on Rebecca's findings. Sam had attended such meetings before and the lawyer's 'findings' had amounted to very little. He had no doubt that she was doing her best and possibly her love for Matthew spurred her on to greater effort, but Sam had little faith in the discovery of new evidence. When he himself had attended part of the trial on those days that he could gain admittance, for there was always a long queue of salivating spectators who had already found Dreyfus guilty, all the testimonies against his friend had seemed foolproof, and the witnesses did not falter under grilling cross-examination. It had all sounded thoroughly rehearsed. The defence, on the other hand, such as it was, was far from convincing. On the basis of the judge's summing-up, and the cold efficiency of the prosecution, Sam thought that even Dreyfus would have pronounced himself guilty.

But Matthew did have news, and when they met at their usual café on the river he seemed excited. He no longer looked about him for eavesdroppers, and if he was recognised, he was pleased to acknowledge it. He looked like a potential winner with a few cards up his sleeve.

'She's been tracing the witnesses,' Matthew started right away. He paused when the waiter approached and he quickly gave their order. 'Most of them are at university,' he said, 'though two of them are in the army. The interesting one is James Turncastle.'

'Here's our coffee,' Sam said. 'Hold it.'

The waiter laid their coffees on the table. Sam lit a cigarette.

He was ready to listen. 'What about Turncastle?' he said. He could hardly utter the name for it was Turncastle's testimony that had been the most damning.

'He's in a psychiatric clinic. He's had a breakdown.'

'Interesting,' Sam said. 'Is there anything more on him?' Where is this clinic? And what kind of breakdown?'

'He's somewhere in Devon. That's all we know. Rebecca's tracking him down.'

'We must not be too optimistic,' Sam said. 'The breakdown need not have anything to do with the trial. But it's worth investigating.'

'There's something more,' Matthew said. 'Eccles.'

'What about Eccles?'

'You remember you thought he was an enemy? Or at least Alfred thought so. And I told you that his testimony was exemplary? Rebecca wondered why you were doubtful. And Alfred too. So she did a bit of investigation on Eccles. No findings so far. But there are certain questions.'

'Like what?'

'Eccles's holiday resorts. Regular ones. Austria, West Virginia, Marseilles. He said he had friends in those places. What kind of friends? Rebecca smells a clue and she's ferreting.'

'I see no connection. Do you?'

'I'm willing to believe there is a link and I'm sure Rebecca will find it,' Matthew said.

They finished their coffee.

'I'm seeing Alfred later today,' Sam said. 'Any messages?'

'Just love and loyalty. But no mention of Rebecca. Not yet anyway. Though I suppose it will be known soon enough. We bumped into Susan the other day. Quite by chance. We were in the supermarket, Rebecca and I, and we met over the frozen peas. We didn't speak, but she looked none too pleased. I hope she'll have the sense not to seek for divorce. She can be a very jealous woman.'

'Are you sure you don't want me to talk to her?' Sam asked.

'No. I don't want to make a production of it unless it becomes absolutely necessary. Thanks anyway.'

They parted, Matthew to Rebecca's office and Sam to the prison.

There he found his friend deeply depressed and from his mood, he gathered that he had begun to write the story of his fall. He felt sad for him. He had no news to cheer him. The substantial American offer would, in any case, leave him indifferent, and Rebecca's probings were not to be spoken about in fear of raising his hopes.

'What about a game of chess?' Sam suggested. As he said it, he heard its silliness. It was like offering a sweetie to a crying child.

'I can't concentrate,' Dreyfus said.

'Is it the book?' Sam asked.

'It's so damned unfair. Here I am, saddled with a life-sentence for something I didn't do.' He started to shout. 'I'm innocent. D'you hear me?' He grabbed Sam by the collar. 'D'you hear me?' he said again.

'I hear,' Sam said sadly. 'But don't you give up hope. Matthew has found a new lawyer.' That much he was not forbidden to tell. 'She's looking for new evidence.'

'She?' Dreyfus asked.

'Yes. A woman. But a very experienced one,' he lied. 'And one who doggedly believes in your innocence.'

Dreyfus sat on his cot and put his head in his hands. 'I despair,' he said.

Sam went to sit by his side. He put his arm about his shoulder but he could think of nothing to say. He recalled sitting at his own mother's bedside after the doctor had told her that there was no hope for a recovery. He had sat silent then. Any words of solace would have been an obscene mockery.

'I'm finding the writing difficult,' Dreyfus said after a while.
'I'm coming close to the trial and I find the story absolutely
unbelievable. When I write it as fiction, and sometimes I see it
that way, it passes for a novel. But then suddenly, in the middle
of a sentence, I realise that it's not fiction at all and I look
around me and I see this cell and the bars on my window and
I know that it is all real. And the fiction is reality. Incredible. I
have a wife I cannot hold, and children who are growing up out
of my sight. I am forbidden family and freedom. And I have
done nothing wrong. Nothing.'

He shouted his despair. 'Nothing. Nothing.'

Sam let him cry himself out, and found it pitiful to view. He
felt as helpless as Dreyfus himself. He wanted very much to
read what Dreyfus had written to date, but suddenly the book
seemed totally irrelevant. All that mattered was a monumental
miscarriage of justice.

Slowly Dreyfus composed himself. Sam dared a suggestion.

'Would you like to read your latest chapter to me?' he asked.
He thought that in the presence of a listener, his friend could
distance himself from his narrative and thus feel the urge to tell
his tale to the end. It was worth a try. And Dreyfus was willing. He crossed to his desk and gathered together some papers.
Then, without looking up, he started to read.

Sam listened, less to the matter of the work than to the
manner of its reading. For Dreyfus had assumed a totally
detached air, as if the story he told had happened to somebody
else. His tone was uninvolved, almost to the point of indifference. Sam felt that the reading was remedial, and satisfied, he
concentrated on the matter. And that pleased him.

When the telling was over, Dreyfus said, 'I must get on with
it.'

Sam rose. It was a good time to leave. 'I won't disturb you,'
he said. 'It's good. Very good, and it has to be finished. I like
being read to. Can we do it again on my next visit?'

'Come soon,' Dreyfus said. 'I'll have a new chapter to read to you.'

On his way back to his office, Sam resolved to visit his friend on a regular basis, simply to be read to. He wouldn't ask for the manuscript. He would listen to it on site. He knew that the life of any writer was an isolated one, but it was at least occasionally punctuated by contacts with society. Poor Alfred was doubly isolated, dwelling in a relentless loneliness, compounded by the injustice of it all.

Once in his office, Sam made a phone call to his wife. And when she answered he didn't know what to say. He had phoned simply to hear her voice, to affirm that he had a listener, to acknowledge that he had two children, and a life outside his work.

'Just phoning to say hello,' he said helplessly. 'I'll be back early. We can all have dinner together.' How many blessings could Dreyfus count, he wondered. But he could think of none at all.

18

During the half-term break I spent time preparing for the visit
of the Headmaster of an American public school whom I had
met briefly on one of my lecture tours while I was still at
Hammersmith. Dr Smithson was a sound Anglophile, steeped
in English history and cultural heritage. He had heard of my
appointment and had written to ask if he could come and see
the workings of what he had heard was England's finest school.
I was happy to invite him and his wife to be our guests. I
arranged an inspection of the school in the hands of sundry
masters, as well as a buffet supper for them to meet other
members of staff, while Lucy set up a tour of the surrounding
countryside, pock-marked with history. I looked forward to the
return to school-work and especially to a report of the skiing
holiday.

According to Eccles, the boys had made great improvements
with their skiing, and had thoroughly enjoyed themselves and

were loath to leave. He laboured the success and pleasure of the holiday and I thought he protested too much. The boys looked well enough, and when I had the chance, I casually asked each one of them how they had enjoyed themselves. Their answers were uniform and, I suspected, rehearsed.

'We had a wonderful time,' each of them said. With the exception of George, who gave me the same rehearsed answer but in a tone that suggested that his time had been anything but wonderful. He seemed sullen and faintly troubled, and over the next week I watched him closely. I often saw him with young David Solomon. Indeed he consorted with no one else, and though I delighted in that friendship, its exclusiveness gave me some concern. Moreover, George no longer seemed to be taking the Eccles's teas. I was convinced that something had gone radically amiss on those Austrian slopes, but I had no clue as to its nature. All I could do was to keep my eyes and ears open.

The Smithsons arrived the following week, and kept to the itinerary that I had planned for them. I spent much of my time guiding them, and clarifying the workings of the English public school system. Dr Smithson's enthusiasm was infectious, and for the duration of his visit I shelved my concern regarding George and the skiing party. But it jogged me once more on the morning after the Smithsons had left. I was returning to my study after a staff meeting, and I saw George loitering near my door. I asked him what he wanted. He stared at me like an animal caught in a trap.

'Nothing, sir,' he said quickly. Then he slithered past me down the corridor. I had a very heavy programme to fulfil that day to make up for the time I had lost during the Smithson's visit, and I thought no more of it.

Over the next few weeks, my work became routine. I attended chapel from time to time and paid my weekly visit to the Jewish assembly. We were approaching Passover, which that year fell very close to Easter. The minister was telling the story of the festival of the unleavened bread and the hurried exodus out of Egypt. And I thought to myself how, in its essence, that story has been repeated throughout our calamity-lurching history, and how Egypt dwells in many lands, how Pharoah has many names and speaks in sundry tongues.

A few weeks later – we were already approaching the Easter vacation – I again found George loitering outside my study. This time I was determined to question him. But as I approached, I saw James Turncastle walking quickly down the corridor, and I watched as he reached George, put a strong arm about his shoulders and hurried him out of my reach. The incident disturbed me, and again I knew not why.

The following morning, as I was working in my study after assembly, a knock came at my door. It was matron. She looked very flustered.

'Sir,' she blurted out, 'George Tilbury is missing. He hasn't answered to the register and . . . and . . .'

'And what, Matron?' I asked, hearing my thunderous heart-beat.

'His bed hasn't been slept in.' She was almost weeping. 'And all his clothes are still there.' Then she broke down completely.

'We must start a search,' I said. I tried to hide my agitation but my heart was full of foreboding. 'I'll call the upper school to assembly in hall.'

This was quickly done and, within ten minutes of Matron's call, I was appraising the boys and some of the staff of George Tilbury's disappearance. Dr Reynolds took charge of the search of the grounds and outbuildings, while I myself led a party of boys about the school proper. We arranged to meet again at lunch-hour, unless George had been traced before that time.

'We have to find him,' I told them. I tried to hide the panic in my voice.

They set off, the grounds search-party, while I led my troops through the nooks and crannies of the school. At lunch-time, we reassembled. There had been no sightings. I ordered the search to be continued throughout the day until darkness fell. And by then it was clear that George Tilbury had simply disappeared.

At this stage I find it hard to go on writing. I've tried to read aloud what I've written, but without a listener, I know with certainty that it is not fiction. George Tilbury went missing on that day, and nothing would ever be the same again.

19

Rebecca Morris had traced James Turncastle's Devonian aunt. She had located the clinic where James was being treated but she had failed to gain admission as she was not his next of kin. The receptionist had given her the name and address of James's aunt, to whom enquiries should be directed. Rebecca did not write for an appointment, for she feared a refusal. So she went in person. She found that Miss Turncastle lived close to the seashore, in a richly appointed villa surrounded by a vast and well-laundered garden, but there were no forbidding iron gates, nor the sound of dogs. A gardener noted but ignored her approach as she drove up the gravelled drive and rang the single bell in the middle of the oaken door. A uniformed maid answered her ring and asked her what she wanted.

'Could I see Miss Turncastle?' she asked.

'Is she expecting you?'

'No. But I called on the off-chance. I'm a friend of her nephew James,' she said. She knew she was taking a risk but she could think of no other reason for wishing to see her.

The maid invited her inside and told her to wait in the hall. Rebecca looked around the panelled walls. There was little to indicate the nature of the character who dwelt therein. The maid returned quickly and almost begged her to follow. Rebecca had the impression that Miss Turncastle had not received a visitor in a long while.

She was sitting in a stiff upright chair in the drawing-room, although she was surrounded by comfortable loungers. It became her, that seating, Rebecca thought. She wore a rigid look on a face that was a stranger to a smile, her upper lip curled in perpetual disdain, and her nostrils quivered faintly. The woman fairly stank of piety.

'You're a friend of James,' she said. She did not invite Rebecca to take a seat. She wished to assume the position of cross-examiner.

'Yes,' Rebecca answered. She would not elaborate unless she was called upon to do so.

'A great disappointment to his parents, that boy,' Miss Turncastle said. She sniffed as punctuation. 'My brother gave him everything.'

Everything except love, Rebecca thought. She waited for Miss Turncastle to continue. She needed to know as much as possible about James, and his aunt was very forthcoming.

'I volunteered to care for him while they were abroad,' she said, 'and it was a thankless job I can tell you. The boy has no gratitude.' Rebecca wondered what he should be grateful for. But Miss Turncastle was about to tell her.

'I gave him a good home in the holidays. No shortage of food, and he's not a small eater. He had his own room and he didn't have to do a thing for himself. He sulked most of the time. Didn't seem to make any friends. Understandable I suppose,' she concluded. She still had not offered Rebecca a seat. 'Now, what is it you want?' she said.

'I heard that James was ill. I wanted to know what's the matter with him, and how he's getting on.'

'I don't know whether you can call it ill,' the woman said. 'They say he's had a breakdown, though he could of course be putting it on. He's a bit of a liar, our James.'

'But why *should* he have a breakdown?' Rebecca insisted.

'Well if it really is what they say it is, it's probably guilt. It's always guilt, isn't it, a breakdown. Guilt.' Miss Turncastle relished the word, donating it at least three syllables. 'He's got plenty to feel guilty about.'

Rebecca felt that at last she was getting somewhere. 'Like what?' she asked.

'Like what? I've already told you. Of letting his father down. Isn't that enough for a breakdown? I don't know how the boy can live with such guilt.'

Rebecca wanted to grasp the woman's turkey neck and screw it tight. She was tired of standing and wondered whether she dared take a seat. But she was too cowardly.

'D'you visit him?' Rebecca asked.

'I've been once,' the woman said, 'but he didn't welcome me. I shall not go again.'

'What about his parents?'

'I've written to them of course and told them about the situation. They've asked to be kept informed and I shall do as they wish.'

Rebecca saw no point in staying. She was not prepared to be the receptacle for Miss Turncastle's spleen. She was depressed too. There was no hope of a clue from James. But she would find some excuse to keep in touch with the clinic. For her part she did not wish to see Miss Turncastle again.

'I must be going now,' she said.

'The maid will show you out,' Miss Turncastle muttered.

She did not move one inch in her chair. She simply sat there and waited for gratitude.

Rebecca was glad to return to her car, if only to sit down. But she didn't dawdle. She wanted to get out of those grounds as quickly as possible. It was only when she was a few miles beyond the Turncastle estate that she turned into a lay-by and conducted a sad board meeting with herself. It could well be, she accepted, that Miss Turncastle was right. That an over-whelming guilt had precipitated James's breakdown. But the poor boy could feel guilty about many things, and his rotten father was only one of them. She needed to feel that James's guilt was connected to the Dreyfus trial. She had to think in those terms, else her quest was futile. She remembered that she had a psychiatrist acquaintance. She would enlist his support as soon as she returned. She drove out of the lay-by and speeded towards London. She wanted very much to be with Matthew.

As he had promised, Sam went again to the prison for an updated reading. And it was just as well. For in no other way would his friend have continued his narrative without believing that it was fiction. For worse was to come. And Dreyfus knew it.

20

I needed to know whether George had gone back to his home but I was wary of phoning his parents as I did not want to panic them. But after our fruitless search I could postpone it no longer. I would ascertain that George had not gone home – for some reason I doubted that easy solution – then I would alert the police.

Sir Henry himself answered the phone. I came straight to the point. I saw no reason for a preamble, nor could I have fashioned one.

'Is George, by any chance, at home?'

'Of course not,' Sir Henry said. 'Why did you ask?'

'He seems to be missing,' I said, though there was no 'seems' about it.

'Missing?' he shouted at me, as if it were I who had lost him. 'Since when?'

Then I heard Lady Tilbury's voice. 'What's the matter dear?'

Then a pause. Then a scream.

'Since when has he been missing?'

'We don't know,' I said. 'His bed wasn't slept in last night.'

'Have the police been informed?'

'I shall do that now,' I said. 'I wanted to ring you first. But we've been searching all day.'

'I'm leaving now,' Sir Henry said. 'I'll be at the school in a couple of hours.' He put the phone down before I could say any more. In any case, there was nothing more to say. I looked at my watch: 7.30. It was going to be a long night.

With a sinking heart, I dialled the local police station. Perhaps I should have informed them earlier, as soon as George had been reported missing. But at that time I had harboured a faint hope that he might be found and I didn't want a production made out of it. I had the reputation of the school in mind. I was wrong. I should have called them right away. God help me, but they wouldn't have found him. I know that now. But they should have been given a chance.

Very soon, three members of the local police force, all in plain clothes, arrived at the school, and in their presence George's disappearance assumed an altogether different colouring. It was suddenly attached to crime. I called the policemen into my study, together with Dr Reynolds, and after a few preliminary enquiries they outlined their plan of campaign. An official search would go out in the morning at first light. The small lake on the boundaries of the school grounds would be drained. Many pupils, especially those in George's house, would be questioned, as well as his teachers and Matron. They asked permission to start with the teachers straightaway.

'Perhaps we could start with you, Sir Alfred,' they said.

Dr Reynolds rose to go. 'I shall be in my study,' he said.

I was alone and I felt if not accused then certainly responsible. I answered their questions freely, for I had nothing to hide. I realised that, although I felt a special attachment to

George, I knew very little about him. I mentioned that I had seen him on the day before when he was loitering outside my study. But I didn't teach the boy and probably knew less about him than the other masters. 'Mr Eccles will help you there,' I added.

The interview was of short duration. I had told them all that I could. Then I directed them to Dr Reynold's study and told them that he would introduce them to other teachers, as I had to wait for George's father, who would be arriving within the hour.

'An unpleasant business,' one of the inspectors said. 'Always is with children.' His voice was laced with pessimism. I dreaded the arrival of Sir Henry.

But there were worse arrivals in the shape of two reporters from the local newspaper. They had received a tip-off from the station and lost no time in scooping the story. I couldn't deny them an interview, but played it down as well as I could. I knew that it was now only a matter of time before the invasion of the national press. The reporters ferreted round the school for a while, and I didn't stop them, as matters had already gone far beyond my control. Lucy was concerned as much for me as for George. She made a cauldron of hot soup to keep the inspectors on their toes, and she even doled it out to the reporters. All the while she said nothing. She had caught their pessimism. She did not even talk to me, for she knew that we both feared the worst.

Sir Henry Tilbury drove past the school and came straight to my house. I took him into the drawing-room. I was glad that Lady Tilbury was not with him.

'Did anything happen to upset him?' was Sir Henry's first question. 'Was he bullied in any way?'

'Not as far as I know,' I said. 'And I would have noticed bullying. Mr Eccles might know more.'

I don't know why I kept referring to Eccles. With no logical reason, I sensed that he held a key. 'Only yesterday,' I said, 'I saw George hanging about outside my study, and I had the feeling he wanted to tell me something. But he must have changed his mind. In any case, a friend of his came along and they both walked away. Perhaps it was nothing at all,' I said. But in my mind, I felt it was a key of sorts and I blamed myself for not insisting that he talk to me. 'The police are in the school now,' I went on. 'I'm sure they'd want to talk to you, and you to them.'

'May I phone my wife?' he asked. 'She's frantic with worry. She insisted on staying at home in case George turns up. But she's there alone.'

'Of course,' I said and, pointing to the phone on the table beside him, I left the room. I couldn't imagine what words they would find to say to each other. Where were the words for 'no news', a 'search party', 'divers', and the 'draining of a lake'. No words at all. Just a silence of shared despair.

I went to the kitchen, carrying that same silence with me. I noticed that Lucy had been crying and her tears irritated me. They seemed to have come to a premature conclusion. I shed no tears, but I have to confess that I shared her worst fears. It was clear that no one of us would go to bed that night. Later the two reporters tapped on our door to say goodnight and to give thanks for the soup. Then they rushed away to file their stories. I would make a point of not buying the local paper in the morning.

The inspectors were still interviewing. I invited Matron into the house. I knew she would not be able to sleep, so she paced our kitchen as a change from her own. In time the inspectors left and what remained of the night was absorbed unnoticed into the day. At morning assembly I announced George's disappearance to the whole of the school and the chaplain offered up prayers for his safe return. And after assembly the inspectors returned. The school routine was totally disrupted but I accepted that necessity. There was an air of excitement amongst the boys owing to the thrill of survival. Sir Henry had joined the search party and I was relieved that an event had interfered with his silence.

I felt powerless, and I shut myself in my study for longed-for privacy. And I phoned Matthew. I caught him just as he was going to work, but he gave me time to listen to my story. Even then, surrounded as I was by society, I needed a listener. Matthew said nothing, but I sensed his horror and sympathy down the line. When I had finished, he offered to come down. I told him there was nothing he could do, but that I would keep him informed.

But he didn't need me as a courier. The story was splashed soon enough across the lunch-time edition of the London evening newspaper. 'CABINET MINISTER'S SON MISSING' was the headline and beneath it a photograph showed Sir Henry at the centre of the search party. During the day the reporters came in their hordes, and from all over England. They carried their notebooks and cameras and thinly veiled enthusiasm. Amongst them there was a television film crew. They found enough boys willing to talk to them, but few teachers volunteered and Matron gave them very short shrift and told them to go back where they had come from. I handed them a prepared statement which provided nothing more than the facts that they already knew but I could not avoid the photographers. It seemed to me that the person of young George Tilbury was slowly disappearing under a cloud of reportage. Somewhere, out there, George was wandering, either in body or in spirit, but the search and the lake-draining had grabbed the headlines and the cause was obliterated in its effect.

Lady Tilbury arrived later that afternoon and Lucy comforted her as well as she could. She had left someone in the house in case George made any contact, with instructions to phone the school immediately. And every time the phone rang, which it did frequently that day, she inhaled with hope, only to breathe out her terror. After a remedial cup of tea, which cured nothing, she insisted on joining the search. From reports from the outside I knew that divers had entered the lake and I was loath to escort her to the lakeside to find them drawing a blank, or worse, making a discovery. But she insisted. So I took her there, muttering all the while about not giving up hope, and trying to imbue my voice with some confidence.

She joined her husband at the lake and I noticed a clutch of photographers at the ready, their fingers on the trigger, waiting for the kill. I turned away with some excuse that I had people waiting to see me and I returned to the school.

Night fell with no findings, and the search was planned to include the village and the nearest town. By the morning Scotland Yard had joined in the enquiries. And more inspectors visited the school.

Over the next few days while George's disappearance was causing more and more concern, a number of boys and some teachers were asked to go down to the station to make statements to the police. I noted that all the boys called were of the Eccles group. Eccles himself was not summoned though I'd noticed that even during the disruption of routine he had still managed to host his tea-parties in his study. David Solomon was the only outsider who went down to the station. And that was understandable because he was George's friend. Yet I noticed a certain reluctance in his gait. It lacked the willingness and even the eagerness of the others. He looked at me as he was led away, and gave a sad shrug of his shoulders. Of the teachers, there were two. Smith of geography, with whom I had a distant relationship – he rather disapproved of my constant availability to the boys – and Jones from maths in the lower school, with whom I'd had little contact.

George had been gone for over a week, and the search party were running out of places to look. Sir Henry and Lady Tilbury had returned home and sat together in silence waiting for the knock on the door. Term was nearly over and I tried to reorganise our old routine. But in going back to regular lessons and assemblies it seemed that we had written George off, that his disappearance was a mystery that was never likely to be solved. No clues had been found, no arrests had been made. There were not even suspicious rumours around. But something was different. Very different. And it disturbed me. I noticed that, at my lunch-table, some of the chairs were empty. Eccles and Fenby were faithful regulars, as was Dr Reynolds, my deputy. But Smith, I noticed, was eating amongst the members of his house, and Brown from chemistry was nowhere to be seen. When I spoke at assembly every morning, I referred to George's disappearance with prayers and hopes for his safety. And while I spoke, I heard rustling in the hall, and murmuring, and even at one point, a grunt of disdain. Dr Reynolds called for order, but I was completely unnerved, and when it was over, I went straight to my study, and for the first time in my life I was afraid. More than afraid. Terrified. And I didn't know why.

Now of course I know. Which is why I can't write any more. I cannot face the words of what must now be written. I shall wait for Sam to come and listen to it all.

They have brought me my supper, but I have no appetite. I am glad when the prison governor comes to my cell. He drops in to see me from time to time. He has brought me something, he says. And he hands me a piece of paper, a poem written by his ten-year-old son and it is dedicated to me. I read it with gratitude. It's about injustice and how truth will conquer. But most of all, it *rhymes*. I am suddenly elated. Beyond my walls there are still children who find joy in verse. There are still writers and poets and painters outside, who know the meaning of the spaces between words, who see the undrawn images, who hear the unnotated sounds, and somehow that thought creates for me a company of which, with luck, I may become a part. I am crying with the pity of it all. The governor puts his hand on my shoulder. 'Thank your son,' I say. 'I will treasure his gift. Tell him it has given me hope.'

Sam came yesterday and he listened. And I knew that I had to go on.

21

It was the last week of term and I was glad of it. For I was still very frightened. I tried to ascribe the hostility I sensed around me to the need for someone to blame. George's disappearance had rocked the school and, as headmaster, I was the obvious target for their rage, pain and bewilderment. I hoped that by the beginning of the summer term, time would have healed their wounds, and this hope helped to get me through. Every morning, at 9.30, the police would phone me with an update on the George investigation. It consisted of three words, and it never varied. 'No further progress.' I kept in constant touch with the Tilburys simply to commiserate with their fears. It was the waiting that was so painful. Sometimes I thought that a breakthrough of any kind, even of the worst, would have been a relief. I had cancelled all end-of-term festivities. Nobody complained. I hoped to see the term out in a solemn and dignified manner.

Then the bombshell dropped. Though, as I discovered later, it had been slowly falling for some time. It was a Wednesday and I sat in my office waiting for my regular 9.30 call. My phone did not ring. At ten o'clock I thought of phoning the station myself and asking for my daily conduit Inspector Wilkins. I gave him till noon, but still he had made no contact.

So I dialled his direct number. A woman's voice answered.

'Can I speak with Inspector Wilkins?' I asked.

'Who's speaking?'

'Sir Alfred Dreyfus,' I said. It was a name of which she must take notice. There was a pause. Quite a long one, and I heard a rustling of papers. Then the woman came back on the line.

'He's out I'm afraid, and I don't know when he'll be back.'

I put the phone down. I felt uneasy. I had the feeling that Inspector Wilkins was not out at all, that he was sitting at his desk miming his absence to his clerk. I don't know why I was frightened. I felt like an innocent stag who, hearing with his inner ear the rustle of leaves and the cocking of a barrel, runs for his life into the camouflage of the forest. And I bolted, back to my house, and my safe haven. Or so I thought. For the news that was to await me there only served to augment my fears. We settled down to lunch, Lucy and I.

'Any news?' she asked.

'None,' I said. 'The same message. No further progress.' I lied to her because I didn't want to show my unease. Halfway through lunch, Clara, our cleaner, arrived. She always came late on a Wednesday. Wednesday morning was her shift for preparing meals-on-wheels. She was all of a fluster.

'Have you heard anything?' she said, hinting that she herself had information.

'No, nothing,' Lucy said. 'There's been no progress.'

'There's a rumour going round the village. They say a body's been found.'

'Oh my God,' I said. 'Where? And is it George?'

'I don't know,' Clara said. 'That's all I heard. I asked around but no one knew anything. It was just a rumour I suppose.'

I wondered whether the discovery, if there was one, had anything to do with my lack of daily bulletin. I went back to school soon after lunch and I kept my ears open, but the rumour had not spread that far. I waited at my phone for the rest of the day, hoping that Inspector Wilkins would call, but hoping too that he wouldn't. At six o'clock, I went back to the house. The children were home from school and Lucy was preparing supper. I noticed that the table was set for five. Another tremor. Anything non-routine frightened me. I was about to ask Lucy who was the fifth diner, when Matthew came into the kitchen.

'Surprise?' he asked. 'I got a few days off work, so I came down. Susan and the children arrive on Saturday.'

I was delighted to see him of course, as I always was, but the timing of his visit seemed ominous. For some reason I saw it as a move of pre-emptive support and I wondered why I was going to need it.

'Any news?' Matthew asked.

'Nothing,' I said.

It was Lucy who mentioned the rumour, but I said that I gave it no credence. The village was rife with gossip and gossipers and they were possibly so fed up with the lack of progress they had invented their own. Matthew suggested we go down to the village pub for a drink before dinner. 'Perhaps we can pick up some more rumours,' he said.

I was wary of going. I felt that by showing myself in public I was placing myself in the firing-line. I don't know why. I had absolutely no cause on earth to feel accused. It was preposterous even to think about it. I dared not share those fears with Matthew. I barely admitted them to myself. So I agreed to go with him for a pre-prandial drink. I half hoped that the rumour was true, that the body found, God forgive me, was that of young George Tilbury and that the police could once and for all find his murderer.

The pub was crowded and full of loud whisper. I expected a silence to fall as soon as we entered, but though we were noticed the hum was interrupted only to greet us. Matthew was especially welcomed since he was an occasional visitor and they asked after Susan and the children. I noticed a few of my staff around the bar, and they acknowledged me with a smile. One even offered to buy me a drink. But somehow their smiles and bonhomie instilled me with the same fear. No one spoke of the rumour; it was obviously a stillborn hearsay. We had one more drink and then I suggested we leave since supper would be ready. I did not want to announce our departure, so I whispered 'goodnight' to the landlord and we made to leave. As we reached the door, the landlord shouted 'goodnight, Sir Alfred' across the bar, so our departure was public. Once outside, I lingered a while, fully expecting a sudden silence to fall, but the hum continued as before.

We took a short cut through the grounds. The front of school was in darkness, which did not surprise me for the dormitories and staff quarters, including my own house were at the back. But as we passed I noticed that one front light was switched on and that shadowy figures filtered the uncurtained windows. I knew that room to be Eccles's study and I don't know why my unease returned. But during the evening, I relaxed once more. Lucy had made a special supper and I opened a good bottle of wine. We played with the children for a while until Matthew said he was tired and needed an early night. The children were bedded and Matthew settled in his room. We held our silence, Lucy and I, until the telephone screamed an interruption. I thought it must be a tardy call from Inspector Wilkins with the day's bulletin. I rushed to answer it, but as I picked up the receiver, the purr of the dialling tone whistled past my ear.

'It was nobody,' I said to Lucy. 'Probably the wrong number.'

Why did I think it was the right number and that whoever it was on the end of the line was checking on my whereabouts? We went to bed early that night, Lucy and I. It was a way of avoiding the silence between us. But I couldn't sleep. I kept thinking of that light in Eccles's study and the shadows that crossed the window-panes, and somehow it was all linked with that heinous Eccles wink that I had never forgotten. Eventually I fell asleep, exhausted by fear.

(Oh Sam, Sam. Please come and *listen*.)

I woke up suddenly and for no reason. My alarm clock showed 6.15. The house was very quiet. Lucy was sleeping soundly. I heard the tweeting of a bird and a distant cock crow. Through the window I could see the crowns of birch trees in full leaf. I felt suddenly joyful to be alive.

The knock on the front door was not polite. It was thunder. I leapt out of bed, and so did Lucy. We stared at each other and I saw fear in her eyes. I heard Matthew leaving his room. Then the knocks came again and I hoped they wouldn't wake the children. I tugged on my dressing-gown and leapt down the stairs, hoping that whoever it was wouldn't knock again. Lucy and Matthew were by my side before I opened the door. Two men stood there, one of whom I recognised as Inspector Wilkins. Mercifully they were in plain clothes. They clearly had news of George and I made to invite them inside. But I didn't have to. They invited themselves and shut the front door behind them. We stared at each other.

'Sir Alfred Dreyfus?' Inspector Wilkins said.

I wondered at his sudden formality.

'Of course,' I laughed. 'You know that very well.'

'Sir Alfred Dreyfus,' he said again, and there was no hint of a smile anywhere, 'I am arresting you on the charge of the murder of George Tilbury. You don't have to say anything, but anything you say will be . . .'

I was convinced I was watching television or perhaps even playing a starring role in a crime series. I heard Lucy scream and I felt the handcuffs around my wrists and I still thought it was television and I wanted to switch it off. It was much too early in the day to be watching the box. I felt myself being led away. I heard Matthew say that he would get me a lawyer, and Lucy whisper, 'This is monstrous.'

I did not look back at the house. It did not occur to me that I would never enter it again. I was led to an unmarked car that was waiting in the driveway and noticed that my own car was not there. 'My car's gone,' I said.

'We've taken it away,' the Inspector informed me. I looked back at the school and noted that Eccles's light was still burning. And in that moment I knew that it was not television, and that I was being charged with young George Tilbury's murder.

I sat between my two silent captors during the ten-minute drive to the police station. Few people were in the streets, but none of them seemed to take note of the car. As we drew up outside the station, Inspector Wilkins asked, 'Would you like a blanket to cover your face?'

'Whatever for?' I said. 'I've nothing to hide.' I don't know what I expected them to say, but in any case, they made no response. I was practically dragged into the station, and during my passage, I imagined the apologies they would offer me when they realised their terrible mistake and I weighed up the pros and cons of forgiving them. I was Sir Alfred Dreyfus still.

I was taken to a desk and told to empty my pockets. But I had none, since I was still in my pyjamas, so that routine was quickly dispensed with. The handcuffs were removed and so was my watch, for which I had to sign, and I was led to an interviewing room. My two captors sat opposite me. One of them turned on a tape-machine and spoke into it, giving the time and the names of those present. I said at once that I was saying nothing until my lawyer arrived.

'Do you not want to hear the evidence?' Inspector Wilkins asked.

I was beginning to hate that man. 'No,' I said firmly. 'I shall wait for my lawyer to advise me.'

Wilkins's side-kick then said, 'Interview terminated,' and once again he gave the time which was barely a minute after we had started. I was shown to a cell by another policeman, this one in uniform.

'You'd better get used to it,' he said as he let me inside. Then, more kindly, 'Have you had breakfast?'

I couldn't answer him. I was beginning not to understand anything at all. I sat on the bunk that stretched along one wall and very much wanted to cry. I thought of Lucy and the children. They would be at breakfast by now. I wondered how she would explain to them my absence. And Matthew. What was he doing? How was he feeling? Was he sharing my own sublime indignation? I hoped he would contact Simon Posner, a good lawyer who knew our family well. He would be as horrified as I.

Soon my guard brought in a breakfast tray. I was surprised at my appetite. The food was wholesome but tasteless, and it sat-isfied my hunger. I even relished the large mug of tea, and for a moment, I saw myself as a convict and I laughed. I imagined retelling the story to my children and I could picture their wide-eyed amazement. I looked at my wrist and realised that I had no way of telling the time. It would be quite exciting, I thought, to live without a watch, to check on time's passing with the rise and setting of the sun. I couldn't understand why I was having such gentle and benign thoughts, while inside myself I raged with fury. And that fury was fatiguing. I lay down on the bunk and shortly must have fallen asleep in an effort to make up for my so rudely interrupted night. When I was woken by the guard, I automatically looked at my wrist. I didn't know how long I had slept. It was still light outside and I was hungry. I reckoned it must be lunch-hour. But the guard told me it was only eleven o'clock and that my lawyer had arrived. I was still muzzy from sleep and I wondered why a lawyer had come to see me. Then I looked at my surroundings and I knew.

I was led to an interview room where Simon was waiting. I was glad to see him, and he gave me an equal welcome. The guard withdrew and shut the door. We were alone for whatever advice he had to give me. I sat down opposite him.

'Forgive my attire,' I said. 'They got me out of bed.'

'Matthew is bringing in a suit,' Simon said.

'Then at least I can go home dressed.'

'I don't think so.' Simon laid his hand on my arm. 'It looks bad, Alfred,' he said.

'What looks bad? What evidence have they got for heaven's sake? They haven't even found the body. What are they looking for? A scapegoat?' Suddenly that word sounded particularly Yiddish, as if it had been coined for no other race.

'They've found the body,' Simon said.

'Where?'

'That's the terrible point. It had been buried in your garden in Kent.'

A deafening sound rang in my head. Simon's words hit me like shrapnel. I curled with the wounds. In my mind my child-hood village was host to only two graves, two sacred plots, and our cottage garden bore the fruits of what they had tended, and where Matthew and I had played with our children. Now it was sullied entirely, and their memory tarnished. 'How dare they!' I almost screamed.

'It's hard evidence,' Simon said. 'It points the finger at you.'

'Rubbish,' I said. 'There has to be more than that.'

'There is,' Simon said, 'but as yet I've had no time to assess it. All I know is that some of your boys have made statements accusing you and offering proof. I've not seen the statements as yet, but I gather that they are pretty damning.'

I don't know why, but at that moment I sensed that Simon was not the right choice for my defence. He showed little appetite in proclaiming my innocence, and his pessimism worried me. Now, in hindsight, I know I should have heeded those warnings.

Suddenly I felt ill. I could actually feel the colour draining out of my face. Simon poured me a glass of water. I had entered a nightmare.

'When will you see these statements?' I asked.

'I shall study them in the next few days while I prepare your defence. Meanwhile you are due to appear in the magistrates' court in the morning. I shall be with you. You will be formally charged with murder and asked if you plead guilty or not guilty. You will reply "not guilty". Then you will be remanded in custody and probably be sent for trial at the Old Bailey.'

'Simon,' I said, unbelieving, 'you're my friend.'

'And will continue to be so,' Simon said. He rose. 'There's one thing I must ask you,' he said. 'It's a mere formality.'

'I know Simon,' I said. 'Did I do it? And the answer's no. Absolutely not. So you can defend me with a clear conscience.'

'Thank you, my friend,' he said.

I was led back to my cell and given a tray that passed for lunch. I must have dozed off again, for I was woken by my supper tray, though it was still light, and sardonically wished a good night. I didn't expect to sleep at all and I wished I had something to read. But my fatigue surprised me, a fatigue fed by despair and utter bewilderment. And a terrible sadness. I wept for young George and I cursed whoever it was who had taken his life, and doubly cursed him for his choice of burial ground.

I was woken by birdsong, but it did not elicit that joy I had felt as I lay in my own bed at home. And the thought struck me for the first time that this day might be my last of freedom for a very long time. The guard brought me my breakfast, together with my suit and toilet bag and, when I had eaten, he took me to the cloakroom where he watched me wash, shave and dress.

The magistrates' court was reached through an underground tunnel that led from the station so I was not obliged to appear on the street. But even from the inside I could hear the hum of the crowd. And it was a hostile hum, a lynching hum, and I was afraid. I was handcuffed once again and led into the court. The sudden light blinded me and I could not at first see the faces of the crowd, but after a time of adjustment, I noted that the court was filled to capacity. I looked among the faces for Lucy and Matthew, but I could not spot them. The magistrate and his two side-kicks took their seats on the bench.

'Will the prisoner stand?' somebody said.

I obeyed, and as I did so I identified a number of my pupils in the front row and wondered who had given them permission to leave the school. I felt that I had already lost my headship, and I could not help but think that it was Eccles who had given them leave. Behind them, I caught sight of Lucy and Matthew and I thought that they had come to take me home.

'Sir Alfred Dreyfus,' the magistrate said, 'you are charged with the murder of George Tilbury. Do you plead guilty or not guilty?'

'Not guilty, my Lord,' I said, as I had been instructed. It was, in any case, the truth. Simon asked for bail, but it was refused as he had expected. The case against me was presumably so strong that the magistrate feared I might abscond. I was sentenced on remand to remain in prison until my appearance for trial at the Old Bailey. Then I was led down. I looked back at Lucy and Matthew, and Lucy blew me a kiss. Matthew mouthed something; I think it was 'courage'. Then I was once more handcuffed and led to the court door that opened on to the street. Without my permission, my head was draped with a blanket and I felt myself suddenly in the open air, guided by two strong hands. It was only a few steps to the waiting van but in that short transit I heard catcalls and shouts of 'murderer'. And, as I was driven away, there were angry shouts and bangings on the side of the van. I had been charged with murder. I had not been tried. I had not been found guilty. Yet the mob had made up their minds.

Their verdict had been fuelled by rumour. Rumour that I was a Jew. At the time, I wondered at its source. Now I know that it was one of Eccles's men who dropped that explosive word into the crowd, and it had spread like delicious wildfire throughout the throng.

They vented their spleen on glass and stone. That night the nearest synagogue, some twenty miles away, was partially destroyed by fire. And the Jewish cemetery, not far distant, was vandalised. Swastikas were painted boldly on the tombs.

I don't know what prison I was taken to. It wasn't this one. That I know. I know that it was on the outskirts of London and I think it was a makeshift place because of prison overcrowding.

It was a waiting time and I resigned myself to it. For I still lived in hope. I couldn't imagine on what evidence I could be found guilty. But those outside had already given their verdict. Matthew, I heard, had been made redundant with a suitable pay-off. Lucy and the children had been obliged to move out of the school house. Dreyfus was already a cursed name. The site of young George's burial had become a magnetic attraction, and cars pulled up outside our parents' cottage and disgorged their gaping sightseers. In the tourist trade our childhood village now ranked with Canterbury Cathedral.

But what broke my heart, and what I shall never never forgive, was what those vandals did to my parents' last resting-place. Despite the Jesus that protected them, their tombs fared no better than those of their kind who were buried according to the Mosaic law. For like those, they were swastika-daubed, and the protecting arm of Jesus was chopped off at the elbow. As a finishing touch, red paint had been smeared on the stone wound.

The lie that my father and my mother had lived all their lives had now, once and for all, exploded.

PART THREE

22

I digress. I postpone. My mind wanders and my hand follows
into a nightmare sketch of my trial. I fool myself into thinking
that a drawing will set the scene for what I have now to write,
that it will facilitate the flow of words. I am setting the scene so
that I know where I am. But I hoodwink myself. I know exactly
where I am and the terrifying purpose of my being here.
Nevertheless, I set the scene. And not only that. I must dress

for the part. I put on the suit that Matthew has delivered to the prison. I must look respectable. Above all, I must look innocent. But for God's sake, that is what I am, suit or no suit. I must speak loud and clear and convey to my audience a belief in myself. So I practise, 'Not guilty, My Lord', as I pace my cell and then I wonder why I am pleading innocence at all, since no one has any reason to accuse me of guilt. Nevertheless, I must look at the jury without fear and I practise that look on my four bare walls.

I am preparing for my trial. I am setting the scene. I arrange the props. I dress for it, and I invent stage directions that have nothing to do with anything at all. Anything, sooner than put it down in words that I cannot find. So I turn on my radio as a further means of postponement. I hear of yet another suicide bomb in Tel Aviv. Four more people killed and countless injured. Many children amongst them. And suddenly I cease to pity myself.

Enough of these doodlings and digressions. I pick up my pen and I hold it firmly, because I know how anxious it is to slip my grasp. But I master it and go in search of those words that are so fearfully hidden.

They came for me as the prison clock struck eight, and I recalled that not so very long ago that same bell tolled the hanging of a poor prisoner who might well have been innocent. I shivered. They took away my untouched breakfast tray. They watched me as I shaved. Although I shaved daily, I rarely studied my face in the mirror. But that morning I looked at myself very carefully, and for the first time in my life I saw how Jewish I appeared. Why that morning, of all mornings, did I acknowledge those features that all of my life I had ignored, in the hope that the beholders would do likewise? And had I gone through life masked, would I still have been rumbled? Did my feet look Jewish? My hands? These thoughts troubled me. And on this morning of all mornings, I knew why. They were simply the pith and marrow of my trial and the nub of the verdict. I put on my suit of innocence and I was ready.

Once in the van, I noticed the time-honoured blanket at the ready and I wondered whom last it had shielded and whether it still smelt of his guilt or otherwise. When the van drew up outside the court, I heard the hissing verdict of the crowd and I was glad of the blanket-cloak. I stumbled into the building like a guilty man.

I had to wait in the basement cell for a while. Simon was already there, and once again he recapped on the charges against me. He smiled a lot, and even offered a few jokes, but I knew they were ruses to cover his pessimism. He rehearsed me again in my 'Not Guilty' plea which, by now, so over-practised, sounded meaningless in my ear. I refused to rehearse it further. We sat silently together. Simon seemed to have run out of advice and it was a relief when the guards came to fetch me.

'See you in court,' he said, as if I had an alternative choice.

I stood between the two guards who each held me by the elbows. I noted that their touch was gentle and I thought that perhaps they were on my side. A desperate man will clutch at any straw. We were faced with a long and narrow corridor. At the end of it, I could see the beginning of a flight of steps. I knew that they led to the courtroom and the dock wherein I would be charged and I suddenly saw them as steps to a scaffold, and I tripped in fear. I felt a tighter grip on my elbows.

'Come along now,' one of the guards said. His tone was kindly, and having no choice I obeyed him. But I tripped again as we mounted the steps. My body pulsed from head to toe with a floundering fear. Again they gripped me, less kindly this time, and I had to be dragged to the top steps and the small platform that led into the dock. It was not a happy entrance. My reluctance to appear already marked me as guilty and my over-rehearsed plea sounded hollow in my ear. I straightened myself as I took my place in the dock but I felt that it was already too late to offset my appalling debut with the stance of innocence. I looked at the rail in front of me. I daren't look anywhere else. I did not trust my face. I did not trust its expression which I feared was beyond my control. In my eye-line I saw the belly of the courtroom and the public gallery, and a sea of indistinguishable faces. I did not want to catch sight of anybody I knew. I was tempted to shut my eyes tight in the childlike hope that I would be invisible. I saw them all stand and I knew that the judge had entered, but I kept my eyes fixed on the rail. I knew I had to be bold. My timid stance, my low-ered gaze, indicated an abundance of shame and remorse. But I felt neither, nor had reason to. So I straightened my back, looked directly at the bench, then at the clerk of the court as he read out the arraignment.

'Sir Alfred Benjamin Dreyfus,' he boomed my name into the courtroom.

I was relieved to hear that I was still titled but that relief was quickly soured by the sound of that middle name of mine, one that I had never had reason to use and had almost forgotten. Benjamin. A name which in Hebrew means 'son of my right hand'. A beautiful name, I thought, though so undeniably Jewish. Whereas 'Alfred' was a count-me-in name, one could hardly get away with Benjamin. I was tempted to look at the jury to gauge their reaction, but again, I didn't trust my face.

The voice of the clerk of the court interrupted my thoughts and I could not help but hear his arraignment.

'You are charged that on April the fourth last, or there-abouts, you did murder George Henry Tilbury. How do you plead? Guilty or not guilty?'

I dried. They say that practice makes perfect. It is not true. God knows I had practised my plea often enough. But the words had gone. Gone from my mind and even I feared, from my heart. For suddenly I didn't know how I should plead. The charge was so preposterous that neither plea would have given it credence. Once again, the clerk repeated his question and again my throat was dry. I looked at Simon who was staring at me, bewildered. Then, like a stage prompt, he mouthed my reply. 'Not guilty,' I repeated out of Simon's mouth, and 'not guilty' again, to make up for the plea I had missed on the first cue. I was not doing myself any good, I knew. What with my feeble entrance, and my plea-hesitation, things did not augur well for my defence. I saw Simon wipe his brow. I had let him down.

The clerk of the court, having dealt with me according to his office, now turned his attention to the jury. I was glad to take the opportunity to look at them for the first time in the safe knowledge that they wouldn't be looking at me, for they were paying attention to the clerk's instructions. They were a grim gathering, one mindful of their heavy responsibility. I was glad to see two black faces amongst them, a man and a woman and I drew a measure of hope from their presence. After all, they too belong to a persecuted race and have been ever since white was the colour of power. And in a way, I thought, their lot was even worse than that of my own tribe, for there was never a remote possibility of their pleading 'count me in'. As I studied them I listened to the clerk's words.

'Members of the jury,' he was saying, 'the prisoner at the bar is charged with the murder of George Henry Tilbury on or about April the fourth last. To this indictment he has pleaded not guilty. It is in your charge to say, having heard the evidence, whether he be guilty or not.'

At the end of his little speech, they all turned to look at me and I turned my head away, although I knew it was a mistake and I pitied Simon for the uphill task that I was preparing for him. I was told that I could sit down, and I was grateful because I was tired, worn-out with fear. I watched the counsel for the Crown, the chief prosecutor, as he rose to his feet. He took his time. It was not that he had difficulty standing. His slow timing was made for effect. He did not stand but rose, as befitted the dignity and power of his office and throughout that movement he kept his eyes on me. This time I did not turn my head. I stared at him with a look of challenge. Perhaps that was a mistake too, but it seemed that whatever I did or however I behaved was neither in nor out of my favour. Once again a sense of helplessness overcame me and I felt my shoulders drooping in translation of my mood.

After the rising was over, the crown prosecutor took an equal time to assume his stance. I could not see his feet, but I imagined that he stood with his legs slightly apart for before speaking he practised one or two swivels, to his right in line with the jury, to his left to face the judge and then in his centre balancing to lay his beady eye on me. I was beginning to hate him.

His first swivel was to the jury. 'Ladies and gentlemen,' he said, 'this case as we all know, has attracted a great deal of publicity both in the press and on television. I want you to put all that publicity out of your minds. It has nothing to do with justice. We are here to grant the accused a fair trial. The case shall be tried on the evidence alone and on that evidence alone, you will give your verdict.'

He now swivelled towards the bench. 'May it please you, My Lord,' he said, 'in this case, I am instructed for the Crown together with my friend and colleague, Derek Chambers. The accused, Sir Alfred Benjamin Dreyfus, is represented by my friend and colleague, Simon Posner, who is assisted by James Windsor.'

I was not happy to hear that Simon was my accuser's friend, but I passed it off as a turn of phrase and hoped that there was no truth in it. His final swivel landed in my eye-line.

'The charge against the accused,' he said, 'is that on or about April the fourth of this year he did murder George Henry Tilbury, and bury his body in the garden of his cottage in Kent.'

He paused to take a drink of water. I knew he wasn't thirsty. The gesture was in line with his affectations of rising and swivelling and, while he was slaking his non-thirst, I took the opportunity to slide my eyes around the public gallery. It was Lucy whom I saw first, flanked by Matthew and Susan. They smiled at me, all three of them, though there was no hiding the alarm that dimmed their smiles. I could see none of my staff from the school and I presumed that they were being called as witnesses. I tried to search out some pupils but could find none, until my eyes rested with relief on young David Solomon, who gave me a smile of that same quality that my family had donated.

The prosecutor returned his glass to the table. 'The case for the prosecution is as follows,' he said. Now he swivelled once more to the jury. 'Ladies and gentlemen,' be began, 'this is the most tragic case. A young boy, young George Tilbury, was viciously stabbed to death. He was of a mere fourteen years, and was never to reach manhood. Was never to enjoy his undergraduate years, was never to fall in love, was never to marry, was never to father children. It is contrary to the natural order of things, ladies and gentlemen, that parents should survive their children, and here we have a heartbroken mother and father whose grief is inconsolable.' Here he paused, which gave time for the jury, the audience and myself to agree with every word that he had said. He now swivelled towards me with an accusing stare. 'Sir Alfred Dreyfus,' he said, 'this man whom you see in the dock, stands accused, and in the opinion of the Crown Prosecution, stands rightly accused, of George Tilbury's murder. Now why, you may ask, should anyone want to murder a young and innocent child? The answer in this case is simple greed, self-aggrandisement and overweening ambition. Hardly enough, you might think, to justify murder. But if you add to all these reasons the spur of evil, evil incarnate, and nothing less my friends, you will understand, with equal amounts of sorrow and horror, how this tragedy came to pass.'

He slaked his non-thirst once more, though this time I may
have been wrong. It is more than possible that he was thirsty.
His natural flow of saliva was not sufficient to irrigate his outburst of histrionics. He drank deeply, as if he really needed
to, and I could swear that all the court drank with him in
sympathy.

'Sir Alfred Dreyfus, the accused,' he went on, 'is a highly
educated man who has achieved honours in his field and who
has been awarded a knighthood by the Queen for his services to
education. He has served as master and headmaster in fine
schools, the finest of all being that of his present incumbency.
Indeed he has reached the very peak of his profession. Yet this
man, this accused man, ladies and gentlemen of the jury, this
forty-eight-year-old man, has lived a lie every day of his life.
Not a lie by commission, ladies and gentleman, but one rather
more heinous. He has lived a lie of omission. In other words, he
has hidden the fact that he is a Jew. Now you might well say to
yourselves, "What is wrong with that? If a man chooses to pass
as a Gentile, that is a pity, but it is his business, and there is
nothing criminal in his intent." And you would be right, members of the jury. But if he fails to disclose his identity, and
indeed finds all means at his disposal to hide it in order to
achieve the headmastership of the finest school in the land, of a
Church of England establishment, if he conceals an identity
which would be unacceptable in such a renowned school, if, I
repeat, he is at such pains to hide it, pains to the point of
murder, then I think ladies and gentlemen, that we are here
dealing with a monstrous crime. He is a cunning man, the
accused, and his subterfuge was so arch, so manipulative, that
he might well have got away with it were it not for the bewildered, innocent and God-fearing George Tilbury who, on
discovering the disguise, decided to bring it out into the open.
And paid the ultimate price for his faith.'

I could not help but admire the man, and I was clearly not

alone. I dared to take a look at the jury and I found them all gazing at him with reverence. I forbore to look at the spectators, and I certainly dared not glance at Simon for I feared he could in no way match his adversary's oratory.

Another glass of water for my accuser. The slow swallow, the clear relish, and the dramatic laying down of the glass. 'Now, my Lord,' he turned to the bench, 'I call upon my first witness. Mr James Turncastle.'

23

I must stop now. I cannot write further. I cannot bear to hear in my heart the echo of the tissue of lies that came out of a mouth of one I had looked upon as a son. I cannot bear it. Moreover, I feel ill. Seriously ill. My heart pumps and my head throbs to its rhythm. And although I have nothing to look forward to in my life, except for its miserable duration in this wretched abode, I still am anxious for my health. I don't want to die. My innocence forbids it. I want no posthumous pardon.

I call the guard. I shout for him. I am frightened. They bring me the doctor. He is a kindly fellow who, I dare to hope, believes in my innocence. He orders me to the prison hospital. 'For observation,' he says. 'You'll be in a ward with others,' he whispers to me. He thinks I am suffering from abject loneliness, and maybe he is right.

As soon as I am put into a bed, which lies between two other prisoners, I feel slightly better. But I am wired up to a heart-machine, my blood pressure is taken, my pulse and my temperature. I lie in that bed for three days, under constant observation, and at the end of it my rage subsides. I do not want to go back to my cell. The writing awaits me there and I am not sure that I am ready for it. I have grown used to company, to the sound of others' voices, others' groans, others' sighs, and even to the occasional exchange of words. The man on the right-hand side of me is a lifer too. He tells me his name is Martin. He knows mine.

'You're famous,' he says.

I don't have to ask what he's in for. A lifer is almost always a murderer. I wonder whether, like me, he is innocent. But I don't ask him. Having been in solitary for so long, I have never learned the prison jargon, nor its etiquette. I know there are some questions that must never be asked and I imagine that the question of innocence or guilt is one of them. But on my second day of observation, Martin volunteers.

'I killed my wife,' he says.

'Why?' I ask, because I sense that some reaction is expected of me.

'She was getting on my nerves,' Martin says.

I don't know why, but I want to laugh. In everybody's life there must be numerous people who get on one's nerves. Hardly enough to justify murder.

'D'you ever feel sorry?' I ask.

'No, never,' he laughs. 'Didn't start living till I came to this place. Never 'ad so many mates. Right old social club in 'ere. I'll miss them.'

'Are you being released?' I ask with a touch of envy.

'In a way, I s'pose I am.' He laughs again. 'No mate,' he goes on, 'I'm kicking the bucket. Got cancer. A couple of weeks they give me. You got to accept it. Life just isn't fair.'

Well it certainly wasn't fair to his poor old wife, I think. But despite everything, I feel sorry for him.

'Just not fair,' he says again. 'Copped a rotten judge, I did. Just my luck. One of your people 'e was.'

I let it pass. The man was dying. There is no point in arguing with him. He will not be a threat for much longer.

'What did you do outside?' I ask, hoping to change the subject.

'I was a brickie,' he says. 'My boss was one of yours too,' he says. 'Jesus, they're everywhere, aren't they.'

'Not too many of them here,' I cannot help saying and that shuts him up a bit, but he leaves my pulse throbbing. I know that in this man's company it's not likely to subside. I look at him and I see that he has gone to sleep, and I marvel at how innocent he looks and I wonder how I look when I am sleeping. A distant clock strikes eight. It is already past my prison bedtime. The nurse comes and again he takes my pulse, my blood pressure and my temperature. He gives me something to help me sleep and I am grateful. I take the night drink and feel already drowsy. Martin is groaning in his sleep, and now he looks less innocent. He seems restless. His hands grope at nothing outside the sheet, and I note that his feet shiver under the covers. I turn my back to him and lie on my side and in the morning I wake in exactly the same position. I have slept so deeply that it takes me some time to remember where I am, and why I am there. I turn around to see if Martin is awake. His bed is empty. And stripped. And I know that he has died in the night while my Jewish back was turned. I cannot help but mourn his passing. In the old days, he would have been hanged. And perhaps that would have been kinder. Instead he was condemned to a very loose noose, and a drop of painfully slow descent, until in a final spasm he could legitimately bite the dust.

Despite my distress, I eat a large breakfast and when the doctor comes later that morning he pronounces me well enough to return to my cell. And I am ready. The writing is waiting for me. With Martin's death, the world is minus one anti-Semite. But that is no cause for celebration. There will never be a shortage of Martins. But as he said, 'Jesus, they're everywhere,' I must go on writing to prove that the likes of Martin are right. We *are* everywhere. And what's more, we are not going to go away.

24

I watched as James took the stand. I thought of Lucy and wondered what she must be thinking but I knew that she shared with me all the regrets for the affection and care we had shown to this sadly deprived boy. His very presence in the box as a witness for the prosecution testified to his gross abuse of that affection and to his ingrate disloyalty.

In view of his youth, the Judge did not oblige him to take the oath. He asked him if he knew the difference between right and wrong, between a lie and a truth.

James nodded.

'Say yes or no,' the Judge said.

'Yes,' James said firmly. 'I know the difference.'

After the formal declaration of his name and residence, which latter James gave as his Devonian toe-hold, the prosecutor asked him to describe in his own words his relationship with the accused.

'We were very close,' he began. 'He treated me like a son. He took me into his family. I was friends with his children. I looked upon him as a surrogate father.'

So far, so truthful, I thought. But ominous. For his was a preamble that heralded a woeful change.

'When was it that you first had doubts about the accused?' the prosecutor helped him along. 'You may take your time,' he said, assisting him further.

'I was staying at his house one weekend,' James said. 'We were going for a walk and it was very cold. I wanted to go back up to the school to fetch a jumper. But Sir said I could borrow one of his, and he told me where to find one. I went to the drawer and in among the sweaters I found a piece of silk. I pulled it out to look at it. It was white with blue stripes and there were silk tassels on each end. I knew what it was. I'd seen it in films. It was a Jewish prayer-shawl and I wondered what it was doing in Sir's drawer. I didn't mention it to Sir, but it worried me a bit.'

It was true that I had a prayer-shawl, but James could never have seen it for it was locked in a chest. When I had first found it after my father's death, I was bewildered. And deeply moved. I had never seen my father wear it. Indeed he had no cause, since to my knowledge he had never entered a synagogue. I presumed that the prayer-shawl had belonged to my grandfather and that my father, as a boy, in his flight from France, had stuffed it into his meagre luggage. A prayer-shawl is not an item one can easily abandon, for such desertion is tantamount to a premature burial of its owner.

'Why did it worry you?' I heard the prosecutor say.

'Because I suspected that maybe Sir was a Jew and I wondered what he was doing as headmaster at our school.'

'Why should a Jew not be a headmaster of your school?' the prosecutor fed the response.

'Because it is a Church of England school and it is not the

custom to employ a non-Christian. And certainly not as a head-master.'

'Was there anything else that aroused your suspicions that the accused was of the Jewish faith?'

'Yes, sir,' James replied. 'One Sunday morning when I was staying at his cottage, I was going to the bathroom and I passed Sir's bedroom. The door was slightly open. I heard murmuring in a language I couldn't understand. I peeped through the crack in the door. I know I shouldn't have, but I was curious and I saw Sir bobbing up and down and praying. He had a little box on his forehead and his arms were bound with strips of leather.'

I couldn't help smiling. I have never in my life seen a set of phylacteries except in pictures of old engravings, and they were attached to young post-bar mitzvah boys in a seminar, or to old Rabbis in a stetl. I assumed that young James, at someone's prompting, had studied a book on Jewish ritual and I wondered what he would come up with next.

'And were there any other indications which led you to believe that the accused was a Jew?' the prosecutor said.

I fully expected James to trot out the prayer fringes that I supposedly wore and I was right in my assumption.

'Another weekend,' James said, 'and again it was a Sunday. It was very hot and Sir suggested a swim in the lake. While we were undressing at the lake's edge, I noticed that he was wear-ing a sort of silk belt with fringes hanging down. I thought it was odd for a man to wear such an accessory, and I said noth-ing about it. But I found out later what it was, and by that time I knew for certain that Sir was a Jew.'

'Could you explain to the court what these things were? You could start with the little box on the forehead.'

'They're called phylacteries,' James said. 'The box contains texts from the scriptures and Jews put them on every morning to pray. Except on their sabbath.'

'And the fringes?' The prosecutor's tone was deeply friendly.

'They are an essential garment for orthodox Jews and they are worn from birth.'

Our James had certainly done his research, I thought. He had handed out three undeniable proofs of Jewish identity.

'Thank you, Mr Turncastle,' the prosecutor said.

I caught sight of Lucy. She was shaking her head in emphatic denial. Matthew's face wore a look of abject disgust and Susan's head was lowered as if she had seen and heard enough.

'Did your relationship with the accused change after your discoveries?' the prosecutor gently prodded.

'Yes,' James said. 'But I didn't know what to do. I wanted to tell him that there was nothing wrong in being Jewish but he ought to come out with it. I knew that he would be dismissed if it were known to the school, but it seemed to me to be an unfair deception.'

'Did you ever try to talk to him about this?'

'I was afraid,' James said. 'I knew what it would cost him to come clean.'

'So you kept all this to yourself.'

'No,' James said. 'That's the terrible thing. I confided in George. George Tilbury.' His voice broke convincingly on the dead boy's name, and I thought what a consummate liar James had turned out to be. He had never to my knowledge been George's friend. Indeed, apart from the encounter outside my office, I had never seen them together. I wondered who had prompted James in his testimony. Who had rehearsed him over and over again. Who had suggested the pauses in his evidence, the break in the voice, the look of sorrow. I thought that if only I could pinpoint his mentor, I could find the key that would unlock all this deception and prove my innocence once and for all.

'Take your time,' the prosecutor was saying. 'I know this must be very painful for you. Tell us what George said when you told him.'

'He was horrified. Just like me,' James said. 'But he didn't want to talk to Sir either. But like me, he thought it should be known. So he said he would tell his father and his father would deal with it.'

'Then what did you do?' the prosecutor asked. 'And take your time.'

'I was very fond of Sir,' James said. 'He'd been like a father to me.'

Again a voice break. The boy was undoubtedly a star.

'I thought I'd better warn him. It was the least that I could do. So I went to his study and I suggested that he resign or it would all come out anyway. George would see to it.'

Now James started to cry. I don't know how he made those tears, but they were pretty convincing.

'I think,' he blubbered, 'that if I hadn't mentioned George, he would still be alive. It was all my fault.'

And then he broke down completely.

At this point the Judge intervened. He called for an adjournment for lunch and ordered the court to reassemble at two o'clock.

When he had left, I was taken down and confined to a small cell. A lunch tray was brought to me, and shortly afterwards Simon arrived.

'How are you feeling?' he said.

'How d'you expect me to feel? The boy's a liar.'

'He'll break, don't worry,' Simon said. 'I'm going to break him if it's the last thing I do.'

'What more can he come up with?'

'I don't know,' Simon said. 'I don't know what my learned friend has up his sleeve. But no one's going to believe a word of it.'

I wished that Simon sounded more confident. He could not conceal the lacing of doubt around his words.

'Eat your lunch,' he said. 'I'll see you in court.'

He was clearly in a hurry to get away and I had no questions with which to detain him. Or rather, I had too many questions. Far too many. But I knew that they were all unanswerable. I dreaded going back into the court. I dreaded further allegations and raked-up evidence. For I was powerless. I could only shake my head in enraged denial.

But soon enough they came to fetch me and I stood once more in the dock. I feared that I had lost my legitimate look of innocence and that one of fear had taken its place, and that that fear could only point to culpability.

When the court was reassembled, James once more took the stand.

'Mr Turncastle, do you feel able enough to continue with your evidence?' the prosecutor asked kindly.

'I do, sir,' James said.

I realised that James had never once looked at me during his testimony. I hoped for his glance to see how long he could sustain it, together with the stream of lies that he was pouring forth. So I stared at him, willing him to turn, and to be appalled at his gross betrayal. But he was too much of a coward for that. He kept his eyes fixed on the prosecutor, with occasional glances at the jury to convince them of his integrity.

'You were talking to the accused in his study, you were saying,' the prosecutor went on. 'What day was this?'

'It was April the second. I remember because it was my seventeenth birthday.'

It was the first piece of honest testimony that he had given. April the second was indeed his birthday. But not a single card or present. No acknowledgement from any quarter that he had ever existed. But Lucy had remembered. She had given him a leather-bound Shakespeare as a present. No mention of that of course. James's memory had been brainwashed.

'April the second,' the prosecutor repeated. 'And you warned the accused that George Tilbury would tell his father. You begged him to resign. What happened then?'

'He said there was no need for it,' James answered. 'He said that everything would be all right as long as I kept my mouth shut. And then I said, "What about George?" And he said again that it would be all right. I reminded him that George's father was a cabinet minister, and he said that there was nothing to worry about.'

'How did he look when he was saying these things? How did he behave?'

'He seemed nervous,' James said, 'and he told me to leave. He said that he had things to do.'

'What things?' the prosecutor asked pointedly.

'I don't know,' James said.

'What did you do then?'

'Nothing,' James said. 'I tried not to think about it. I saw George later on, but I didn't tell him anything. I hoped it would all die down and solve itself somehow. The next morning I saw George at breakfast, but I still didn't say anything. After breakfast, George went to his classes and so did I. I missed him at lunch because I was late. I had to do some work for Mr Eccles. Then after lunch, at about two o'clock, I passed Sir's house and I saw him walking towards the car. And to my surprise, I saw that George was at his side. Sir's arm was around George's shoulder. They were talking and it seemed to be friendly enough. So I wasn't worried. I thought Sir was going to explain things to him. Then they both got into the car and drove off.'

'This was at two o'clock on April the third, you say?' The prosecutor was anxious to stress time and dates.

'Yes,' James said. Then after a pause, 'I never saw George again.'

I waited for the voice-break, but this time it was not forthcoming.

'Would you like a rest?' the prosecutor asked kindly.

'No,' James said. 'I want to get it all out.'

'We come now to the next day. April the fourth. What happened then?' the prosecutor asked. 'And you may take your time,' he added, for he knew what was coming.

'It was very early in the morning. My room overlooks the driveway of Sir's house. I was woken by the sound of tyres on gravel. I looked at my watch. It was three o'clock. I went to the window and I saw Sir getting out of his car and going into his house.'

'Was he alone?'

'Yes,' James said.

'You had last seen him leave his house with young George at two o'clock the previous afternoon. And you saw the car return without George at three o'clock the following morning.'

'That is true, sir,' James said.

The prosecutor turned to the jury. 'So the prisoner was absent from the school premises for thirteen hours.' He hoped that they would draw their own conclusions, having gauged the return journey to Kent. The prosecutor swivelled once more, this time coming to rest at Simon's stand. 'Your witness,' he said and there was no hiding the contempt and pity in his tone.

Simon rose quickly. His tempo was going to be very different. No swivelling for him. No glasses of water. No histrionics. Neither would he allow them in his witness. He came straight to the point.

'Let's talk first about the prayer-shawl,' he said. 'And then let us talk about the phylacteries. And then let us talk about the fringes. Are you aware Mr Turncastle, that you have picked upon the most salient symbols of Jewish orthodoxy?'

He waited for a reply, but James must have thought the question rhetorical, because he didn't immediately answer.

'Did you hear my question?' Simon asked.

'Yes,' James said.

'Then I await your reply.'

'Yes, sir,' James said. 'I am aware of those things.'

'It seems to me, Mr Turncastle, that you have chosen these symbols with a great deal of care. As if you had researched them. As if you had read a book on Jewish ritual practices and have put them forward to support your suspicions of my client's faith. What was the book called, Mr Turncastle?'

'I didn't read it in a book,' James said.

'Then someone must have rehearsed you.'

'No they didn't,' James said.

But I noticed that his voice faltered and I delighted in this first crack in his credibility.

Now it was Simon's turn to give pause. He turned and stared at the jury. 'Our witness does not seem too sure,' he said. Then turning back to James, he said, 'May I remind you that the symbols that you have chosen to finger my client's faith are those of very orthodox Jews. Pious Jews. Practising Jews. Jews who do not shave, who are never bare-headed. Jews with cover of a hat or a skull-cap. Would you look at the prisoner and tell me if he has a beard?'

James was thus forced to look at me and as he did so, I pitied him, for clearly it was painful for him to look me in the face. It was but a glance but it was more than enough for him, for quickly he turned to face the court.

'No,' James said.

'And would you look once more and tell me whether his head is covered?'

Again a furtive glance.

'No,' James said.

'Then it is highly unlikely that my client made use of any of those tokens and that you have lied about seeing them at all.'

'No,' James said. 'I did see them. On my honour.' He was a little boy again, a lying little boy trying to get himself out of trouble, and though I thought that Simon was doing a creditable job of destroying the boy's evidence, I could not help but pity him.

'And as to the ludicrous bathing story,' Simon went on, 'I suggest that, like all your fantasies, it is pure fabrication. An orthodox Jew, one who puts on a prayer-shawl, one who wears fringes, dons phylacteries, one who is bearded and hatted, such a Jew does not bathe in a public place that is open to women as well as men. And if your little book on Jewish ritual told you that he did, then that little book was wrong.'

James was silent. He even hung his head a little.

'Now let us come to the day before George Tilbury's disappearance was reported. You say that at two o'clock you saw the accused walking to his car in the company of George Tilbury.'

'Yes, I did.'

'It was in the middle of the day. There must have been a number of people walking around. Going to lessons. To sports. Yet nobody else has come forward to testify that they saw George Tilbury in the company of the accused. *And* with his arm about his shoulder. Surely others would have noticed that?'

'I didn't see anyone else about,' James said.

'And as to the car which came back at three o'clock in the morning of April the fourth, there are other students whose rooms overlook the headmaster's house. That noise, the tyres on gravel, if it was loud enough to wake you, is it not strange that others did not hear it and come forward to corroborate your vision the following morning? Because you probably dreamt it all, did you not, Mr Turncastle?'

James made no reply and I almost heard his whole evidence crumbling.

'No further questions,' Simon said. Then very slowly he returned to his seat.

The judge rapped his desk for silence, though there was very little noise in the court.

'Court adjourned till tomorrow at ten o'clock,' he said.

So ended my first day at the Old Bailey. I was taken away through the back door of the court and, despite my means of

exit, there was a mob there too, together with a posse of photographers. Again I was glad of the blanket-shield, though I
could not close my ears to the cries of 'murderer' and 'scum'.
Back in my cell that night, I found it difficult to sleep. Despite
Simon's partial demolition of James's testimony, I was not
hopeful. I sensed that I had already been found guilty, and if
better liars than James were to be witnesses for the prosecution,
then I was indeed condemned.

And the first witness of the following day confirmed my
fears.

'Call Police Constable Derek Byrd,' an usher shouted.

The witness entered from the side door of the court. His face
was fairly familiar; I had seen him foot-patrolling in the neighbouring town and we had acknowledged each other as a mere
formality. He had a cruel face and hair so closely cropped that
it was almost shaven, and his jowls were heavy with superiority.
He did not look at me which wasn't easy for him since I was in
his direct eye-line, and I knew instinctively that he, like James,
had been schooled in fabrication. He took the oath, which I considered pretty audacious, then gave his name and ashamedly his
rank, below which it was impossible to sink.

'Would you tell the court,' the prosecutor said, 'of your
duties in the early hours of April the fourth last?'

PC Byrd coughed to clear his throat. He was nervous I
thought, and though I was convinced he was about to deliver a
parcel of lies, I knew that his uniform gave him a certain credibility.

'I was called out to investigate a break-in in a tobacconist's
corner-shop,' he said. 'As I made my way to the premises, I saw
a saloon car driving rather fast down the main road in the
direction of the school. As it passed me, I was surprised to see
the accused in the driving seat. It was his car. I had often seen
it. I looked at my watch and noted the time as 2.40.'

He had said it all in one breath. He had clearly learned it by heart and did not trust himself to pause at any time during his recital. When he had finished, his jowls jutted even further. I think he expected some applause.

'No further questions,' the prosecutor said. And at once Simon got to his feet.

'Constable Byrd,' he said, 'you say you saw a car driving at speed down the road in the early hours of April the fourth.'

'Yes, sir,' Byrd said.

'You say the time was 2.40.'

Again, 'Yes, sir.' Byrd was happily safe with the monosyllable.

'You say you were called out to investigate a break-in at a tobacconist's corner-shop.'

'Yes, sir.' Byrd was still happy.

'Yet there is no record at the station of any report of a break-in at that time,' Simon said. 'We too have investigated. No report at all. How d'you account for that, PC Byrd?'

The constable was flummoxed. 'They must have forgotten to put it down,' he said feebly.

'I don't think they forgot at all. There was simply nothing to put down. There had been no break-in, and no reports of one. You were certainly on duty that night, but your beat was on the other side of the village, far away from the main road. So I suggest you didn't see the car at all, much less the prisoner in the driving seat. No further questions,' Simon said quickly. He gave a wave of his hand as if to confirm that PC Byrd's testimony was pure poppycock.

I felt that Simon was doing rather well and a sliver of hope comforted me. But that soon dissolved at the sight of the next witness, whose appearance at my trial stunned me. Anthony Ellis, the maths master from my old school in Hammersmith. I did not remember him for his teaching abilities, which were pretty mediocre, but how could I forget his presence in the staff urinals on that shameful day? I have already written about that ignoble incident, and I have no intention of spelling it out once again. But I had to listen to it, as Ellis unfolded with some relish, the story of my deception. He told it with much elaboration, using such phrases as 'indecent exposure', and 'flashing'. I heard sighs of disgust from the courtroom and I knew that I was damned. I could see the lurid headlines of the morning papers. I daren't look at Ellis, so I can't be sure that he was looking at me. But I suspect he gave me a leer of triumph. Ellis had very much wanted the headmastership at Hammersmith and this was his splendid revenge.

At one point in the testimony, Simon rose with an objection.

'My Lord,' he said, 'I submit that this account has nothing to do with the trial. The prisoner stands accused of murder. The witness's story has nothing to do with that. It is totally irrelevant.'

'My Lord,' the prosecutor interrupted, 'I am simply trying to establish the fact that the prisoner was at pains to publicly pass himself off as an uncircumcised Gentile. It is germane to my argument.'

'Proceed,' the judge said, and Simon had to sit down. But mercifully, he did not cross-examine and I was grateful that the subject would not be aired yet again. In any case, what Ellis had said was true, and apart from my own testimony, possibly the only truth spoken during the whole of my trial.

The prosecution's next witness was Smith from geography.

'Could you tell the court of your first meeting with the prisoner?' he asked.

I had forgotten that first encounter, but suddenly I recalled it with fear. My chickens had truly come home to roost.

'It was at a dinner at the school,' Smith said, 'before the prisoner was appointed headmaster. We were in the library and the talk turned to our childhoods. He said that he was a country boy and that he had been brought up in a village in Kent. He talked about the village church and the fact that his parents had been married there. He added that he himself had been baptised in that same church.'

'And, in the light of what we now know, how do you regard that conversation?' the prosecutor led him on.

'I think we were grossly misled,' Smith said with some indignation.

The prosecutor gave much pause while he swivelled slowly around the court. Returning to Smith, he said, 'And now would you give your account of the events at the school on the morning of April the fourth.'

'I heard about George Tilbury's disappearance when Sir announced it to the staff and upper school. He organised a thorough search. It seemed to me odd that he had not immediately informed the police. When I mentioned this to him he said he didn't want police interference until he'd spoken to George's parents. He hoped that George would be found before spreading panic.'

'How did you view this delay?' the prosecutor asked.

'In the light of the evidence revealed,' Smith said, 'I think it was possible that Sir wanted time to get rid of the body before informing the police.'

'Thank you,' the prosecutor said. Then to Simon, 'Your witness.'

'You say, Mr Smith,' Simon said, 'that the prisoner delayed calling the police because he wanted to give time to have George Tilbury's body hidden.'

'That is right, sir.'

'You say that that is your opinion. Simply your opinion. May I remind you, Mr Smith, that the witness-box is not a platform on which you may state your opinions. It is a platform for facts. No further questions.'

I felt that Simon's cross-examination was timid and unconvincing, despite his strut back to his seat, and in the light of Smith's opinions, coupled with Ellis's facts, my already threadbare hopes for acquittal were dashed. And the testimony of the next witness did nothing to revive them.

His face was familiar and I placed it in our childhood village, and when he gave his name and the nature of his work, I recalled him immediately. He was a Mr Clerk, a verger at Canterbury Cathedral, who lived with his sister in our village. Neither of them were particularly liked in the community. They were uppity and they did not mix. No one had ever been inside their cottage, but there were rumours that it was like a museum, housing a collection of sorts though no one knew exactly what that collection consisted of. There was a whisper too, that they were rather more than brother and sister.

I was not pleased to see him. He took the oath then stared at me. I looked away, fearful of his testimony. He told the court that on the evening of the third of April, at about nine o'clock he hazarded, he was walking through the field at the back of our cottage and he had noticed that a large hole had been dug in the garden.

'I assumed there was a problem with the drains,' he said, 'and I thought no more about it. I was working late that night – Cathedral work –' he added for the benefit of the jury, 'and I didn't retire until 11.30. As I drew the bedroom curtains, I saw a figure in the prisoner's garden, and I noticed that the hole had been filled up.'

'Did you recognise the figure?' the prosecutor asked.

'No. It was dark and the view from my window is oblique. It was possibly a man, but in all honesty I couldn't describe him further.'

This admission gave his sworn evidence the stamp of utmost credibility. I looked at the jury and I saw that they were impressed.

'And what did you do then, Mr Clerk?' the prosecutor was chatty.

'It puzzled me a little,' the virtuous verger said, 'but I

thought no more about it. It was when I heard of the location of the body of George Tilbury that I saw fit to go to the police and tell them what I had seen.'

Mr Clerk gave the impression of being an innocent and upright citizen. His evidence was cut and dried. He spoke as if he had done his duty. I looked up to the public gallery and caught sight of a woman whom I recognised as his sister. I noticed that she was smiling. And suddenly I gathered in my mind all those witnesses who had testified against me, and I sniffed the undeniable smell of conspiracy.

'Your witness,' the prosecutor said, and to my horror, Simon declined.

I don't know what he could have said to question the verger's story, but his refusal to discredit it simply let it lie and remain acceptable. I wondered whether he was beginning to doubt my innocence. Mr Clerk stepped down from the box, and as he was leaving the courtroom he looked up to his sister for her approval.

I was glad that an adjournment was called at that time for it gave the jury something to dwell upon. But after lunch, the plot thickened, a plot fashioned by a person or persons unknown and fashioned with meticulous detail.

The next prosecution witness was one Albert Cassidy, who owned a hardware store on London's Tottenham Court Road. I had never seen him before in my life, and I was thus unnerved when he looked at me with a nod of recognition. Then I knew that he too was part of a conspiracy. He told the court, and under that laughable oath, that he was serving in his shop at three o'clock on the afternoon of April the second when a gentleman came in and viewed a collection of knives along a shelf. 'I saw that he picked up a selection,' he said, 'and tested the blades and points with his thumb. There was no other customer in the shop at the time, so I was able to see him very clearly. After about five minutes' perusal, he made his choice and paid

for it at the counter. It was a wide kitchen knife with a short-
ish handle. And very sharp. It cost twelve pounds and eighty
pence. Stainless steel,' he added in the judge's direction. 'I
made out a bill. When I saw the photograph of the prisoner in
the paper, I recognised him as my customer and I handed the
bill to the police.'

He'd learned it all by heart, I thought, and had gone over it
as diligently as I had practised my 'not guilty' plea, and it was
as much a lie as my rehearsal had been the truth. The bill,
Exhibit A, was passed to the bench, and I felt my knees melting. Had I been on the jury, I would, with little hesitation, have
found myself guilty, and when Simon again passed on cross-
examination, I knew that I was doomed.

Neither did he cross-examine the following witness, Mr
Cassidy's assistant, who swore to have seen me in the shop at
the knife shelf. By now I was totally without hope. I was certainly in London on that day. It was known that I went to a
meeting of school inspectors. It was also known that that meeting was due to finish at lunch-time. These facts were known to
the staff members. And of course Lucy knew them too. I
searched for her in the body of my court, and spotted her
immediately. The look on her face was strange. I'd not seen it
before and it frightened me. It was a look from which all trust
had been drained and I feared for a moment that she doubted
the stated purpose of our London trip and that she wondered if
she'd been persuaded into coming along in order to provide an
alibi for at least part of the day. I wanted to scream, 'It's not
true. It's not true. Nothing of this is true.' Just for Lucy's ears.
I had suffered some desperate moments in the course of my trial
but that moment was the most desolate of them all.

The next witness was Inspector Wilkins, the arresting officer.
I harboured no more hope of him than I did of any of the other
witnesses. Truth in that courtroom would have been an intrusion. But Wilkins proved the exception.

'What information led you to arrest the prisoner?' the prosecutor asked.

'I received a telephone call at the station. The caller would
not give his name and the line was untraceable. He stated that
he had seen a man burying what looked like a body in the
garden of the accused's country cottage. I asked him if he could
describe the man, and he said that he was of medium height
and probably in his forties.'

'In other words,' the prosecutor said, 'that could well have
been a description of the prisoner.'

Inspector Wilkins was indignant. 'That fact did not occur to
me at the time,' he said. 'It could well have been a description
of thousands of men.'

'What did you do about the phone call?'

'We get many hoax calls at the station, and I am wary of
those which are untraceable,' the honest Wilkins replied. 'But I
was disturbed by the location he had given. I could not overlook
that call. I decided to examine the site. And in doing so, we discovered the body. I arrested the prisoner a few hours later.'

'Thank you, Inspector,' the prosecutor said.

Simon did not cross-examine. He knew that Wilkins was
telling the truth. If there was indeed a conspiracy to frame his
client, the Inspector played no part in it. He had done simply
what he had to do.

The prosecutor then called his final witness and I knew he'd
saved his last for the clincher. I did not know the man but he
wore a policeman's uniform of a respectable rank and announced
himself as being attached to the Kent Constabulary. He stated
that, together with forensics, he had minutely examined the
prisoner's car. He had found no traces of blood or fibres, but
there were fingerprints. Apart from those of the prisoner, there
were fairly newish prints of young George on the dashboard.

'Was there anything else?' the prosecutor asked, knowing full
well there was plenty else to condemn me.

'There was a button,' the witness said. 'It was discovered at the back of the front passenger seat. On exhumation of the body it was found to match the missing button on George Tilbury's school blazer.'

For a moment I sensed that I was reading a thriller, and one that I found totally convincing. I was anxious to read to the end and hear with pleasure of the miscreant's punishment. Then suddenly I heard my name, 'the prisoner', in reference to the ownership of the car, and I shivered with the knowledge that I was the protagonist in those pages, and that it was not fiction at all.

As the damning evidence was passed to the bench, the prosecutor said with a certain satisfaction. 'If Your Lordship pleases, that concludes the case for the prosecution.'

And then I started shivering. I began to imagine that I was guilty, and I strove to keep that thought within the bounds of fantasy. Young George was indeed a threat to my continued headmastership. He had to be disposed of. I couldn't use the word 'kill'. Not even in my fantasy. But I was able to imagine his body in my arms, and the stray blazer button that had come adrift. Then his burial in my cottage garden. And on that sacred ground my fantasy faded, and I saw myself with George's blood on my hands and I cursed my frail imagination that it was so limited. I felt a sudden sweat on my forehead, as I shivered with an ice-cold fever. I gripped the hand-rail, and with what seemed the last of my voice, I screamed aloud, 'I did it. I murdered George, God forgive me. And I don't know how or why.'

I watched my sweating fingers slip their grasp as I folded to the floor of the dock. As I lay there, I heard Simon's voice in the distance. 'I would ask Your Lordship to disregard those last remarks. My client is delirious and under great stress.'

But Simon did not sound convinced. Perhaps he thought that, at long last, I was telling the truth.

I heard no more. I felt some cold water on my face and I heard murmurings from the court. I felt myself carried and laid down on a bench somewhere and I heard the guard whisper that the judge had called an adjournment. As I slowly came to myself, I recalled with horror those thoughts that had triggered my collapse. And I feared that they had little to do with fantasy. Perhaps after all, I *had* killed the boy and it was so terrible that I had blocked it from my memory.

25

In all, the Crown prosecutor had taken just over two weeks to present his case. I have not given it in detail. I have omitted all the legal jargon and the interruptions of the judge on a point of law. Though my life was at stake, I found them tedious and I would not wish to burden my reader with these irrelevancies. I am concerned only to give the gist of the prosecution argument. And it was damning enough. I couldn't imagine how Simon was going to handle my defence. Finally, it came down to my word against theirs, and theirs was altogether too powerful. Moreover, I had no doubt that my fainting fit at the end of the prosecution's case was a solid pointer to my guilt and to my unbearable remorse.

It was a Monday when the case for my defence opened. I waited to be taken into the court. I fully expected Simon to visit me, but it was not until I stood in the box that I caught sight of him. Although he smiled, I felt he was avoiding me.

It was my turn to go into the box and to find a thousand words that all meant innocent. I took the oath and I took it with fervour, for rarely could the truth, the whole truth and nothing but the truth be sworn with greater zeal. Again Simon smiled at me.

His first question struck at the heart of the matter.

'Sir Alfred,' he said, 'what is your religion?'

I was relieved that he had given me the opportunity to speak aloud on a subject hitherto confined to the whisper, the under-tone, the murmur, those intonations of rumour and suspicion.

'I am a Jew,' I said. For the first time in my life I felt a certain pride in that declaration, though I was careful to conceal it. 'My parents were born in Paris, and during the German occupation of that city it was unwise to parade such a faith. They managed to escape, but almost all their family was left behind.' I thought I might tell the court about my grandparents and the ovens, but their memory was sacred, and I would not exploit it for my defence. 'They came to England,' I went on, 'where I was born. But they did not practise our faith. But we never converted. I am a Jew,' I said, 'and I have never denied it.'

At that moment somebody coughed in the courtroom. He might simply have been clearing his throat but, hounded as I was, I could be forgiven a touch of paranoia. And I took that cough as a sign of somebody's suspicion. Then anger seized me.

'Am I being tried as a Jew?' I asked. 'Or as a murderer?'

Simon gave a hint of a smile. He was not displeased by my outburst, but he had to be seen to restrain me.

'The charge is murder, Sir Alfred,' he said quietly. Then quickly he posed his next question.

'Tell the court about your relationship with the witness James Turncastle,' he said.

'I felt like a father to the boy,' I said. I went on to detail the deprived background that demonstrated the lack of interest or love from his parents. I spoke of how he played with my own children and how he had spent the weekend at our cottage in Kent. 'He was one of my family,' I said.

'Can we talk about the items that James Turncastle allegedly found on your person and in your home. The religious items.'

I said that I certainly owned a prayer-shawl. I had found it in the cottage after my father's death. But it was not kept in a drawer. It was in a locked chest in my study. As to the phylacteries and fringes, I had never possessed such religious tokens. I added that although I was a Jew, and had never denied it, I was not a practising one.

'James Turncastle stated that he was a close friend of George Tilbury,' Simon said. 'Would you say that that was true?'

'No,' I answered. 'I never saw them together. James had friends, but young George wasn't one of them. The only time I saw them together was the day before George disappeared. I saw George loitering outside my study and I was about to ask him what he wanted when James appeared and whisked him away. I had the impression that George wanted to tell me something and that, whatever it was, James did not want it known.'

'Now let us examine your whereabouts on the day or night of the murder of George Tilbury,' Simon said. 'The afternoon of April the third. The prosecution witness James Turncastle has sworn that he saw you driving out of the school at two o'clock, and that George Tilbury was in the passenger seat. Is that true?'

'Partly,' I said. 'I did indeed drive out of the school at two o'clock, but I was alone.'

'Where were you going?'

'I had an appointment with my dentist. It was my six-monthly check-up.'

'What time was your appointment?'

'Half-past two. It is written in my diary, and no doubt also in Mr Tweedie's appointments book.'

'And what happened at the dentist's?'

'I had to wait a while and Mr Tweedie did not see me until ten to three.'

'And then?'

'He examined me and found nothing amiss. So he simply cleaned my teeth and by three I was out of his surgery.'

'And then?'

'I drove straight back to school. I had a paper to prepare for the *Times Educational Supplement* and I worked on that for the rest of the day.'

'Thank you, Sir Alfred,' Simon said in an attempt to boost my confidence.

'Now we come to the testimony of PC Byrd who stated, on oath,' he stressed, 'that on the morning of April the fourth, at 2.40, he saw you driving on the main village road in the direction of the school. Where were you at that time?'

'I was in bed,' I said. It sounded so simple, so virtuous and so boring. But truth is all of these things, and the banality of truth was all I had to give.

'Why didn't you inform the police immediately of George's disappearance?'

Again the truth. 'I wanted to look for him. I felt he couldn't be far away. But after a whole day of fruitless search, I informed his parents. And thereafter the police.'

Simon then continued with the matter of the hole in my Kent cottage garden, the hole that one moment was a hole and shortly afterwards was a hole no longer. I swore that I knew nothing about it and that the last time I had visited the cottage was some weeks before George's disappearance.

By the time Simon handed me over for cross-examination, I had gained a little confidence, but that small gain was quickly wiped out by the Crown prosecutor. He itemised one by one every fact of my testimony and suggested that in all aspects, I was an out-and-out liar. I could do nothing but deny his accusations. 'No,' I kept saying. 'That's not true.' Over and over again, as I had once rehearsed my mantra, 'not guilty'.

At the close of his grilling, he swivelled towards the jury and shrugged his shoulders in contempt. I stepped down, and my knees were melting.

I was relieved to see Mr Tweedie take the stand. I had no doubt that he would confirm my alibi. Which he did, promptly and with no hesitation and in almost the same words as I had given in my defence. His honesty was so evident that the prosecution for once, did not cross-examine.

What I write now is unbelievable. The prosecution had taken over two witness-packed weeks to arraign me. My paltry defence was over in little more than a day. Apart from Mr Tweedie, Simon had scraped two defence witnesses from the bottom of the barrel. And neither could give more than character references. Eccles was the first to appear, and I felt that if my life depended on somebody like Eccles, Eccles of that never-forgotten wink, then it was indeed lost.

I listened with some fascination to his testimonial. He said that I was the ideal headmaster, a man of integrity and principle. That I was renowned and revered as a teacher and as a disseminator of educational methods. My work in the English school system had been duly recognised and honoured. And deservedly so. Then he really went over the top. 'Above all,' he said, 'I consider him a close and loyal friend and I cannot imagine in my wildest dreams that he could have committed the crime of which he stands accused.'

The prosecutor did not even bother to cross-examine. He simply shrugged his shoulders as if he knew that Eccles had somehow been planted. Eccles was followed by Fenby, whose testimony was melancholy but patently sincere. Even so, the prosecutor ignored him. After Fenby had stepped down, there was a hushed silence in the court. Everyone seemed to be waiting for Simon's next move.

He rose reluctantly and addressed the judge, 'My Lord,' he said, 'that concludes the case for the defence.'

There was a gasp around the courtroom. He might as well have thrown in the towel and conceded that his client was guilty as charged. The jury sighed with relief. They possibly reckoned they could all get home in time for supper, for the verdict seemed quite clear. But first they had to endure the closing speech for the prosecution and the defence's summing-up, as well as the judge's charge to the jury before they could adjourn and return with their verdict.

But at this point, the judge called for a late lunch-break and I was taken down to the cell once more. As I left the courtroom, I noticed Mr Eccles scurry out of the door as if he had urgent business to attend to. I tried to be grateful for his glowing testimonial, but somehow that too, was redolent of conspiracy. I saw nothing of Simon during that lunch-hour and I assumed that he was preparing his summing-up. I left my tray untouched. I had appetite for nothing. I knew I was condemned and I saw no point of even returning to the dock. But in time they came to fetch me.

I shivered on the stand. I was convinced that my freedom, truncated as it had lately been, was now well and truly over. Yet I harboured hope. I had to. For even if the jury were not convinced of my innocence, of which I myself was no longer too sure, they surely must be beset with doubts. Surely the words 'framed' and 'conspiracy' would play some part in their deliberations. They were twelve good men and women true. They would not be cavalier in their judgement. They would doubt, they would hesitate, they would waver. They could not in all conscience declare their certainty. I willed them to doubt. It was all I could hope for.

The judge had not yet entered. The jury were seated and expectant. I looked at the prosecutor, and though he was sitting quite still his face wore a swivelling smile. He clearly expected the verdict he had argued for. Then I looked at Simon, and I was stunned. His head was bowed and his shoulders drooped in despair. I waited for him to look at me and when he did, I saw that his skin was ashen. He shook his head in my direction. 'We have lost,' he seemed to be telling me. 'There is no hope.' I wondered what new piece of evidence had surfaced during the lunch-hour to dash his hopes so thoroughly. And I was soon to learn.

We stood as the judge entered and took his seat. The court was silent. Expectant. It was the last act of the drama. Anything could happen. And it did.

'Before we proceed with the summings-up,' the judge announced, 'the prosecution counsel has made an application for alibi rebuttal. Let the prosecution recall Mr Tweedie.'

My automatic response to this announcement was to seek out Eccles, for I knew that his hurried exit from court was linked with this reversal. But I could not see him. I looked at Simon and he shrugged helplessly.

Mr Tweedie took the stand once more, and once more he took the oath.

'You wish to withdraw your former testimony?' the prosecution asked. His tone was angry. He wished to impress the court that he had no truck with perjury.

'Yes,' Tweedie said. 'I was not telling the truth.'

'And you wish now to correct your statement?'

'Yes,' Tweedie said humbly.

'You stated that on April the third, between two-thirty and three o'clock, you treated the prisoner at your dental surgery. Is that not so?'

'I didn't treat him,' Tweedie said. 'He had an appointment at 2.30. I was expecting him. But he didn't turn up. I waited for him until three o'clock. And then I saw another patient.'

I was stunned. Tweedie, like the rest of them, was a bare-faced liar. I ran my tongue along my teeth, hoping to trace some vestige of his cleaning. But I felt only fur on my tongue, and I thought perhaps that Mr Tweedie was right. That for some reason I had missed my appointment and that the man was telling the truth.

'So although the prisoner claims that you treated him on that day,' the prosecution insisted, 'you are saying that he did not turn up for his appointment. That you did not see him that day at all?' He wanted to make the damning evidence perfectly clear.

'That is correct, sir,' Tweedie said.

The prosecutor swivelled to Simon. 'Your witness,' he said, with infinite pity.

Simon dragged himself to his feet.

'Mr Tweedie,' he began, 'I have in my files a statement that on April the fourth, at 2.30, you treated Sir Alfred at your dental surgery. You signed that statement in my office before his trial. Do you agree that you signed that statement?'

'Yes, I did,' Tweedie said.

'And now you have suddenly seen fit to withdraw that statement. Could you explain why?'

'That statement was a lie,' Tweedie said, 'and I decided to tell the truth. It would have been on my conscience.'

'Your conscience?' Simon queried, surprised that he had one at all.

'Do you realise,' he went on, 'that your initial statement was therefore perjury, a criminal offence?'

'I do, and I regret that,' Tweedie said.

'Then why did you lie in the first place? If indeed,' Simon added, 'it *was* a lie?'

'The prisoner was my friend,' Tweedie said. 'I did not want to let him down.'

'I'm sure my client will value your friendship.' His tone of sarcasm was the best that he could do. Then he turned and walked back to his seat. I felt sorry for him. He was soon obliged to offer his summing-up for my defence, and in view of that last-minute evidence, I couldn't imagine what words he could cobble together. I watched him as he drank from a glass of water.

The prosecutor then swivelled into position for his summing-up. It was surprisingly short. He was clearly convinced that the jury needed little persuasion on his part.

'During the course of this trial,' he said, 'we have clearly established and provided a motive, an essential in any charge of murder. But to provide motive is not enough. We need evidence, hard evidence, that the prisoner is guilty. And that we have in plenty. We have been told by reliable witnesses that young George was seen in the company of the prisoner at two o'clock on the afternoon of April the third. And young George was never seen again. We have evidence that the prisoner bought the murder weapon in London on April the second. We have a witness who saw the hole in the prisoner's garden in Kent, that hole in which young George was found to be buried. The prisoner's car was not seen in his driveway until three o'clock on the morning of April the fourth, the day that George's disappearance was announced. That car was about its business for thirteen hours, ample time to drive down to Kent, dispose of young George and bury his body. And then to drive back to the school. Damning evidence had come from forensics: the fingerprints of the victim on the dashboard of the prisoner's car, and the torn-off blazer button that was found on the passenger seat. But the most incriminating evidence of all is that of Mr Tweedie, who withdrew his first testimony made on the basis of friendship and finally told the truth. That the prisoner's alibi was false and that he had not kept his dental appointment. What further proof do we need, ladies and gentlemen of the jury, to find the prisoner guilty as charged?'

On the basis of the evidence that he had outlined, I couldn't see how the jury could come to any other verdict but guilty.

I watched Simon's reluctant rising. As he walked towards the jury box, the hopelessness was clear in his tread.

'Members of the jury,' he began. 'This case revolves on the supposition that Sir Al.red Dreyfus went to great pains to hide the fact that he is a Jew, in the knowledge that if that fact were known he would lose his position as headmaster of the school. A man would hardly kill for that. Not a man of such reputation and integrity as Sir Alfred Dreyfus. The prosecution has presented no evidence that Sir Alfred has ever denied that he was a Jew. It is true that he has never advertised it, but I am sure that if ever he had been called upon to state his faith, he would have done so in honourable fashion. But ladies and gentlemen of the jury, he was never *asked*, so where is the evidence that he denied it? To kill a child is the most heinous crime. Nobody would gainsay that. But to kill a child for the sake of a *job*, even though that job was possibly not recoverable, that ladies and gentlemen, is inconceivable. Unimaginable. Sir Alfred has two children of his own. He knows what it is to be a father. He is not a man to inflict such grief on another parent. He is as broken by the tragedy as any of us.

'Let us examine the evidence that has been brought against him. Does it not seem to you to be rehearsed? All of it? How well James Turncastle had learned his part. How diligently had PC Byrd studied his lines. How Mr Cassidy had learned it all by rote. How Mr Clerk knew his lines without need of prompt. I venture to suggest that even the officer from the Kent Constabulary was tutored in his part. Indeed, all of them were amateur actors, drilled acutely for their opening night. To say nothing of Mr Tweedie's suspicious change of heart. Ladies and gentlemen of the jury, does not all this play-acting seem to you like a conspiracy? Can you not sniff the intrigue behind it? The machinations that lie behind the plot? For that is what I am suggesting to you, ladies and gentlemen, that Sir Alfred Dreyfus is innocent and that for some reason he has been framed. When Sir

Alfred says he is not guilty, those words come from the depth of the soul, laced with bewilderment that he has been charged at all. I ask you to listen to his words, ladies and gentlemen. "I am not guilty," and to hear them resound with the man's innocence. Poor George Tilbury is dead. Brutally murdered, and his body heinously planted in Sir Alfred's country garden. There is someone who walks free today, through the streets, through the parks, the marketplace; perhaps he even sits in this courtroom, he who has young George's blood on his hands. But that blood is not on the hands of Sir Alfred Dreyfus. Listen to his plea, "I am not guilty," and let it echo and resound in your hearts as you reach your decision, and pronounce the only verdict that is true and just. That Sir Alfred Dreyfus is innocent.'

I thought it was a splendid try. At that moment, I even thought I stood a chance of acquittal. The conspiracy theory was certainly one to be seriously considered.

The judge's summing-up centred mainly around points of law with which I will not burden the reader. It seemed fair to me, and in no way did he lead the jury. He summarised the speeches for both the prosecution and defence, but he made no comment on either. When he had finished, he instructed the jury to retire.

It was five o'clock when they left the courtroom. Five o'clock in the afternoon. The hour of the matador and his kill. And it was 5.30 when they returned. There was now no doubt about their verdict. In fact, on the basis of the evidence against me I marvelled that they'd taken so long to come to a decision.

I was asked to stand, and I clutched the rail in front of me as I envisaged my wretched future. The clerk of the court asked the jury foreman if they had reached a verdict. And at the affirmative answer, he said, 'Do you find the prisoner, Sir Alfred Dreyfus, guilty or not guilty?'

I could have answered for him and in the voice of the whole jury.

'Guilty,' the foreman said.

A cheer went up around the courtroom, and would have continued had not the judge rapped his desk for silence. I looked up at the gallery and caught sight of a figure that was vaguely familiar. He was cheering with delight. His face suggested unpleasant recall. And then I remembered. It was our neighbour in our Kent village, John Coleman, he who spoke such impeccable English. I recalled that Christmas Day in our village when he had made his first visit. I remembered the distaste I felt for him. I wondered what he was doing at my trial, and why he was cheering its outcome. And with such indecent enthusiasm, one that almost signalled a personal involvement. The echo of his cheers, and his grin of delight, would haunt my nights in my cell.

The clerk turned to me and asked if I had anything to say before sentence was passed. I had nothing to say, except for my time-honoured mantra, and I saw no point in uttering it any more. I shook my head. I was too stunned to speak. I was in a quandary as to where to look. I didn't think I wanted to see Simon again and I was afraid to look at my family. So I looked at the judge. I had no feelings for him. He was simply a man who was doing his job.

'Sir Alfred Dreyfus,' he said, and I was surprised that he still thought me worthy of title, 'it is my solemn duty to pass on you the only sentence that the law permits for the crime of wilful murder. The sentence of this court is that you will go to prison for life and I recommend detainment for at least fifteen years.'

I did a quick sum. I would be of the age of sixty-two on release. I would possibly be a grandfather. More possibly I would be divorced and I wondered who would be around to visit me. And Matthew was the name. I sought his face in the body of the court, and lit on it immediately. I shut out Lucy on his one side, and Susan on the other. I saw only Matthew, and I knew that I would see him age along with me and that he would lighten my loneliness with his presence. I returned the smile he gave me as I was taken down. And then, blanketed, I was brought to this prison, and to this cell.

My first visitor after the verdict was the prison chaplain. He said he had come for a chat. Not a talk. A chat. He was being matey. I took one look at the cross that dangled from his neck and I asked him politely to leave. He was miffed I think, so I apologised.

'I'm sorry,' I said, 'but I'd be happier to see a rabbi.'

'I'll see what I can do,' he said.

And a few days later, a rabbi paid me a visit.

'I've never had call to come to this place,' he said.

I sensed he wanted me to feel ashamed of myself, having so let him down as to break his record. I was angry.

'I have shamed nobody,' I said. 'I want you to know that I am innocent and unless you believe that, sincerely and honestly, then I have no use for your visits.'

'If you say that you are innocent, then I must believe you,' the man said.

'But *do* you believe me? In your heart do you believe me?'

'If that is what you say,' he parried.

'I think you believe the verdict of the court,' I said.

He was silent, and that silence of his was answer enough. I told him to leave. He made no protest. I think he was relieved to get away.

Matthew was my first real visitor, and I fell into his arms. At first we said very little to each other. We sat side by side in silent bewilderment. Then for no reason that I could understand, he laughed. It was a bitter laugh but a laugh nonetheless. I asked him what was so funny, and he told me that I had hit the headlines. Then he gave me a resumé of world reaction to my trial. The French papers, it seemed, had recalled my namesake, but had made no mention of his proven innocence. The German press wavered, as one might expect, but some papers applauded the verdict. One of their correspondents suggested that, since my crime was committed around Easter, it was a replay of the ritual murder that Jews were rumoured to carry out prior to their Passover feast. And the Austrian press, in follow-my-leader fashion, agreed. The Vatican condemned me outright, and it was their report that most offended me. How dare that office, which in its time had happily shipped my people to the ovens, which had provided Vatican passports for the murderers' escapes; how dare they offer an opinion? Only the Dutch and Scandinavian press questioned the fairness of the verdict, and suggested a conspiracy that called for further investigation.

I shared Matthew's bitter laughter, and we were silent once more. Matthew clearly found the visit as painful as I, and he made to leave long before his allotted time. He said he would come again soon. Lucy too, and he would arrange to bring my children. 'I'll get you out of here,' he said. 'I promise.'

He turned quickly away, then rushed back to embrace me. I watched him go, and I felt more sorry for him than I did for myself.

A week later, I received my first prison letter. It came from the offices of the Palace and I knew without reading it what news it conveyed. I let it lie for a while on my cot, recalling the joy I had felt when I had first received a letter from that same source. I opened the envelope. I knew I had to confirm what I already suspected. The letter informed me that, in view of the verdict against me, I had been stripped of my title. Dear Lucy is plain Mrs Dreyfus now.

And my name is Case.

PART FOUR

26

HM Prison Wandsworth
London SW18

21 October 1997

Bernard Wallworthy, Esq.
Jubilee Publishing
London House
Sen Street
London W1

Dear Mr Wallworthy

What now, Mr Wallworthy? Where do we go from here? I
have come to the end of my version of the 'affair'. Yet I refuse
to accept that there is no more to say. I dare not. I shall not

allow myself to believe that I shall linger in this cell for the rest of my natural life. Today it is my birthday. I am fifty years old and it is the second birthday that I have marked in this place. I no longer say 'I am not guilty'. I should never have said it in the first place. Guilt never came into it. Never. I am innocent. That's all there is to it.

Here I sit, Mr Wallworthy, in the same cell allotted to me a year ago. You are entitled to imagine that I am familiar with it. But you would be wrong. I do not know it well, simply because I have never examined it in its particular. Until the moment of that unbelievable verdict I had looked upon it as a temporary dwelling, a stop-over to my freedom. But now that view is no longer feasible. For it relied on hope of which, at present, there is little vestige. I have paced my cell often enough but never with its footage in mind. Its width and its length have served as rhythms for my words of hope and despair. Now, as I pace, I count. I measure nine feet in length, and six across, a generous enough area, I think, for a grave.

My family are coming to visit today. Matthew too, though Susan and the children have gone to see her mother. I'm sorry about that. I haven't seen Susan for a long while. The governor has set aside a room for us to be together and to eat the special tea that Lucy will have prepared. My children aren't children any more. I am missing out on them growing up. I fear they are strangers. Peter is sixteen now. He's in his final year at school. With his name it could not have been easy. I am very proud of him. But I can only tell him so. There is no way I can show it in daily contact, in touch, in caress, in teasing. Perhaps now he is too old to tease, too old to laugh at my silly jokes, and much too young so courageously to have endured his name. They assure me in their letters and visits that much is being done on the outside to secure a new trial. But they will come this afternoon with no news of progress. They will bring with them their hopes, their faith, their trust, and I shall be expected to share their optimism. I shall try, though in my heart I despair.

But I must pick up my pen. I must. Without it I close the final door on my escape, and I shall go to my grave, my innocence unproved. Somewhere I shall have to find the words for my fading hopes, and words too to feed my rage. For it is the waning of that rage that I fear, for if that dissolves, lethargy will take its place and with it, a permanent state of melancholy. So I shall pick up my pen again and wish it all speed on its perilous way. Bear with me, Mr Wallworthy.

Dreyfus

27

My family were due to visit me. Apart from Matthew's short call after the trial, it would be their first time since the verdict. And frankly, I was dreading it. I felt so deeply shamed.

I was led to the visitors' room and seated at a table to wait. For the first time I viewed my gaol companions, and for the first time they viewed me. I felt that they were waiting for the arrival of my visitors. I have learned that you can tell a lot about the nature of an inmate by the visitors he receives. I hoped that mine would be dressed simply, that there would be no ostentation. Though none of my family are given to *haute couture*, I remember being deeply anxious about their attire. The fact that I had been condemned to this place for the rest of my life seemed of minor importance. What mattered most at that time was the general appearance of Lucy, my children, Matthew and Susan. I was ashamed enough of myself and presumed that they would be equally ashamed of me and I hoped to God that it would not show.

As I waited I noticed the others chatting to each other with a certain bonhomie which I both envied and feared. I envied their merriment but at the same time it worried me. They were old-timers, inured to their confinement, resigned to it, wholly institutionalised. I feared that in the course of time I might become a veteran too. I felt I ought to apologise to them for my misery. In fact I felt the need to apologise to absolutely everybody for simply being there at all. I didn't know where to look. I was frightened of catching the eye of other inmates, so I looked at the table-top. I stared at it. I viewed the scratched vinyl of its cover, worn with the sweat of men's hands as they waited for visitors who perhaps never came, or for visits that they would have been happier to do without. And I thought of all the funerals of kin that were unattended, of all the weddings of sons and daughters shrieking with an absent guest. And I thought of all the marriages that had dissolved over that vinyl and I found myself forgiving Lucy for leaving me. And then I saw her, or at least her hand across the table as it covered my own. I looked up and she was smiling. I felt suddenly so sure of her but at the same time I sensed that I had no right to such loyalty. And I have to confess that as I looked into her face I began to dislike her a little.

I looked at them all in turn, my children, Matthew and Susan, and I wished that they would all go away. I think that they must have sensed my unease.

'Are we too many for you?' Matthew asked, and how could I tell him that just one of them was too many and that I wanted to be alone and bury myself in my shame.

'You are innocent,' Lucy whispered. 'We all know that.'

'That's what makes it so difficult,' I said.

Peter pulled up chairs around the table, and we sat there positioned for a round table discussion, but we were a group in search of a subject.

'You mustn't lose hope,' Matthew said after a while. 'We'll

work for an appeal. There's a positive feeling abroad that justice has not been seen to be done.'

I was bewildered by his terminology. He was already talking like a lawyer, that dear brother of mine who had never talked very much at all and whose conversation was one of monosyllabic loving. I wanted to embrace him. I swallowed the lump in my throat.

'Talk to me Peter,' I said. 'And Jeannie. What are you doing with yourselves?'

And then I regretted my question. What on earth could Dreyfus children be doing at this time except keeping themselves to themselves, shielding their ears from the taunts and insults that must be echoing their footsteps wherever they turned?

'You know I'm innocent, don't you?' I said to them.

They nodded in unison.

'Never forget that,' I told them. 'It will help you on your way. I've done nothing of which you would be ashamed.'

'You don't have to tell us,' Peter said.

'What can we bring you?' Lucy asked after a while.

'I don't know yet what I'm allowed. But books, if it's possible.'

I was glad when the bell rang to signal the end of the visiting hour. It was too much of a strain for all of us.

'Don't worry,' Matthew kept saying. 'We'll get you out of here.'

He was desperate to comfort himself and I wished that I could console him.

When they had gone, it occurred to me that during the whole hour Susan had not once opened her mouth. And I knew from her studied silence that sooner or later, and in her own way, she would betray me.

28

Rebecca Morris had been very busy. Over the past months she had uncovered many leads. But she was a barrister with a living to earn. She needed a private eye to follow up her investigations, so with Matthew's permission she hired a detective. She gave him much ground to cover and many suspects to follow, but her one lead, and in her mind possibly the most fruitful of all, she kept for herself. She would make it her personal business to investigate James Turncastle.

A psychiatrist acquaintance had given her an introduction to the social services centre in Devon. She visited the centre claiming she was doing research on after-care facilities offered to psychiatric patients. She owned to being a barrister and said that she wanted to specialise in the laws pertaining to mental health. She was invited to accompany one of the centre's workers to the clinic where James was a patient. It was the only psychiatric hospital in the county, so she ran no risk of being side-tracked. During her visit she took care to make no mention of James and was at pains to point out that her enquiries were general. To this end she investigated the histories of a selection of patients and on subsequent visits she talked to those whose backgrounds were known. It was not until her fifth weekly visit that she casually included James in her research. In his file he was diagnosed as a depressive. His family showed no interest in his welfare and apart from an aunt who lived locally and who had come only once he'd had no visitors since his arrival. He was a voluntary patient but he seemed to have little appetite to discharge himself. When such a discharge had been suggested, he had attempted suicide. He was treated to daily therapy but showed himself to be surly and incommunicative. There was the occasional tantrum which waned as quickly as it flared.

Rebecca asked one of the nurses if she could talk to him.

'I wish you luck,' he laughed. 'But you'll be doing most of the talking.'

She was taken to his room.

'Visitor for you, Jamie boy,' the nurse shouted at the door, and Rebecca entered and shut the door behind her. She saw only the back of him. James was sitting in a chair facing the window. He made no response to the nurse's call. For one who rarely had a visitor he was strangely incurious. He neither turned his head nor made the slightest movement in his chair. Rebecca walked over to his side, introducing herself and declaring her purpose. She was careful to avoid the social worker's jargon. She knew how off-putting it could sound.

'I thought we could have a little talk,' she said.

'Go ahead,' he muttered without moving.

She looked at his profile which was all that he granted. Its contours were chiselled out of melancholy, and she felt sorry for him. Very gently, she started on her questions. He was distinctly incommunicative. He volunteered his name and his age, and considered those offerings more than generous. Then he turned his chair so that his back was towards her. It was his sign for her dismissal. She asked if she could come again, but he made no answer.

But Rebecca persevered. She took a fortnight's leave from her law practice and drove down to Devon, booking a room in a hotel hard by the hospital so that she was able to visit James every day. She had become a familiar face to the hospital staff, and she was given free passage. For form's sake, she visited other patients, but most of her time was spent with James. She asked him no more questions. She simply talked to him, telling him stories of her own work and the more interesting cases that she'd worked on. Occasionally she invited him to offer an opinion, or even advice, and very slowly, James thawed. By the second week of her stay, the monologue had dissolved into a dialogue of sorts and it seemed that James even took pleasure in their conversations.

It was the last day of her leave. They were sitting in the window-bay in the common lounge, and in the course of one of her courtroom stories, Rebecca dared to drop the name of Dreyfus.

It was a quiet afternoon. An old lady was knitting an endless scarf that draped about her feet and only the unrhythmic click of her needles, as she dropped a stitch and bred some more, could be heard in that unhinged silence. A few roses rested quietly in a vase on the table. For the still time being. Until the vase struck Rebecca, hurled at her shoulder, the rose-thorns caught in her cheek, and the green water and broken glass at her feet. James stood by the window, rigid on his feet, his hand in the air still poised for the throw. And he was screaming. The haggard sound that came from deep in his throat was not sustained. It cut out to give respite and then tuned in once more. Its siren was a morse code SOS. Rebecca stared at him and noted the bulging muscle on his raised arm. She wanted to approach him, but his rage was bursting with strength and she feared that he might well kill her for the terror raked by that name in his mind. She stared as two nurses crossed her vision and gently held him and led him from the room. She watched as they trailed him away and listened to his despairing sema-phore as it faded into a stuttering silence.

Rebecca shivered with a burdensome sense of responsibility. She knew that she had broken him, and with one single word had possibly achieved the breakthrough sought by months of therapy. She sat down and nursed her bruised cheek. The room was still silent. James's outburst seemed to have made no impression. Apart from the clicking needles, the entire space was blind, deaf and mute. She closed her eyes and once again she heard his screams, though she knew that by now James had been sedated, but his screams still fidgeted in her ear. She wondered whether their hypodermic had erased the Dreyfus name or whether James would wake with the dead weight of it on the tip of his parched tongue. She felt a none too gentle tap on her shoulder. She looked up and saw a nurse, one whose face was not familiar.

'You are wanted in the office,' she said. Her tone was abrupt and Rebecca expected a severe reprimand. Matron was waiting for her and she came straight to the point.

'We do not think it a good idea for you to visit Mr Turncastle again. You clearly disturb him. Heaven knows what harm you have done.'

Rebecca was enraged. The woman showed absolutely no interest in the matter that had ignited James's screaming. She simply wanted to be rid of the one who had caused it. But Rebecca sat down indicating that she had no intention of leaving.

'Don't you want to know what started it all?' she asked.

'I know that your visit distressed him,' Matron said, 'and that's all I need to know. Now I must ask you to leave.'

'You are right,' Rebecca said. 'I know I have disturbed James.

But I think that disturbance marks a significant breakthrough. I want to see his therapist.'

Matron gave her a look of mild contempt. 'I'm afraid that's impossible,' she said. 'You're not even a relative. You have been free to come and go these last few weeks. We have given you ample licence. Now it is over. You will not be admitted again.'

'I'm not leaving until I see his therapist,' Rebecca said. She crossed her legs and assumed a comfortable position.

A while passed with silence between them. Rebecca took a notebook and pen out of her briefcase and started to write. She wrote nothing of importance but it was a signal to Matron that she had no intention of going away. The silence continued and when Rebecca turned over a page Matron knew that something had to be done. She picked up her phone and said that Dr Field was wanted in her office. As she replaced the receiver she said, 'I have to tell you that this is most irregular.'

Rebecca didn't respond. There was no point in salting wounds.

Matron went to the door of her office. She clearly wanted a word with Dr Field before the meeting. She approached him as he walked down the corridor.

'It's that Miss Morris,' she said, 'the one who disturbed James Turncastle. She insists on seeing you. And she refuses to go away until she does.'

'I'll sort her out,' Dr Field said roughly. He was in no mood to discuss his patient with that interfering woman who had caused such havoc. He would give her a piece of his mind. He strode into the office while Matron withdrew with some relief to the staff kitchen to swallow her defeat in a cup of tea.

'What is it you want?' Dr Field asked as he entered the room.

'How is James?' Rebecca asked. First things first, she thought.

'None the better for your interference,' he said.

'I'm astonished,' Rebecca said. 'You're his doctor. Are you not in the least bit interested in the reason why he lost his cool? Do you not think it might be valuable information regarding James's treatment?'

'Madam,' Dr Field said on his guard, 'James's treatment depends solely on what I learn from James himself. What outsiders tell me is irrelevant.'

Rebecca stood up. 'Irrelevant or not, Dr Field,' she said, 'I intend to let you know. I disturbed him today because I let fall a name which is possibly the very core of his depression. I just thought you ought to know.' Rebecca had occasionally been obliged to consult with therapists while involved in a law suit. She found them often unreliable. They tended to know everything and they were never wrong. When in doubt, they sought refuge in psychobabble, as she expected any moment from Dr Field.

'Do you know what transference means?' he asked with a sneer.

Rebecca ignored the question and gave another in return.

'D'you know what the name Dreyfus means?' she asked.

He was flummoxed. He knew the name of course but clearly he'd never connected it with his patient, and Rebecca wondered what in God's name the man had been doing for the last twelve months of James's hospitalisation. She gathered her papers together. 'Remember the name, Dr Field,' she said with some scorn. 'It was that name that tipped James over the edge. Remember it. It might well come in handy.' She left the room before he could begin to vent his spleen. For he was indeed furious. The woman had had the crass impertinence to tell him how to do his job. But he was also angry with himself and his niggling nudge of incompetence.

Rebecca returned to London only partially satisfied. She sincerely felt she'd made some headway in James's treatment but was sad that she was now declared out of bounds. She had expected much from his story and had pinned her faith on getting to its truth. Now that truth might or might not be revealed to Dr Field and there was certainly no way that Dr Field would divulge it. And certainly not to the person who set him on the right track in the first place. She hoped that her private eye would have made some fruitful discoveries.

And he most certainly had. He had brought back stories from Austria which spelt out the first clues to a conspiracy, and what he'd discovered in Marseilles had confirmed those clues.

'We're on our way,' he told Rebecca. 'And how was James?'

She had to tell him that the trail had gone cold. And she told him why. But the private eye was elated. 'You've established the link,' he said. 'That's what's important. Something will come of it. It's bound to. We must just be patient.'

'Tell that to poor Dreyfus,' Rebecca said.

29

When I returned to my cell after that first family visit, I fell into a deep depression. I wanted to cut myself off from my family. Or rather I wished that they would abandon me. I wanted them all to go away, to leave the country for a faraway place, to change their names and begin a new non-Dreyfus life. Their absence would, in some measure, relieve me of the catastrophe I had wrought in their lives. I would urge them to leave, I decided. I would insist on it. And, if they refused, I would refuse their visits. I had worked myself up into such a state of determination that I began to shout aloud. 'Go away. All of you. Just leave me alone.' The grill clicked on my door and a pair of eyes checked that nothing was amiss. I was not attempting suicide; I was not frothing at the mouth. And above all I was not dead. Therefore nothing was amiss. The grill closed with scorn on my frenzy.

I don't know how I weathered the next few days. My

depression did not lift. Occasionally I was thrust into company. Meal-times in the dining-hall, I noticed that I was ignored. No one approached me with offers of friendship or communication of any kind. On the contrary, I detected a distinct hostility, which upset me greatly. If I was bent on ridding myself of family, then I certainly would need friends of a sort. Even amongst the men of this wretched company with whom on the outside I could never have associated. But I would have to lower my sights. I would have to consider a radical change in my values. Innocent as I was, I would have to behave like a criminal. Moreover I would have to think like a criminal. But as yet I had no guidelines. I must prepare myself for education. I would mix. Yes, mix. And hopefully merge.

To this end I decided to avail myself to the exercise period which hitherto I had forfeited. With some trepidation I allowed myself to be led to the exercise yard. It was already full. A ball game was in progress, a game which seemed to have no rules but rather depended on the one player outdoing the other with swearing and curses. The actual ball seemed an irrelevancy. Some men were jogging, and even this exercise involved swearing soliloquies. The playground was abuzz with blasphemy.

I hung around the wall for a while. Perhaps I was waiting for a passing word, or a simple nod of acknowledgement. I noticed that several of the men nudged each other and pointed me out. At least I had been noticed. I decided to circle the yard at a trot. It was, after all, an exercise yard and there was little point in leaning against the wall. So I set off, and as I circled I felt their eyes on me. They were not kindly eyes and I felt threatened. So I decided to sing to myself to allay my fears. And out of my mouth, as from nowhere, except from out of two thousand years of memory, came a tune that my mother had sung to me when I was a baby. Her own mother had sung it to her. That Yiddish song was the sole Jewish legacy my mother could not deny. My grandmother's song, that not even the ovens could

stifle. I imagined her face as I sang it to myself, and with her I
mouthed the odd Yiddish word that I could remember and for
some reason that recollection gave me so much joy that for a
moment I forgot where I was and why. And even who, that
prime source of my pain. And as I sang, recalling more and
more words, I was shipped back into that Paris apartment, long
before the time when she went to buy milk and when my
grandfather went to look for her. I kept running and singing the
while. Then I heard a shrill whistle and I stopped in my tracks.
A Gestapo's whistle, which sound punctuated their fears in
their last Parisian days. Then I looked around me and saw
where I was, and knew why I was there and my name no longer
escaped me. The words were gone from the song and so was its
melody, as I was hustled back into line on the way to my cell.
And once there I could not recall the tune, much less those
occasional words and even my grandmother's face had become
a blur. But I did not lose heart. I assured myself that visits to
the exercise yard would rekindle that memory. But never again
was it so strong. The tune returned, but fewer and fewer words
and I could never forget who and why I was, as I had so bliss-
fully on that magic morning of my first exercise sortie.

The hostility of the other men was constant. It occurred to
me that I might make the first approach with some innocuous
question referring to the weather or the food, uninflammable
topics. It would be a start. At the next meal-time I made my
way to my usual table. It was where I had been deposited on
my first visit to the mess-hall. It was a small table, smaller
than the others, seating about ten of us, and it was placed near
the door and the guards who stood there. Its size and placing
had not seemed of any special importance to me, but one
dinnertime I was to understand its difference from the others.
I sat with the other men, and after a while I broke the silence
with a fatuous comment on the weather. To my surprise my
remark elicited a response. Not from one, but all of them. It

seemed they were as eager for exchange as I. But the theme of weather can be quickly exhausted and after a short while silence was bound to take over. I noticed one of the men open his mouth to speak, but he thought better of it. Then the man next to him nudged him.

'Go on,' he said. 'Ask him.'

'Ask me what?' I asked, happy that a possible conversation was in the air.

'You're one of us, aren't you?' the nudged man whispered.

I was puzzled. I was certainly one of them in that I was a prisoner. But the man couldn't have meant that. His 'one of us' pointed elsewhere. For a moment I thought that all my table companions were Jewish and they were cementing me into their tribe. But none of them looked Jewish. Indeed a couple of them sported crosses about their necks. I decided to play safe. 'Of course I am,' I said. 'I'm a prisoner, like all of you.'

The men grinned. I'd clearly not understood. 'Isn't that what you meant?' I said feebly.

Then one of them leant across the table. He was sitting opposite me and as he leant forward, his silver cross dangled over his plate.

'We're all child-killers,' he whispered.

I thought I was going to cry. I am not a man much given to tears. Indeed I could count on less than one hand of fingers how many times I have wept. With tears I mean. I don't count the lumps in my throat. There were tears when my father died and I think that was the last time. But now I felt the heat behind my eyes and I knew that the tears would fall and I didn't care. I would be crying for young George Tilbury whom I did not kill. I would be crying for the company I was forced to keep, for the small shameful table that accommodated us like lepers, and the guards on hand to shield us from violence. I let the tears flow. I wanted to tell them that I was innocent but I feared they would laugh in my face. I felt dirty in their company and I shuddered at the thought that I would have to break bread with them for the rest of my life.

I left the table and asked to be taken back to my cell, pleading a raging headache and the need to be alone. The guard told me to wait, and I had to sit there while the tears streamed down my face.

'It's all right,' the man with the cross said. 'We all feel sorry sometimes. Then we forget about it. Good days. Bad days.' He turned to the table. 'Isn't that right, men?'

They nodded their agreement and tucked into their pudding. They had enrolled me into their club. Whether I liked it or not, I was one of them. A barely paid-up member but with all the privileges of a pariah.

Once back in my cell, I dared to wonder what had become of me. And my grandmother came once more to my mind together with her melody and the smattering of words. And that memory brought me a strange peace and I wondered how I had ever contemplated sending my family away.

Despite the hostility that surrounded me, I steeled myself to my meal-time company and to my lonely trotting around the exercise yard. One morning, during the exercise period, I thought I might indulge in something more strenuous than my gentle running. I would stretch myself, touch my toes perhaps, or at least try. I am not by nature a physical man. I play no sports. I take walks occasionally, and sometimes I swim, or I used to in my days of freedom. But I have never seriously tested my body. I thought this might be a good time to remedy many years of neglect and I rather looked forward to it.

I found myself a place at the end of the yard. I was sure that it would not be crowded. My mere appearance in the yard sent the other men scattering. I faced the wall. I did not wish to face the men. I was a little nervous of my gymnastic abilities and I did not want to view their scorn. For a while I jogged on the spot, flexing my muscles and holding my grandmother's song in my ear. Then I tried my first bend. Keeping my knees straight, I was not able to reach my toes. My fingertips achieved a mere mid-calf. But I was not discouraged. I would practise. I would give myself a target. By the end of the week I would caress my toes with ease. I took a deep breath and tried again. I fared no better on the second turn but the strain was less and I was encouraged. I tried a few more times and I heard a rustling behind me.

'Want some help?' a man said.

I heard the sneer in his voice and then I felt a savage kick on my buttocks and my toes obligingly met my hands for the first time. I tumbled painfully on to the hard ground and viewed with terror the two pairs of heavy black trainers in my eye-line. I shifted a little only to view four more pairs and I knew that I was surrounded. And then the battery began. Their kicking was brutal, frenzied and in perfect rhythm with their curses. 'Child-killer,' they kicked, and 'Scumbag Jew'. These oaths were repeated over and over again, for even in the lexicon of cursing they had limited vocabulary. I lay there helpless and in worsening pain and as I listened to their fulsome rebuke I wondered how they viewed themselves. Would they have kicked themselves with that same fury knowing that they were killers? Would they have tortured themselves for their lack of remorse, those men who had killed their wives, murdered their business partners, tortured their enemies and mangled their remains? Did they think well of themselves, well enough to forgive those who had similarly offended? It occurred to me then that the child-killing had nothing to do with their rage. Guilty or innocent, it was the Jew and all that he stood for they were kicking. And I, writhing on the ground, was the representative of that cursed race on whom to vent their scapegoat spleen. I was not surprised when the 'Child-killer' abuse was gradually withdrawn and 'Scumbag Jew' wholly took over, confirming my view that, killer or not, in my Jewish skin I happened to be a handy butt for their sublime frustration. I wondered if I had to endure their punishment until the whistle blew or whether perhaps I should show some kind of resistance. I decided on the former, hoping that they would grow bored with such a defenceless target. And indeed they soon tired. The kicks grew desultory and the curses wearied too. And I lay there with throbbing prints of their canvas jackboots pulsing through every pore of my body. The pain was tempered with the relief that the torment was over, together with a small sliver of gratitude that they had left my face alone. I marvelled that, in the abject wretchedness of my present state, I could still cling to my vanity.

I lay there until the whistle blew. The two guards had not once moved from their sentry position. But they had witnessed the whole spectacle, and no doubt had viewed it with approval. I tried to stand, but I did not trust the alignment of my limbs. I managed slowly to get to my knees, then I felt two strong grips on my elbows as I was raised from the ground. The guards had taken their time. Without a word, they helped me back to my cell, and though I did not look at their faces I knew that they were smiling.

It was a relief to lie on my cot and let my pain rage and slowly subside without witness. For the whole of that day I lay there. I ignored the lunch and the supper bells. My pain forbade movement. My absence would no doubt gratify my tormentors. They would link it with cowardice. But oddly enough I was not afraid. I would rejoin them once the pain had ceased. I would not be kept from the exercise yard. It must have been my innocence that gave me courage.

The following morning I forced myself to rise and rejoin the community. I was driven more by hunger than heroism. My body ached but I forced myself to walk erect. I made my way to my sordid table and I was surprised at the friendliness that greeted my arrival. And offended by it too, for I did not want to be counted amongst them.

'We don't go out for exercise,' one of them said. 'We do press-ups in the cells.'

'They're not going to stop me,' I said.

This only served to increase their admiration. I had the sour impression that I was about to be appointed their leader. So I said no more. I could not even smile at them. I wanted them to hate me because I was not one of them. But they would never believe that. In their eyes I had murdered a child as they had done, and as such I qualified for their club. Membership was obligatory.

After breakfast I took myself to the exercise yard. I was aware of glances of surprise and as I made my way to my corner I heard the phrase 'ready for seconds'. I was not fazed and I thanked God for my courage. I hummed my grandmother's song and I decided to begin with my trotting around the yard. The ragged ball game ceased, as did the press-ups and general exercises. I had an audience. In silence they watched my unhampered run and heard my joyous song and after my second lap they returned to their own work-outs and for the rest of the exercise period they left me alone. I felt I had scored a small victory. Back in my cell I lay my throbbing body on my cot, and the relief was sheer joy.

For the next few weeks I dined and exercised with the scum I was forced to associate with and by then I thought I had made my point. Thereafter I exercised each day alongside my cot, and my meals were brought to my cell. During my short time in prison, the governor had already befriended me. Occasionally he would come to my cell to check on my welfare. I think he must have believed in my innocence. He brought me news from the outside and sometimes left me a newspaper. I think he understood my need to be alone. I had never reported my beating, but he must have heard about it and he was concerned for my safety. So he granted my request though it was uncommon. For a while I relished my privacy, but I could not deny that I was desperately lonely. But the thought of the company on offer was sickening enough to lift that depression. The days passed very slowly but counted as nothing when measured against the fifteen years that was my term. Lucy's regular visits and the family news that she brought cheered me for a while and then only served to remind me of all the living that I was missing. But I still had hope. I still could not believe what had happened to me. It was a farce, and I smiled sometimes until I caught sight of the bars on my window.

And then one day, my life changed. I did not know it at the time but now in hindsight I realise how much that visitor turned my life around. Sam Temple came to see me that day. I have to confess I did not take to him on the first meeting. Perhaps in my desolate state I would have taken to nobody. But then I think he found me faintly resistible too. I was short with him, and possibly rude. I was deeply out of practice socially and when he had gone I regretted my coolness. But I *did* start to write. It might have been because I had nothing else to do. But once started I had a purpose. I had found a way to prove my innocence. Or so I thought. Since that time, I have had moments of deepest doubt, sensing the futility of my pursuit. But in the main the writing itself has given me – may I say – joy, and the occasional magic moment in which my prison bars can play no part. Sam has been a frequent visitor, and I venture to say, a close friend. He has met my family and is in constant and generous touch with them. Above all, he is a listener, a sympathetic ear. He clears my mind of its confusion of reality with fiction. In many ways, I owe him my survival.

They have just brought me my supper on a tray. My body aches but I know I shall sleep well for tomorrow Sam is coming, and I shall read to him and he will listen.

30

Ronnie Copes, Rebecca's private eye, had surpassed himself and enjoyed a pretty good holiday into the bargain. For he had travelled widely. His first port of call was at a little village in the Austrian Alps. Pre-investigation led him to the village where Eccles had taken his students on their regular skiing trips, and with little difficulty he had also located the Viennese family with whom James had stayed during his term's leave from school. On the pretext of looking for a week's lodgings, Ronnie called on them. He was offered a room and moved in straight-away. During the course of that week he ingratiated himself with the family. Frau Müller was English, and had been born in Sheffield. As a young girl, on a skiing trip to Austria, she had fallen in love with her ski instructor and they had married. Only once had she returned to Sheffield, but she no longer had any interest in her place of birth. 'Vienna's my home now,' she told him 'and I am very happy here.'

She had two children, she said, both married now and living in Münich. She had shown him photographs of her family. Amongst them there was a portrait of a young man in uniform.

'That's Peter,' she said proudly of her husband.

Peter, when Ronnie met him, never ceased talking of the 'good old days'. 'I thank God that my children have inherited that sense of honour, of patriotism, and know of the glory of those days that will come again.'

Ronnie Cope left the Müllers before the week was out. But he had stayed with them long enough to gather a fund of information which he found both fascinating and disgusting at the same time.

His next port of call was Marseilles, and using clues that he had picked up from the Müllers he located Eccles's friends. In their company, he played the part of the disgruntled Englishman irritated by the hordes of immigrants that flooded his country and by the unscrupulous power of the Jews who seemed to run everything. Poor Ronnie practically choked on his every syllable. He was warmly welcomed into their circle, and that Marseilles sojourn proved even more fruitful than his stay with the Müllers.

From Marseilles he took himself off to the Appalachian mountains in Virginia, honed in on his prey and dug up information which confirmed his earlier findings.

The little village in Kent, the site of George Tilbury's burial, was Ronnie Cope's last port of call. From the investigative view, it had turned out to be a gold-mine. He had the names of those locals who had borne witness against Dreyfus in his trial. Spending most of his time in the local pub in the guise of a tourist, it took two weeks of intensive ferreting to investigate them all. Yet not one of them suspected that they were being subjected to scrutiny. Ronnie returned to London triumphant and presented all his findings to his impatient employer. Rebecca was delighted. Ronnie's discoveries represented a major breakthrough in her searchings. They almost had enough evidence to warrant an appeal. But one piece was missing. A major piece. James Turncastle. She had no evidence that his story, should he even wish to tell it, would confirm any of Ronnie's findings. All she knew was that the young tormented James Turncastle had Dreyfus on his mind.

It was some months since she had last seen him. She had made roundabout enquiries and had learnt that he had been discharged from hospital shortly after her last visit. But she had no idea where he was. A letter to his Devonian aunt had elicited no response and even Ronnie, with all his ingenuity, could find no trace of him. They both feared that James had left the country. She sifted through all their findings to date and put them in a suitable order for presentation, for she had already begun to draft a letter to the Home Secretary asking for an appeal and as she read it over the gaps in the evidence were plain enough. Only James could corroborate what they had found. But the new discoveries were rich enough to share with Matthew. She would tell him that evening at home. For home it had become. Some months ago, Matthew had moved into her flat. Their relationship was no longer clandestine though, by some fortunate omission, it had not reached the press. Lucy shared their happiness with sealed lips, as did Sam Temple, who visited them often. If Susan was aware of Matthew's move, her lips were sealed too, but in shame and jealousy. Dreyfus was still ignorant of Susan's betrayal but on his regular visits to his brother Matthew sensed that Dreyfus knew of the rift, but did not want to reveal that he knew. For he never asked after Susan and Matthew volunteered no information on her well-being.

That evening over supper Rebecca itemised all the new evidence that Ronnie Copes had collected. She was hopeful she said, but insisted that Dreyfus should not be told of the new developments. 'If I cannot get James,' she said, 'we don't have a watertight case. This is presuming James is willing to tell his story. And moreover to testify in court. He could be anywhere. Who knows?'

'You could try his parents,' Matthew said. 'Perhaps by now they might have shown some interest in him.'

'I've already done that,' Rebecca said. 'They say they don't know where he is, and they don't seem to care.'

Half of that was true. His parents certainly didn't care but equally certainly, they knew where he was. They had never seen his apartment but had bought it over the telephone through an estate agent. A luxurious one, sumptuous enough to square the most guilty of consciences. As it had done for them. The stunning living-room, the Italianate terrace, the formal dining-room, the sanitised bedrooms and showers redeemed their lifelong parental neglect. The tasteful Swedish furnishings, the silver and the plate settled their debts of love withdrawn, and the absence of telephone, fax or e-mail spelt out in clear terms their taboo on communication.

As James rattled around the apartment, viewing each separate pay-off, he slowly began to pity them. During his sojourn at the clinic, his rage against his parents had subsided. Gradually he had freed himself from their reluctant hold, a hold that he himself had nurtured and colluded with. Now they were a mere couple in another part of the world, pursuing their selfish ways, and very slowly, he had begun to savour his own freedom. That achieved freedom that comes with the nonchalance of being unsired. The freedom of being one's own person, of never having to crave approval or to live in terror of its withdrawal. A consummate freedom, he tried to convince himself, yet he knew that it was not entire. That the road to his absolute relief was not a freeway. There were parking bays for reflection, roundabouts for second thoughts, and perhaps a closed lane or road-block that would stop him in his tracks. As long as he stayed in his luxurious apartment, he felt safe. He risked no obstacle. But occasionally, in brave moments, he would take himself to Rebecca's chambers and he would hang about outside and look up at her window. The occasional sight of her, cemented his feet to the ground. He dreaded the temptation to move towards her, to tear down the final obstacle to his freedom. He knew that one day he would have to find the courage to confront her, to unburden himself of the very last dregs of his conscience. But each time he turned and walked away he consoled himself with the thought that he had made certain moves towards that final confession. Since leaving the clinic he had made enquiries. He had read the newspapers and eavesdropped on sundry grapevines, he had heard that she was working on an appeal, he had found the address of her chambers. He had learnt about Matthew, the brother of that man whose name he still could not utter in fear of the pain that it would breed. He knew as much as he would ever know from behind closed doors. He had done his homework, and comforted himself with the facts that he had gleaned and hoodwinked himself into believing that research was all. But as the weeks passed he found he could not stop himself from leaving his flat almost daily, and from loitering outside those windows behind which that unspeakable name chimed with equal echoes of hope and despair. Yet still he cemented his feet to the ground.

The unspoken name, whose parcelling rotted so unjustly behind bars, became a daily waking thought, and James's sortie to her chambers turned into an addiction, and he knew that in time the name would have to be spoken aloud.

One day he even made it to the entrance of her building but at the lift his feet refused, and he fled back to his stand on the street corner. The following day he managed to call the lift, but he faltered when it arrived. It took him a further week to actually enter the lift and take himself to the fifth floor, the site of the offices that echoed with that name, but his hand was firmly on the 'down' button.

But the following day he forced himself into the lift, and on to her floor, and outside her very offices, his hand knocking on her door. Suddenly he found himself inside, and facing a woman at a desk who asked his business. He stammered Rebecca's name because he had to say something, and with a sublime relief he heard that she was in court.

'But you could wait,' the woman said. 'Miss Morris is expected shortly.'

'I'll come back,' he said, and fled to the door.

He had tried, and the attempt itself was a minor triumph. His steps towards the lift were jaunty. He pressed the down button and waited. The lift silently settled on the fifth floor and the door slid aside like a gentleman. To let out that face he had never forgotten, that mouth from which still hung that grievous name. And now he seemed to see it, the clear letters, the D, the R, the E, the Y, though he needed no more. They faced each other in unavoidable confrontation. Rebecca wished to embrace him, to hold him for her own relief and for his courage. But instead she put out her hand.

James took it. It was the first instalment of his confession. It would be done. It would be out. It would be over. He would have spoken that name, that name he had so often confused with 'Father'. And sometimes, not even confused, but truly believed. For that name had loved him as a son.

'You've come to see me?' Rebecca asked.

'I've come often,' he said. 'This time I've been caught.'

'I think you wanted to be caught,' she said.

She led him into her office. 'Sit down and tell me how you are.' She decided that she would not broach the Dreyfus subject. She would wait in the hope that James would volunteer. She would not risk that loaded name a second time.

'I'm better,' James said. 'I left the clinic four months' ago.'

'And where are you living now?' she asked.

'In Fulham,' he said. 'I bought a flat. Or rather my parents bought it for me.' He gave a hint of a smile.

'Then you're in touch with them again?'

'No,' James laughed. 'They just sent me the money. Money, if you have it, is the easiest thing to give. It costs less than caring or loving.'

There was no bitterness in his voice. He had come through his pain and distrust. He now seemed to view his parents as a sick joke.

'It's really lovely to see you again,' Rebecca said. 'I missed our little get-togethers. After the last one, I didn't think I'd see you again.' She hadn't meant to make a reference to it, and she feared his reaction. But he was smiling.

'That was a turn-up for the books,' he said. 'But as you know, I'd had a breakdown. But for some reason, after that visit, I started to get back on my feet again.'

Rebecca could have told him the reason and she thought that she might with some justification send his therapist a bill for her services.

'And what are you doing now?' she asked.

'I have lots to do,' he said. 'That's why I've come to see you.'

Rebecca thought he might have come to see if she could get him employment of a sort. 'Are you looking for work?' she asked.

'Nothing like that,' he said. He paused for a while. 'I have unfinished business.'

She wanted to ask him if it was Dreyfus business as she fully expected but she was still afraid of the name.

'Oh, it's all so complicated,' he said.

'Start at the beginning,' Rebecca urged him. 'I have time.'

'I heard you were working for an appeal,' James said. 'That's why I'm here.' He took a deep breath. 'Now it's out,' he said. 'You've no idea how often I've rehearsed that line.'

'You have great courage,' Rebecca said. 'And all my respect.' She could not wait to get home and tell Matthew, for it looked as if young James was about to come clean, and was about to blow the whistle on the conspiracy.

'Suppose I take you out to eat?' Rebecca suggested. 'I know a very quiet place, not far from here. Italian. That suit you?'

James smiled. 'I love Italian,' he said.

It was a lengthy supper. She wined and dined him as her ears tingled to his tale. Every single word confirmed Ronnie Cope's findings. But his personal contribution to the dire conspiracy was astonishing. He seemed relieved when it was all told.

'I want to testify at the appeal,' he said. 'I have to do it. Then I can start living again.'

Rebecca asked him if he would come back in the morning and tape a statement of what he had told her. James was more than willing to do all that he could to clear his own troubled conscience. She watched him walk away from her and she thought she heard him singing.

'*Now* you can tell Alfred,' she said to Matthew when she reached home. 'And I shall work on the papers to send to the Home Secretary. At last,' she said, 'we have reason to hope.'

As he had promised, James turned up early the following morning, and taped his statement. And Matthew went to visit his brother.

31

I don't know how to begin. There have been many times when I have found it hard to pick up my pen. My despair forbade it. Now, at that moment, after Matthew's visit, the pen still resisted me, but now it was prompted no longer by despair, but by simple joy. I wanted to dance and sing, and indeed I did so continually, since Matthew had left. I was intoxicated with the smell of my possible freedom. I was ready to forgive. I was ready to forfeit my rage. But I knew I had to guard against both for a time. There was yet one more hurdle to clear: the Home Secretary's go-ahead. But Matthew had said that the evidence of a conspiracy was so telling, so undeniable, so multi-witnessed, that a refusal was unthinkable. But the Home Secretary was a Jew. I would prefer him to be a Gentile. I could not help recalling that it was a Jewish judge who sent the Rosenbergs to the electric chair. Another 'count me in' Jew. God help me, but we are a crazy people.

I waited. I can't remember how I spent the next few weeks. Matthew visited often, but simply to report that they were still awaiting the Home Secretary's response. He was optimistic, as always. So was Lucy who had been so careful not to raise my hopes. I wanted to talk to them about what I would do when I was free, but Lucy refused that topic.

'I have to tell you something,' Matthew said.

I feared for a moment that there was some hiccup in the proceedings, that there was a delay or a hint of a refusal to an appeal. I must have paled, for Matthew hastened to add, 'It has nothing to do with the appeal. It's about me and Susan. She left me shortly after the verdict. She changed her name and Adam's and Zak's as well.'

'I think I must have known,' I said, and I was relieved that Matthew had finally told me. I made to embrace him with my sympathy. 'I'm very sorry,' I said.

'There's no need,' he told me. 'I see the children regularly and I'm living with Rebecca. Have been for the past year. We're very happy together.'

'And how is Susan?' I asked, though in my heart I didn't care how she was.

'Angry,' Lucy donated.

We were silent then, and in our silence, Susan was exiled from the family.

When they had gone, I started once more on my story, but I could not find the words for waiting. There were days when my hopes were so high, I simply bided my patient time to my release. But there were days too when I was so full of despair, that I resigned myself to my cell for the rest of my natural life. And so I wavered between these two extremes, and while dwelling in the one, I could never envisage the other.

It was during this time, this uncertain time, that Sam came to see me. It had been almost a month since he had last visited and I had missed him. He had warned me that he was going to

America for a while so I shouldn't wonder at his absence. Yet I did. I couldn't understand why he had to leave me, and sometimes I was angry with him. But I was overjoyed to see him again.

He came into my cell and made himself at home on my cot. That's what I liked about Sam. My cell had never offended him. I think, God forbid, given some misfortune, he would have made a comfortable prisoner. He was full of graphic stories of his American visit but first he had to talk about the possible appeal. Matthew had filled him in on the latest developments and he was bursting to share with me his joy and his hopes.

'The book gets longer,' he said with a sly smile. 'It will have chapters we only dared dream about.'

Then I realised that I had entirely forgotten about the book. It had been a useful and sometimes happy time-filler but soon, hopefully, its purpose would no longer be feasible. Sam must have read my mind.

'The book has a larger purpose now,' he said. 'With luck it is no longer therapy. It is a protest against injustice, against prejudice, corruption and persecution. All of those things. And they go beyond the Dreyfus case. They have a universal compulsion. You have to finish it, whatever the outcome of the appeal. You *owe*, my friend.' He smiled then, and told me how excited the American publishers were, and how they looked forward to the finished manuscript.

'I'll do my best,' I told him. Then he felt free to tell me about New York. I had been there only once, in my halcyon days, when on a lecture tour. As he was speaking, I made plans to revisit New York as soon as I was free. And in my mind I plotted my itinerary. And so engrossed was I in my own arrangements that slowly I ceased to hear Sam's stories. Until he asked me a question relating to his tale, and I had to confess that my mind had been elsewhere.

'You're planning your freedom,' he said.

There was a note of warning in his voice and it depressed me. 'I can dream, can't I?' I said.

'Know them as dreams,' Sam told me. 'Just for the time being.' Then, after a pause, 'I've come to be read to,' he said.

I had written much since Sam's last listening visit, all through the days before Matthew brought me that still half-believable news. In those days I had often wished for Sam's listening ear, for I was still uncertain whether my words lay in the realm of fiction or truth. Now, as I read to him, I knew them for nothing but the truth, every syllable of them, for in my mind was the stubborn prospect of freedom. And because of that prospect I no longer found that truth unbelievable. For if freedom were a possibility, it had to have entailed imprisonment.

When I had finished reading, Sam expressed himself pleased with the work and I think he knew as well as I that I no longer needed a listener.

'We are almost up to date,' he said, 'and with luck your final chapter will deal with the appeal. And even if that is disallowed,' Sam went on, 'you have to write about all the new evidence.'

'I can't believe it will be disallowed,' I said.

He put his arm around my shoulder. 'I agree,' he said. 'But don't dream of your freedom. Dream instead of your confinement, for I think you are close to waking.'

When he had gone, I picked up my pen once more. But, try as I would, I could not find the words for waiting. I sat and stared at my manuscript and soon enough I started to dream. Not of my freedom, as Sam had advised, but of my cell and the bars on its window. And it was a nightmare.

The days passed, with their daily press-ups and toe-touching, the lonely meals and the waiting. Then one morning I awoke with the current date fixed in my mind. May the twenty-first. I don't know how I knew it. I barely noted the change of seasons, leave alone the number of the day or month. It puzzled me, this waking thought, this May the twenty-first that kept ringing in my ear, and I knew that for whatever reason, it was an auspicious day. I knew that something was about to happen. I felt it in my bones. I felt it in my toes as I touched them, in my shoulders as I raised them from the floor. I hurried with my exercises that morning. I did not want to be occupied when whatever was about to happen, would be known. Likewise I hurried with my breakfast and when the tray was removed, I sat and waited. But I could not hurry my waiting. May the twenty-first, I kept saying to myself and I didn't know why. I tried to read, but I couldn't concentrate. I was tired but I was afraid to close my eyes in case I fell asleep and missed out on whatever was about to happen. I stood on my cot and looked out of the barred window. Perhaps I expected to see a fire, or a riot, any event that would make that date memorable. There was nothing untoward to view, yet the date throbbed in my mind.

Once more I sat on my cot and tried to read. My ears were alive to every sound and the silence deafened them. Then suddenly I heard footsteps along the aisle outside my cell and I knew that they would stop at my door. They were the heavy tread of a guard, but those treads muffled another's, treads less rhythmical, shoed rather than booted. I watched my door open and I held my breath. I saw the boots and the black-trousered legs of the guard, then looked up to his grim face as he held the door for the governor's entrance. Although the governor occasionally dropped in to see me, his visits usually occurred in the evening, before lights out. So I knew that this was a special visit and that it had taken place on the twenty-first of May. I heard my heart thumping. He nodded to the guard who withdrew and I rose, trembling, to my feet. I saw the governor's face break into a smile.

'Good news,' he said. 'I was informed this morning that the Home Secretary has allowed the appeal.'

I wanted to embrace him. I wanted to embrace the world. He put out his hand, and taking mine, he shook it vigorously.

'I'm happy about it, as you must be,' he said. 'And I wish you all the very best.' He went to the door. 'Try to be patient,' he said.

'I've waited so long,' I told him, 'I have learnt patience.'

That afternoon, I had three visitors. Lucy, Matthew and Rebecca. I had met with Rebecca once before when she had come to interview me regarding my trial. But this was the first time that I had seen her with Matthew and their pairing pleased me. 'The governor told me,' I said, as soon as I saw them. We hugged each other. We couldn't find words. We had used them all in our desperate waiting.

We were in the visitors' room as a change from my cell. The governor had suggested it. It was clear that the other men knew of the change in my fortunes for they viewed me with even more suspicion and envy. One of them passed by our table.

'Trust you lot to fix things,' he hissed.

I smiled at him and he reddened with rage.

We held each others' hands across the table and after a while I dared to ask when the appeal would begin.

'It will take about a month,' Rebecca said. 'A date will be fixed and then subpoenas will be delivered to all those who witnessed against you.'

'What about Eccles?' I said. 'He spoke up for me.'

'That was his cover,' Rebecca said. 'Eccles too. Especially Eccles.'

'Any others?' I asked.

'A surprise one,' Matthew said. 'Old John Coleman from the village.'

'I can't wait to question *him*,' Rebecca said.

We laughed together, children's laughter. That of innocence while the men around us sniggered and burned with envy.

As Rebecca had predicted, the date of the appeal was set for five weeks hence and the waiting was almost a pleasure. I risked the mess-hall again for my meals and noticed that my table companions were considerably less friendly. They suspected that I was not one of them after all. But I did not risk the exercise yard. I did not want to hobble injured into the courtroom. I wrote diligently during that waiting time and when Sam came to see me, overjoyed with the news, he knew I did not need to read to him.

The evening before the appeal, Matthew came to the prison to deliver my suit. He had not brought the one that I had worn for that terrible verdict. He had brought the suit I had worn on my lecture tours, a reminder of happier days and perhaps those that were to come. I had neither lost nor gained weight, but I had added a little muscle. Nevertheless the suit sat perfectly upon me.

Matthew had news. 'We've lost a witness, I'm afraid.'

'Eccles?' I asked.

'No. Eccles is subpoenaed. He'll be there. It's John Coleman. He disappeared overnight. He's done a bunk, it seems. His cottage in the village is up for sale. Nobody saw him go, and nobody knows where he is.'

'I suspected that man from the very beginning,' I said. 'Nothing very special. I just didn't trust him. That day when he came to tea, he must have been planning my fall.'

'Not you personally,' Matthew said. 'You just happened to be the right target at the right time.'

He embraced me. 'I'll see you tomorrow,' he said. 'We all will. We're all so hopeful. Even Lucy. She almost bought a new hat. Almost.'

I didn't sleep much that night, but I had a fitful dream that my suit didn't fit me. It was much too tight, and I woke up as the buttons burst from their moorings.

My breakfast was brought and I noticed an extra slice of bread on the tray. I was allowed a bath, and the guards watched

me as I shaved and donned my new suit. 'Very smart,' one of
them managed to say, and 'Good luck,' came from the other,
those same two guards who had borne silent and indifferent witness to my playground beatings. But I forgave them, wondering
whether it was still too soon for forgiveness. There was some
time left before I would be taken to the court and I was not surprised to receive a visit from the governor.

'I came to wish you well,' he said. He handed me a copy of
the day's paper. 'Something to read while you're waiting,' he
said.

I scanned the headlines with a sudden and delicious appetite
for news, when my eye caught a title that stunned me: 'ENG-
LISH PUBLIC SCHOOLMASTER FOUND DEAD.'

I knew who it was without reading further. The news excited
me, and without one shred of regret or remorse, I confess to
reading the report with a certain pleasure: 'The body of Mark
Eccles, head of the history department at one of England's
finest public schools, was found late last night in his room at the
Hotel de la Mer, Marseilles. Foul play is not suspected.'

It occurred to me that Eccles's suicide might well be advan-
tageous to my trial, but above all I was satisfied that at least in
one area justice had been seen to be done.

When eventually they came to escort me to the Court of
Appeal, I was in a state close to exhilaration.

Wish me luck, Mr Wallworthy.

PART FIVE

PART FIVE

32

It was a long time since I'd last seen that blanket. I wondered whether it was the same one, oozing the sweat of fear, and contemplated how many innocent or guilty men it had shrouded into court. But this time I would not make use of it. Whatever the banners shrieked outside the Court of Appeal, whatever causes their bearers espoused, I would walk into that courtroom with my head high, as innocent now as I was before. But infinitely less afraid.

As the van slowed down and its engines purred, I heard slogan voices in chorus. And as we came to a stop I heard the words of their chant. 'Free Dreyfus, free Dreyfus.' As I slipped out of the van, I caught sight of several placards declaring my innocence. I shivered with gratitude.

I was led into the chamber. I recalled my trembling gait at my first court appearance, when despair prompted my every faltering step. Now I almost ran into the courtroom. I felt I was about to attend a piece of theatre, assured of the star part and the best seat in the house. I dared not give a thought to its dénouement. For the moment the drama itself would have to do.

Rebecca was waiting there and for the first time in many years I thought about Simon Posner, my erstwhile lawyer, who had so ineptly pleaded my case. Matthew had never mentioned him and I presumed that their friendship had ceased. Rebecca welcomed me. She seemed as excited as I.

'We've lost Eccles,' she said.

'I know. I read about it in the paper this morning.'

'It's no loss,' she told me. 'His suicide could be seen as an admission of guilt. It's to our advantage.'

'Did he have a family?' I asked. I felt suddenly sorry for him.

'None,' she said. 'Just friends. So-called friends. Some of them will be in court.'

Again I sensed that I was going to a theatre. I already knew the plot and most of the cast, but the bit-players, the extras and the walk-ons were all unknown. I could not wait to take my front-row seat.

Once more down a long corridor, but this time I almost skipped despite the two grips on my elbows. I was taken to a seat at the side of the court. Though fenced, it was less of a dock than before. Less isolated, less quarantined, and I regarded it as a rehearsal for my freedom. The chamber seemed small and intimate. In my cell-nightmares the courtroom at the Old Bailey had assumed colossal proportions, bursting at its seams with lies and prejudice, and echoing with the baying for my blood. This room was comfortable, a cosy theatre in the round. The spectators were a neat gathering in the stalls. They were looking at me with a certain curiosity and I returned their gaze unafraid. We all stood for the entry of the three judges and I expected the lights to dim so that the play could begin.

I do not intend to go into the details of the opening procedures. I regard them rather as stage directions, technical
instructions that could hold up the drama of the plot. Rebecca
read the arraignment; to wit that the appellant had been charged
with the murder of George Henry Tilbury. I relished my new
name. I was no longer 'the prisoner'. I was less in other people's
hands.

I looked at the Crown prosecutor, that same old swiveller as
before. But he looked different. He seemed already tired,
dejected, and he bore the face of a loser. He had clearly been
apprised of all the new evidence and he regarded his appearance
in the chamber as a mere formality.

'May it please you, My Lords,' he said, turning to the judges,
'I am instructed by the Crown.' His face fell as if he rather
wished the Crown had not so instructed. Then very quietly, and
with infinite sorrow, he dropped his bombshell.

'The Crown does not oppose this appeal,' he said.

There was a gasp of astonishment around the chamber, and
a murmur too of disquiet. For were they not to be told why the
charge had been dropped, and informed of the evidence for my
clearing? Justice had to be *seen* to be done, and the judges knew
the rules of their office.

'I take note of your opinion,' the Lord Chief Justice said.
'But the decision to grant or to deny the appeal is our responsibility and ours alone. And to that end we will hear the
evidence.'

Rumours about the strange turn of events at the Court of
Appeal had already hit the headlines of the lunch-time press.
The chamber was crowded and it took a while to achieve an
overall silence. Then Rebecca rose and addressed the judges.

'During the course of my submissions, My Lords,' she said,
'there will emerge palpable evidence of perjury and no doubt
that evidence will be referred to the Director of Public
Prosecutions. But my first witness is not subject to that charge.

Two years ago, as a witness for the prosecution, he was not yet eighteen years of age and the judge did not oblige him to take the oath. He is now twenty years old and will give evidence that is sworn. I call James Turncastle.'

I watched him take the oath, and once again I felt that surge of affection that I had held for the boy when he was at school. Despite the years that had passed, I found him little changed in his appearance. Thinner, perhaps, but still with that look of eagerness and curiosity that had so endeared him to me in his innocent days.

'Mr Turncastle,' Rebecca said, 'you will have heard of the sudden death of your history master Mr Eccles.'

'His suicide you mean,' James said.

'Would you tell the court,' Rebecca went on, 'of your relationship with Mr Eccles?'

'There was a club,' James began. 'The Iron Circle. That's what it was called.'

'Tell us about this club,' Rebecca said. 'Who started it? What was its purpose?'

'It's worldwide,' James said. 'But it was started in England about twenty-five years ago by a man who called himself John Coleman. He was sent over from Vienna to found an English branch. His cover was that of an engineer in an industrial plant near Canterbury. He lived in the same village as Sir.'

My heart leapt. I was a headmaster again, and a wave of nostalgia overcame me.

'He recruited members from all over England,' James was saying.

'Was Mr Eccles one of these members?' Rebecca asked.

'Yes,' James said. 'He was a leading member.'

'What was his function?'

'To recruit others into the Iron Circle. Young recruits.'

'What was the purpose of this circle?'

James hesitated. 'It was extreme right-wing.' Then in a

louder voice, 'It was fascist. It worshipped the German model. Hitler was its hero.'

I delighted in the gasp around the court. I knew there was more of the like to come and they were a good audience.

'Could you be more specific about its activities?' Rebecca asked.

'Well, they were against immigration. Whites were all right. But not blacks. The Iron Circle was behind race riots and the murders of Asian immigrants. They burnt their houses and mosques. Not just in England, but all over Europe. And they hate the Jews. They burn down their synagogues and desecrate their cemeteries. They want to make Europe Jew-free. Black-free too. They want a pure race.'

'Did you personally take part in any of these activities?'

'No,' James said. 'I was being trained for leadership. We all were. All of us in Mr Eccles's group at the school. He called us the élite.'

'The élite,' Rebecca repeated and gave pause. 'Tell the court about the skiing trips to Austria.'

'Mr Eccles took our group every Easter. We stayed in a hostel, but Mr Eccles stayed with a family called the Müllers. They were members of the new Nazi party and after skiing we all used to meet in their house and listen to lectures and look at films of Hitler and the Hitler Youth. Mr Eccles sent me to stay with them when I took a term off from school.'

'And what did you do during that term?'

'I spent most of it in Münich with the Müllers' son, going to party meetings.'

'How did you feel about the party?' Rebecca asked.

'At first I was in love with it, its marches and its songs, but I don't think I would have stayed in the Circle for long.'

'Now perhaps you could tell us about George Tilbury,' Rebecca said.

'That was when all the trouble started,' James said. 'One

Easter George wanted to go skiing with us. Mr Eccles didn't want to take him. He was afraid that George would learn too much and tell his father, the cabinet minister. George was too big a risk. But there was no reason why he shouldn't go, at least no reason that Mr Eccles could give Sir. So George had to come. We all tried to hide our secrets from him. He had to stay by himself when we went to the Müllers, but by his second trip he'd sussed it all out. He didn't enjoy that holiday and we were all worried that he might spill the beans. Especially Mr Eccles. And when we got back to school, he told me to keep an eye on him. George told me he was going to tell Sir, and one day I saw him waiting outside Sir's office and I pulled him away. And I went straight to Mr Eccles and I told him that George could get us all into trouble. And Mr Eccles said, "Leave it to me". Then the next day, I heard that George had disappeared and Mr Eccles called me to his study. He told me that there was nothing to worry about. "George has been seen to," he said. Those were his words. "George has been seen to."'

Rebecca turned to face the judges. "'George had been seen to,'" she said. Then she turned once more to James.

'Did you ask him what he meant by that?' she asked.

'No,' James said. 'I feared the worst and I was afraid to be told. He told me to join in the search and to do it thoroughly. I went to join the search party in the field and on the way I saw David Solomon sitting on the wall and he was crying. I went over to him and he said, "George told me all about those skiing trips." He was frightened. "Frightened of what?" I asked. "Just frightened," he said. When I next saw Mr Eccles on the search, I told him about David and he just laughed.'

'Mr Eccles laughed,' Rebecca repeated to the judges. 'George had been seen to, and Mr Eccles laughed.'

None of James's testimony was new to me. Rebecca had read me his statement before the appeal. But I marvelled at his courage. Since his appearance in the court he had not yet given me a glance. But I knew that there would come a time when he would look me in the eye and perhaps even smile. For my smile was ready enough for him.

'Would you now tell the court,' Rebecca urged, 'what happened next. While the search was in progress.'

'It was before George's body was found in Sir's garden in Kent. Mr Eccles asked me to come to his room that evening. When I arrived there were a number of people already there. At the time I didn't know who they were. But I know now since they were all witnesses at the trial.'

'Would you tell the court the names of those present?' Rebecca said.

'There was PC Byrd from the local village, Mr Clerk, the verger from Canterbury Cathedral, Mr Cassidy from London who owned the hardware store and another policeman from the Kent Constabulary.'

'PC Byrd, Mr Clerk, Mr Cassidy and another policeman,' Rebecca repeated slowly. She turned to the judges. 'My Lords,' she said, 'they have all been subpoenaed to appear.' Then once more addressing James, she said, 'Apart from Mr Eccles and yourself, is that the complete list?'

'There was one other,' James said. 'I had not seen him before. But he seemed to be in charge of everything. They called him John.'

'John Coleman.' Rebecca explained to the judges. 'He was subpoenaed, My Lords, but he has disappeared.'

I noticed a small smile flit across the judges' faces and for some reason, I took it as a sign of my acquittal. I sought out Lucy's face in the body of the court. She was smiling too. Matthew sat at her side along with Peter and Jeannie. My family. Those I was soon to go home to.

'Tell the court what happened at this meeting,' Rebecca said. 'And you may take your time.' She knew that what James was about to reveal was the core of the conspiracy against me and she wanted an eager and silent audience.

'Well, this John said that George's body had been hidden. I was stunned. Mr Eccles had told me that George had been seen to but I'd never thought that that meant he'd been murdered. I asked this John man who had killed him. Your leader, he said. He was only obeying orders. It was obvious to me that John had given those orders and that Mr Eccles had been a true disciple. I remember I felt sick. I wanted to leave. I wanted nothing more to do with it. I tried to go but they stopped me. "You are a member of the Circle," John said, "You have your duties." "And what are they?" I asked. He handed me two sheets of paper, and on them were written the testimony I had to give at the trial. I scanned the pages and, to my horror, I understood that Sir was being named as the killer and that they had buried George in Sir's garden in Kent. "I can't do it," I said. "Then you will go the same way as George," John told me. I had to stay there and listen to them. They were all given papers to learn by heart. All except Eccles. He was ordered to defend Sir in the witness-box. That would be his cover. It was all so unbelievable.'

Then, for the first time since he had entered the court, James turned to look at me. 'I'm so very sorry,' he whispered.

I reserved my smile. I didn't think James could deal with it at that time.

'Did you meet again?' Rebecca asked.

'Yes,' James said. 'John said we all needed to rehearse. And that night before Sir was arrested, we had a read-through of our parts.'

I remembered that evening well. I was with Matthew and we were returning from the village pub. I recalled seeing the light in Eccles's window and the moving shadows behind the curtains. The rehearsal, as James called it. The first act of my fall.

'What happened at that read-through?' Rebecca asked.

'John played the part of the prosecutor,' James said, 'and we read out our words to him. PC Byrd read an invented story about seeing Sir in a car at night. And the verger read about seeing a hole in Sir's garden and then the hole was covered. And Mr Cassidy read of Sir buying the knife and the Kent constable read about the fingerprints and the button that was found in the car. All the parts had been written by John and I think he enjoyed being the director. All John had to do was to ring the police and inform on Sir and he had already done that in the morning. We stayed up most of the night and watched Sir being arrested. Then they all drank the champagne that John had brought, and they toasted the memory of Adolf Hitler.' Another sigh from the body of the court and Rebecca allowed its echo.

'Were there any more meetings?' she asked.

'Yes,' James said. 'We met almost every night until the trial. Until we were all word perfect. I knew that Sir would be convicted,' he said. 'We had left no loopholes for the defence.'

'One last question, Mr Turncastle,' Rebecca said. 'Why after all this time did you decide to tell the truth?'

'I couldn't live with it,' James said. 'Shortly after the trial I had a mental breakdown. I attempted suicide. I felt so guilty. Then I was admitted to a psychiatric clinic. After treatment I decided to tell the truth. And tell it aloud for everyone to hear. Because Sir was innocent. He would never have laid a finger on anybody.'

He turned to look at me again and this time I gave him that smile that I had been keeping.

'Thank you, Mr Turncastle,' Rebecca said.

James stepped down. I saw that he was trembling. His gait was unsteady, racked by his long and brave testimony. He clutched at a rail as he walked out of the court and once outside I imagined he slumped on to the nearest chair and wept with his freedom.

The court was then adjourned until the following morning. I was taken down once more, and unblanketed, I slipped into the van. Once in my cell, I sat on my cot and let the tears flow. All those tears from the long months and years had come to the brink of my eyes, all those tears I had firmly sent back to where they came from, now I gave them release. I wept for the years I had forfeited, for the faith of my family, for my future freedom. And I wept for James. But above all I wept for young George Tilbury.

33

Rebecca had wanted to apply for bail. She assured me that in the light of the day's revelations it would be granted. 'You could go home,' she said. But I dissuaded her. For in truth I didn't want to go home. I was frightened. Suddenly I needed the safety of my cell. I felt at home there. I would have been nervous to sit at a table with a white linen cloth and manoeuvre the silver cutlery and bone china. I would have been shy of company, unused to social graces, afraid of questions that I couldn't answer or irritated by those that weren't asked. Above all I feared that there was nowhere else but in my cell that I could write. That my little cot, my barred window, my wooden desk in the fifty-four or so square feet of my little nest orchestrated my every word, framed each phrase, prompted each image, drove my often unwilling pen. I could not envisage writing in freedom but I knew it was the one joy that I would forfeit willingly and I wondered whether all writers had to dwell in a prison of their own making.

That evening, the governor himself brought my supper tray. He had followed the appeal as eagerly as any press reporter. He expressed his pleasure with its progress but he was careful not to discuss it. He left me his copy of the evening paper.

The front page bore a picture of James. Its caption read 'Conspirator Comes Clean'. I was faintly offended by the title. Offended on James's behalf. It made him seem a criminal, but in many ways James had been as innocent as I, misled, gullible, frightened, but innocent still. Page two of the paper carried a picture of Rebecca. Her features were on the edge of a smile that hinted of triumph. I looked at the picture for a while and I tried to recall Susan's face but it was an exiled blur. Half of page three was devoted to a photograph of myself. I don't know where it was taken for no background was visible to provide a clue. I am not by any means a handsome man. My face lacks true proportion. My forehead is too broad, and does not match the length of my face. My ears assume an arrogant prominence and my chin is far too proud. There was a time when I hated my nose, but now as I view it, the length of it, the plain Jew of it, I find it almost beautiful. I looked at the paper and I sensed that I had seen that picture before and I realised it was exactly the same portrait that had appeared on the day of that iniquitous verdict. But now they had retouched it. They had smudged that look of gross guilt it had borne, and feathered it into one of innocence. They had given me a look of incorruptible integrity, and blameless I sang off the page. I did not read the appeal report. Every word of James's testimony still clogged my ears and once again I marvelled at his courage. I hoped that Peter would befriend him. I hoped, I hoped. I wanted it all as it was, but I knew that was impossible.

I lay down on my cot and I allowed myself to think of going home. In my mind I practised my manners; I practised the answers to the questions they would ask. I sat at the head of the dining-room table, my erstwhile place, and I carved the roast and poured the wine. I dwelt on Lucy's face at the end of the table, then on Peter's and Jean's on either side of me. And painfully I must confess that I did not feel at home. I must have sat at that dining-table till the lights dimmed in my cell. I sat there while I slept, and in the morning I remained there still, Alfred Dreyfus, head of household, husband of Lucy, brother of Matthew, father of Peter and Jean. I looked around my cell, at the growing light through the barred window and I knew that when, in time, I would relinquish it, I would be leaving home. God help me, I thought. I have been too long confined.

34

The first witness on the following day was David Solomon. I had last seen him in the public gallery on the first day of my trial. Young David, one of the token Jews in the school. He was grown now, an adult, and after he took the oath, insisting on the Old Testament, he turned to smile at me.

'Mr Solomon,' Rebecca said, 'we have heard from Mr Turncastle that the late George Tilbury told you of his suspicions regarding the Eccles group.'

'Yes,' David said. 'It was after they had come back from the skiing holiday.'

'What exactly did he tell you?'

'He told me that the group were all part of a fascist organisation. And that the group was being trained for leadership. He told me about the evening meetings at the Müllers' that he was not allowed to attend. He didn't know exactly what went on there, but from things he picked up he was suspicious. I told him he ought to tell Sir, and he said that he would.'

'What happened then?'

'Later that day one of the monitors told me I was wanted in Mr Eccles's study. Mr Eccles wasn't my housemaster and I couldn't imagine what he wanted. He was very friendly and he told me I must take no notice of whatever George had said. He added that George had a vivid imagination. I'd never liked Mr Eccles, and I was angry, because I thought George had told me the truth, so I said that if George didn't tell Sir, then I would tell him myself. Then Mr Eccles gripped my arm and said, "If you open your mouth, Solomon, you'll go the same way as George." I didn't know what he was talking about, but I was frightened. Especially when I heard that George was dead. That's why I said nothing at the trial.'

'Thank you Mr Solomon,' Rebecca said.

As he stepped down, David once more smiled at me. He would leave the chamber, and like James, he would sigh with his freedom.

The next witness was PC Byrd. And Rebecca's first question struck the conspiracy chord.

'Police Constable Byrd,' she said, 'are you a member of the Iron Circle? Remember that you are under oath.'

The monosyllabic Byrd hung his head in what he hoped would pass as shame. 'Yes,' he whispered.

'Louder,' Rebecca ordered.

'Yes,' he said again.

'How long have you been a member?'

'Sixteen years,' he said.

'And how did you join?'

'Mr Coleman asked me.'

'And why did you join?'

'He said we could get rid of foreigners. England for the English, he said.'

'And you thought that this was a good idea?'

'Yes,' Byrd said, and with confidence as if he still believed it.

'"England for the English,"' Rebecca repeated to the judges. 'Now let us examine your testimony at the trial,' she went on. 'You said that you were on duty on the morning of April the fourth and you were investigating the report of a break-in at the tobacconists. We have ascertained from local police records that there was no such report at that time.'

'They told me there was,' Byrd said lamely.

'You also said that at 2.40 you saw a saloon car driving at speed down the road towards the school and that you recognised the appellant in the driving seat. D'you still say that was the case?'

'I don't remember,' Byrd mumbled. Then louder and almost hysterical. 'I don't remember. It was a long time ago.'

'Come, come, Police Constable Byrd,' Rebecca coaxed. 'You are too young to claim loss of memory. Now, did you or did you not see a car? And if you did, did you or did you not see the appellant in the driving seat?'

'No,' Byrd mumbled. 'I don't suppose I did.'

'Then why did you swear under oath that these things took place?'

'Well that was my part, wasn't it?' Byrd shouted. 'Those were the words they gave me.'

'Who are they?'

'Coleman,' Byrd replied.

'And you learnt them by heart?'

'Yes.'

'And had lots of rehearsals?'

'Yes.'

'So your whole testimony was a tissue of lies.'

'I was only obeying orders,' Byrd said.

'Of course you were.' Rebecca turned towards the judges. 'He was only obeying orders,' she said. Then back to Byrd. 'Let's talk now about Mr Eccles.'

'I don't know anything about that,' Byrd said quickly, 'I wasn't there. I didn't see it.'

'You weren't where? You didn't see what?'

'You know.'

'No, I don't know,' Rebecca said patiently. 'You tell me.'

'The killing,' Byrd said. 'That happened before I was summoned.'

'How do you know that Eccles did the killing?'

'We were told. He was just doing his duty. He had to, otherwise it would have all come out.'

'What would have come out?'

'About the Iron Circle. And what we were doing.'

'What *were* you doing?'

'I don't know. I was only a minor member. Nobody told me anything.'

Perhaps he expected us to pity him, this poor underling who, without question, simply obeyed orders. Until we remembered that that same plea came out of the mouths of Dr Mengele, Eichmann, Lt. Calley at Mai Lai. But he evoked no pity in the chamber. Simply an urge to spit on him and all of his kind.

'Thank you, Police Constable Byrd,' Rebecca said with infinite politeness. 'You may step down.'

I watched his stooped back as he walked out of the courtroom. Like James, he would make for the nearest seat. And perhaps he would weep too. Not for his freedom, but for his eventual punishment.

Rebecca's next witness was Mr Clerk, the verger from Canterbury Cathedral. She reminded him that he was under oath, and asked him if he was a member of the Iron Circle. He answered proudly that he was, and that he too had been recruited by John Coleman. Then Rebecca asked a question that must have seemed irrelevant to the matter of the appeal.

'I understand Mr Clerk, that you have a special hobby. Could you tell the court what that hobby is?'

'I collect Hitler memorabilia,' he said with a certain pride. 'My collection is widely admired in Europe.' He looked at his sister in the visitors' gallery and responded to the sigh around the court. 'There's nothing wrong with that,' he said.

'Each to his own,' Rebecca told him. 'You are clearly a great admirer of Hitler.'

'Indeed I am. I don't think he went far enough.'

There was a single hiss from the chamber, which was taken up by others and the Lord Chief Justice had to rap his gavel for silence. But Mr Clerk would not be silenced. 'All that nonsense about six million Jews. It's a fairy tale.'

The man was hanging himself with his own rope, but I could not help but admire his courage. He was using the chamber as a platform for his beliefs.

The judge rapped his desk once more. 'You are in danger of being charged with a disturbance of the peace, Mr Clerk. I will have no more of it. Counsel,' he said, addressing Rebecca, 'continue with your examination.'

Rebecca then itemised the verger's previous evidence: the hole that he claimed to have seen in the appellant's Kent village garden, the hole that was suddenly filled in, and his subsequent report to the police. 'Do you still maintain these statements?' she asked.

'Those were the words I was told to say. That was my part. That was the script that John gave me.'

Rebecca turned to the judges and shrugged.

'One last question,' she addressed Mr Clerk. 'Did you know about Mr Eccles's part in all this?'

Mr Clerk barely waited for her to finish the question. The name Eccles clearly lit a dangerous fuse.

'I knew nothing about that,' he shouted. 'Nothing at all. And I say that on oath.'

Suddenly he found the oath a safety-valve and he practically shone with his honesty.

'Thank you Mr Clerk,' Rebecca said. 'You may step down.'

But first Mr Clerk had to look at his sister, and smile at her. He had promoted their cause, and on her behalf as well.

He too would eventually go to prison, I thought, and there he would no doubt find many friends, potential members of his glorious Iron Circle.

The court was then adjourned till after lunch. Again a gentle escort led me to the waiting-room and soon the dull lunch tray was brought to me. I had a sudden craving for a glass of good claret and, as my taste-buds watered, I knew I would soon be free. Rebecca did not visit me that lunch-hour. She was eating with Matthew, Lucy and my children. The thought of such a gathering gave me pleasure, for I already considered Rebecca as part of my family.

The guard took away my tray. 'Not much longer now,' he said. I didn't know whether he was referring to the appeal or the lunch-hour. But his tone was friendly which mattered so much to me. I was on the road to forgiveness, and I no longer found it dangerous.

The first witness after the lunch break was Mr Cassidy from the hardware store on Tottenham Court Road. He owned to being a member of the Iron Circle, and stated that he was recruited by Mr Eccles. He did not hesitate on the name, dynamite as it was. Indeed, he went on to say that Eccles was a close friend of his.

'Was he ever a customer in your shop?' Rebecca asked.

'He bought odd things from time to time.'

'Like knives?' Rebecca asked.

'He might have,' Mr Cassidy parried.

Rebecca let it lie for a while. Then, 'In your testimony at the trial, you stated on oath that the appellant bought a knife in your shop a few days before the disappearance of George Tilbury. Do you still stick to that story?'

'Of course not,' Cassidy almost laughed. 'It was in the script.

That was my part. Coleman rehearsed me. He rehearsed us all.'

Again a helpless shrug from Rebecca. They were all making her work so easy, she hardly needed to have been there at all.

'Did Mr Eccles buy a knife in your shop? You are on oath, Mr Cassidy,' Rebecca reminded him.

'No,' Cassidy said. 'On oath.' And then, as a teasing rider, 'He didn't buy it. I didn't charge my friends. I gave it to him.'

'Did you know what it was for?'

'No. A knife could be for anything,' he said.

'No more questions.' Rebecca dismissed him.

Then Mr Cassidy's assistant took the stand. He was a weedy youth with a pale face pitted with acne. Without looking one knew that his nails were bitten to the quick. In answer to the question whether he was a member of the Iron Circle, he answered that he was on probation but hoped to become a full member soon.

'Did you or did you not see the Appellant in the shop that day?' Rebecca asked.

'I just said what Mr Cassidy told me to say. He said it was part of my probation.'

'But did you see the appellant or didn't you?' Rebecca insisted.

'No,' the lad replied. 'I just did as I was told.'

An Eichmann in the making, I thought, and I despaired.

'You may step down,' Rebecca said.

'Long live the Iron Circle,' the boy mumbled, as no doubt he had been ordered to say, with the promise of full membership. I wondered whether the boy had a mother, and whether she was proud or ashamed of her son. Whatever way, she would be entitled to visit him in prison, where someone would explain to him the meaning of the word perjury.

With the department of ironmongery disposed of, the judges called for an adjournment. I was glad of the respite. I was homesick. Sick for my cell. Again Rebecca offered to ask for bail, and again I refused. My cot would miss me. And my barred window. They were expecting me. I must not let them down.

On my way back in the van, despite my euphoria, I wondered whether my mind was on the turn.

35

I was aware that the appeal might reach its conclusion on the following day, and it was possible that that night would be the very last I would spend in my cell. I didn't want to miss one minute of it. I decided I would not sleep; I would lie on my cot, read a little perhaps and, between paragraphs, absorb my little home. It was not that I wanted to commit it to memory. I was unlikely ever to forget it. Rather I wanted to acknowledge it, every square inch of it, to avow its confinement of months, years, to curse it for its privations and to bless it for its sometime shelter and its prison for my pen. And so I lay awake, my eye wandering from page to corner, to walls, to window, and to the much despair-trodden floor. The dawn light filtered comfortably through the bars, and for its welcome, I sang my grandmother's song.

Breakfast arrived with its extra slice of bread. I dressed quickly. I still needed time to view my cell. It would be an hour before they came for me. Shortly the governor came to visit. He was carrying the morning paper, and as he handed it to me he said, 'I think this means that it is all over.' He put out his hand. 'This is probably goodbye,' he said, and his face was wreathed in smiles.

'You've been good to me,' I said to him, 'and you have my thanks.'

It was a formal parting. It had to be. He was an official. And would remain so after I had gone.

I did not need to open the paper. The news was spread across the front page, half of which was devoted to two separate portraits of Eccles and myself. I resented the juxtaposition. I looked first at myself. Again that guilty picture was air-brushed into innocence. With my allure, I was almost a pin-up. Beside me was Eccles, and as I stared I thought I saw him wink. The Eccles wink that I had never forgotten.

The headline of the report read: SUICIDE LAST CON-FESSION. And underneath: 'A suicide note was found beside the body of Richard Eccles, found dead on Tuesday in a hotel in Marseilles. In it he confessed to the murder of George Henry Tilbury and stated that Dreyfus was innocent. The Dreyfus Appeal is expected to conclude today.'

I felt nothing for myself. My thoughts were with Sir Henry and Lady Tilbury, and I wondered whether the news would be of any comfort to them. Young George would have grown into a man by now, and I imagined that that was all they could be thinking. I wished that Eccles had lived, so that I could have murdered him myself.

Eventually they came for me. Despite my anticipation of freedom, my spirits were low, gnawed by Eccles-loathing. I took a last look at my cell. No nostalgia. No longing. For my sudden indifference was sublime.

36

The first witness of the last day was Mr Tweedie. He looked well enough. He was deeply tanned, a feature which Rebecca quickly highlighted.

'You've been on holiday, Mr Tweedie?' she asked.

'Yes,' he said.

'In Spain, I think. You have a villa there.'

'That is correct,' Mr Tweedie said. He was mumbling. He knew where she was leading.

'How long have you owned this villa?' she asked.

'About two years,' Mr Tweedie admitted.

'Then you must have bought it shortly after the appellant's trial.'

'Yes.' Mr Tweedie had to agree.

Rebecca let it lie. She simply looked at the judges and shrugged.

'You gave two statements at the appellant's trial,' she went on. 'The first was to confirm his alibi, that you gave him dental treatment at your surgery on April the third between 2.30 and three o'clock. Later you withdrew that statement and asserted that the appellant had failed to keep his appointment. I remind you that you are on oath, Mr Tweedie. Now, which statement is true?'

'The first,' he said. 'I treated him at my surgery. He had kept his appointment.'

'Why later on did you withdraw that statement?'

'Mr Eccles suggested it.'

'Are you a member of the Iron Circle?'

'Certainly not,' Mr Tweedie said on his dignity.

'Then why should you be obliged to Mr Eccles?'

'He said he would compensate me.'

'In which way?'

'He didn't say so at the time.'

'Come on, Mr Tweedie,' Rebecca grew impatient. 'How did he compensate you?'

'The villa,' Mr Tweedie said. He had the shame to mumble. He was almost inaudible, so Rebecca repeated 'the villa' for the chamber's benefit.

'Thank you, Mr Tweedie,' she said.

One more witness was to take the stand. The police inspector from the Kent Constabulary.

'You stated at the trial that you examined the appellant's car.'

'Let us say I had it examined.'

'What does that mean?' Rebecca asked.

'It means that I personally did not examine the car. One of my assistants undertook the examination.'

'If you yourself did not examine the car, how do you know that George Tilbury's fingerprints were found on the dashboard? And the blazer button on the passenger seat?'

'That's what I was told,' the Inspector said.

'But you yourself did not find them.'

'No,' he had to admit.

'Then they could have come from anywhere. A set of George Tilbury's fingerprints could have been taken at any time. Likewise the button,' Rebecca said. 'Shortly after the trial,' she went on, 'you took your family on a world cruise. A rather expensive item. How was that possible on a police inspector's salary?'

'The cruise was a present,' he said. 'Is there anything wrong with that?'

'Nothing at all,' Rebecca said. Then, turning to the bench, 'He says it was a present,' she repeated, 'and that, My Lords, concludes the case for the defence.'

It was only eleven o'clock. I dared to hope that I would not have to eat a waiting-room lunch. The Lord Chief Justice called for order, though he had no need. The chamber was muted in the silence of expectation.

'We will now take a short adjournment,' he said.

We stood as they rose and left the chamber. Rebecca crossed over towards me.

'They won't be long,' she said. And she smiled. She knew the verdict as well as I.

And indeed, within ten minutes the judges had returned. We all stood once again until they took their seats. They looked at their leisure, as if they'd been out for a short stroll. I had the impression that they had left the chamber merely to reserve a good table for lunch. The Lord Chief Justice didn't even bother to stand to deliver their conclusions.

'In this case,' he said, 'the appellant appeals against the verdict of murder substantially on the grounds that he was the target of a conspiracy to pervert the course of justice. On the evidence that we have heard, it seems abundantly clear to us that the charge of conspiracy is wholly justified. During the course of this appeal, we have heard evidence that is heart-curdling. There has clearly been a gross miscarriage of justice for which those responsible will pay dearly. Our sympathies go out to the parents of George Tilbury, who have once more had to endure the painful reminders of their tragic loss. And also to the appellant who paid unfairly for others' crimes. The appeal is granted and the appellant is free to go.'

I heard the cheers in the chamber. I felt Rebecca's embrace. Then the huggings of others. Possibly of my family. It was all a blur. I don't recall any detail. Only one thing I remember. I was singing my grandmother's song and the Yiddish slid like silk off my tongue, as I recalled every single word.

PART SIX

37

Now it was all over. But not for Dreyfus. Not for Sir Alfred, as he was again, Palace-redeemed. For Dreyfus there was another trial. Dreyfus versus Dreyfus, that only Dreyfus himself could conduct. Only he could accuse himself; only he could plead his defence, and he alone could pronounce the verdict. And only then, when all that was done, could he walk to the brink with his grandparents. And he would involve his children so that they too would never court the dubious safety of being 'counted in'. Together they would acknowledge their heritage and its long history of triumph and defeat and its infinite sorrow. Together they would close the chapter on denial. And his own parents, by proxy, would reap that multifold harvest.

Along with Matthew, he took his family back to their child-hood village in Kent. He recalled that journey to Paris with his parents, when they had visited the apartment from which they had fled. That same nauseous feeling assailed him as he entered the village. He wanted to make a swift U-turn, for the place sickened him. He saw no beauty in the green fields where he had played as a boy. The village church and all that it stood for was a mockery, but its grounds held his life's blood, his much-loved lineage, albeit hidden with such deception. But now that lie would cease. He had ordered his parents' exhumation.

With Matthew at his side, he approached the graves. They were overgrown, weedy and thistled. He preferred them that way. Their pre-trial neatness, their tended flowerbeds nodded assent to the Jesus that sheltered them. The statue had not been repaired. The arm halted at its elbow, and the red paint still daubed the alabaster decay. Dreyfus and Matthew turned away and left the diggers to their work.

They followed the hearse through the village.

'We will never come here again,' Matthew said.

The rabbi met them at Willesden Jewish Cemetery and there, in peace, he gave their parents a traditional burial. Thus the first station of atonement had been reached.

Dreyfus had planned his itinerary, and in so far as it was possible, he intended to follow his grandparents' unplanned route. And from the very date that they had boarded the cattle-trucks on their way to the ovens. The archives had given that date as July the seventeenth, some four days after their capture. It was on July the thirteenth 1942, that his grandmother had gone in search of milk, and on that same evening, breaking the curfew, his grandfather had gone to look for her. On July the four-teenth, neither had returned. Dreyfus did not know where in Paris they had been caught but he assumed that both had been rounded up in the Vel d'Hiv, or in Drancy. He prayed that at least they had embraced each other before the gas.

Dreyfus and his family set out for Paris on July the sixteenth, over half a century later. On arrival they went straight to Rue du Bac where they tarried a while outside the apartment. From there they made their way through narrow streets to a patisserie which in former days had sold milk. Now it was a hairdressing salon, but it was an obligatory station. From there they went on foot to Boulevard Raspail. No window-shopping, no sightseeing. A right turn took them into Rue de Varenne, thence to Les Invalides. And past it, for Napoleon played no part in Dreyfus's present mission. On to Avenue de la Motte and Boulevard de Grenelle. Here Dreyfus paused. They had been walking in the heat for over an hour. Somewhere along the route they had followed, his grandparents had been captured and their destination was already in Dreyfus's sight. The Vel d'Hiv, on the corner of Rue Nélaton. In the old days, it had been a sports arena, a gathering place for fun. And when the Germans came it was still a gathering place, but there was little fun in it. The Vel d'Hiv was the site of round-up, the Jews' first stop on the way to the ovens. It was in Vel d'Hiv that rumour seriously stirred. Stories had long circulated in Paris about the unimaginable fate of European Jewry, but they were too far-fetched to be believed. In Vel d'Hiv those stories seemed less suspect, less unworthy of belief and, but for the crying of children, there was silence in that arena for to speak that rumour aloud was to give it credence.

Dreyfus led his family towards the site. The arena had been razed to the ground, and in its place stood a branch of the Ministry of Interior but, nevertheless it was a compulsory station. On the site of that shameful pitch they rested, but fitfully, for their memories allowed for little repose.

It had been very hot on the day of his grandparents' capture, unseasonably so, and from stories that Dreyfus had heard, there was but one water-tap in the whole arena. Thousands of Jews were cooped up on that day, and unquenchable thirst carried off many of the old and frail under the merciless sun. Yet death at that place was a kindness, for those who would survive Vel d'Hiv were in line for torture unimaginable. Many contemplated suicide, but were thwarted by the simple fact that there just wasn't enough room. Dreyfus did not know how long his grandparents had struggled in that arena. Their sojourn would have depended on the size of subsequent round-ups and the availability of the trains to take them to their final destination. Towards the end of July, fourteen thousand Jews were deported from Paris, via the Vel d'Hiv stop-over, so it was possible that his grandparents were amongst them.

'I'm thirsty,' Peter said, then regretting it, 'it doesn't matter.'

'It does matter,' his father told him. 'We are survivors.'

They went to a restaurant and had their first meal of the day, and then to a hotel to sleep if they were able. Dreyfus tossed and turned for most of the night. He understood exactly what he was doing, and his quest was almost exhilarating, for he knew that it would lead to a personal freedom. He wondered why he had postponed it for so long. Why he had found it so easy to ignore its need. And he was ashamed that he had lived such a long-term lie, that lie he had inherited from his parents. He would deny his children that false estate. Like himself they would seek out the truth, however unpalatable.

The following day, they took the RER to Drancy, Drancy is a mere suburb of Paris and nowadays of no special significance. But in 1942, Drancy was a name to be reckoned with. For Jews it was the gateway to hell.

It was July the seventeenth. Dreyfus was on schedule. It was on this day, more than fifty years ago that, with thousands of others of their kind, his grandparents were prodded like cattle into the freight-trains that would carry them to the rumours of which they had heard and in which they dared not believe. A short walk from the station was the site of the technical buildings which housed those fearful passengers who waited for the trains. They were built in a U-shape, and were destined originally for lower-class housing. But the Gestapo, on Eichmann's orders, had designated them as a stop-over barracks for the yellow six-pointed stars. The buildings were four storeys high and those who had been thwarted in Vel d'Hiv found room in Drancy to put an end to it all. At the base of the building was a concrete slab, a welcome-mat for those shattered bodies that refused the cattle-trucks to the East. And when their broken relatives had swept away their martyrdom, that same concrete slab served as a playground for the children. No strenuous games. They were too hungry to run or skip. Sitting games and singing. Singing about 'Pitchipoi', that name they coined for the place where the trains would take them, the place where they would find their parents again, and eat together and laugh and sing. Though their parents by now, were ash.

'We're going to Pitchipoi,' they would chant. And believed it, because they had to.

Every day the convoys arrived, as yellow star after star crowded the barracks. The children heard tongues that they did not understand. A babel of Polish, Hungarian and Greek echoed through the buildings but 'Pitchipoi' was a word that everyone understood, and tried to believe that that place was real.

Dreyfus knew from his research into the archives that his grandparents had been gassed on arrival at Auschwitz-Birkenau. The date given was July the twenty-first. It was on that day that he intended to arrive at his last station and to walk to the edge with that past that he had denied. It was a journey of about four days and nights from Paris to the ovens. Matching their timetable he would stay at Drancy until five o'clock in the morning and wait with them on the railway sidings. For that was the time that his grandparents would have embarked on their last journey.

The station was empty and the few night workers who passed on the platforms might have wondered at the curious Dreyfus gathering on the sidings. But none of them were old enough to have a sense of déjà vu, else they would have paused and sickened. The Germans were meticulous about punctuality, and as five o'clock chimed from a nearby church, Dreyfus stepped to the edge of the platform with Matthew at his side and together they recited the Kaddish, that prayer for the Jewish dead. Then they made their way back to Paris and the Gare du Nord to begin their overland journey in the path of their forbears.

From Paris the cattle-trucks had shunted to Compiègne. Thence to Laon and the frontier town of Neuberg. With occasional hold-ups, the trucks rattled the thousand miles across Germany to the East, and finally stuttered to rest at Auschwitz. The journey took almost four days which was the time Dreyfus had allowed for his own pilgrimage. And by exactly that same route. It necessitated many changes along the way, respites that were denied to his grandparents who were cooped, unrelieved, with a hundred and ten others in the wagon, struggling for air and space of which there was none. Taking up precious room were two buckets. One for drinking-water, which after a few hours' travelling was drained dry. The other for a hundred-odd toilet needs which fear had swiftly filled to overflowing. Some passengers, cheating the gas, died on the way, and their bodies were used for seats or leaning-posts. And intermittently there was prayer and song, the former for resignation and the latter for hope. But the ditty 'We're going to Pitchipoi' now carried less conviction, and the children, brainwashed into paradise, sing-songed like weary robots. But there was another song, one of vibrant hope, one that matched the rhythm of the clicking wheels. '*Cela ne va pas durer ainsi*'. This cannot last long. A song that whimpered along the rail-tracks to Buchenwald, Bergen-Belsen, Maidenick, Ravensbruck, Treblinka, Flossenburg, Mauthausen, Lublin, Saschenhausen, Orianenburg, Theresienstadt, Sobibor, all those sad miles of steel cortège, a song sung in Greek, Polish, German, Hungarian, Dutch, Italian, a symphony of suppliant survival that will resound along those rails forever. Four long days of song and prayer, of hunger, thirst and death, so that when at last the doors were opened at the Auschwitz terminal, it was like a deliverance.

Dreyfus and his family stationed themselves at the end of the line at 5.33 in the afternoon of July the twenty-first. The tracks were overgrown with weeds, silent now and almost peaceful. Yet Dreyfus could hear the dogs barking as the truck-doors were slid open. He heard the shouts of the guards and the lash of their whips. He saw the suitcases as they piled up alongside the tracks. His grandparents had had no luggage. The milk, had his grandmother ever found it, had long ago assuaged somebody's thirst. They had arrived only in the soiled clothes they stood in and shortly, denuded of those, they would die naked as they were born. Dreyfus saw the long trail of weary bones, shuffling into line. If they didn't smell the smoke they certainly must have seen it oozing from the distant chimney as the rumours at last found their source and confirmation.

Dreyfus led his family on to the ramp, the site of the selection. One look at his grandparents must have judged them too old and too frail for any practical purpose. His grandfather was beyond work and his grandmother beyond experiment. So they were shifted to the right-hand column along with the children and pregnant women. If the register recorded one thousand and twenty-five persons who were gassed on that day, that figure did not include the many foetuses.

Some in the line fretted for their luggage, and the children wanted their toys to take to Pitchipoi. The guards assured them that their luggage would follow but did not add that it would first be sorted for its valuables and then discarded.

Dreyfus gathered his family and led them slowly towards the crematoria. Much of the camp had been destroyed by the Germans for fear of evidence. But what remained was proof enough of Armageddon. The miles of hastily rolled barbed-wire, the ruins of the four crematoria at Birkenau. The flood lamps that freeze-framed the electrocuted bodies on the wire. In the basement, indestructible, were the rooms for undressing and the shearing of hair, and a few gas-chambers where the pain would explode and thereafter cease.

In the memorial museum Dreyfus saw all that he had read about. He knew about the mountain of shoes, the piles of artificial limbs, the kaleidoscope of spectacles. He knew about all those things. But this was a different kind of knowing. It was a knowledge from which one could never walk away. It was proof. Proof undistilled, unpolluted by metaphor or literature. A heap of children's shoes is exactly what it is, a heap of children's shoes, and the slightest simile diminishes it. They walked around in silence. The horror was beyond commentary.

There was a last station on Dreyfus's pilgrimage, and he and his family made their way to the one remaining oven in the camp. There were many mourners in the chamber, but all were alone, for each grief was private, and the room reeked of survivors' guilt. Dreyfus stood before the oven, his last station, and once again, together with Matthew, he recited the Kaddish. And when it was done, he began his fast. Out of Judaic season, but in the ripeness of his own heart, it would be his Day of Atonement. Or rather, his Day of At-Onement, for at last he could walk with his forbears.

Now his trial was well and truly over. His testimony had been on oath and it was a truth that would fashion the rest of his life, its joys and its freedom, though their burdens would hover forever on the eyelid of sorrow.

38

On his return Dreyfus found a number of letters. One was from his publisher.

17 July 1998

Dear Sir Alfred

I have now finished reading your manuscript, which has given me great pleasure. I have high hopes for it. I notice that you have encountered a great deal of anti-Semitism amongst those who crossed your path. I do hope that you do not count me amongst them. I have to tell you that some of my best friends are Jews.

Yours sincerely
Bernard Wallworthy